SHIELD OF LIFE

Younger Wolf turned to face the remaining Rees. The clearing was full of them, and their tired eyes filled with surprise when the Wolf drew out the stake and drove it into the scorched earth. Binding his leg, he turned at last, holding the Fox lance in his powerful right hand as he steadied the Buffalo Shield with his left.

"I wait my death calmly," Younger Wolf sang softly. "Nothing lives long. Only the earth and the mountains!"

From among the Rees stepped a solitary figure. His chest was marked by the red circles Younger Wolf had seen before, and the three feathers danced lightly from his hair. The Ree chief approached calmly, quietly. His companions held back, cheering him on. He paused twenty paces away and aimed his rifle.

Younger Wolf raised the sacred shield and cried, "Come, Ree, and find your death!"

THE
MEDICINE TRAIL
THE BUFFALO SHIELD

G. CLIFTON WISLER

ZEBRA BOOKS
KENSINGTON PUBLISHING CORP.

for Rex Woodard
remembered friend

ZEBRA BOOKS

are published by

Kensington Publishing Corp.
475 Park Avenue South
New York, NY 10016

First printing: May, 1992

Printed in the United States of America

One

Younger Wolf sat alone on the rocky hillside, watching the sun bathe the valley below in a golden mist. Already the camp dogs were yapping at the celestial intruder, stirring the camp into motion. Soon the pony boys would collect horses for their fathers and brothers. Women would bring water from the river and prepare their cook pots. Life among the Tsis tsis tas would resume.

It was a welcome sight, living proof that the great circle of life continued. Old Cloud Dancer, Younger Wolf's grandfather, had said as much long ago when the two of them had made the morning prayers together. Stone Wolf had been there, too, standing taller and straighter as always.

"One day he will keep the Arrows," the old man had announced.

"Yes," Younger Wolf had agreed. "He's the oldest. Already he sees things."

"He'll soon walk the medicine trail," Cloud Dancer had noted. "It's a hard road, and he'll begin his walk young."

"And what path will I choose, Nam shim'?"

"Choose?" the old man had asked, laughing. "A man doesn't do the choosing. That's for Man Above to do."

"But you know things. Will I be a medicine man like you? As my brother will be?"

"Have patience," Cloud Dancer had advised. "You can't expect to know it all yet. Take boy's steps now. There's time for man's road later."

But the Dancer had climbed Hanging Road atop Noahvose, the sacred heart of the world, when Younger Wolf was but a young man of twenty-two summers. So many of the truths the old man held in his solemn frown and bright eyes had remained unspoken. Cloud Dancer had carried his secrets with him to the other side, leaving only half-remembered words to guide his grandson.

"Keep the old ways," Cloud Dancer had urged. "Let your brother's dreams be a guide to you."

"Yes," Younger Wolf muttered as he fed a small fire and readied his pipe. "Stone Wolf's dreams carry great power."

But while admiration and respect for the Arrow-keeper flowed through every particle of his being, Younger Wolf often lamented his own fate. Was he always to be the younger? Was it enough to walk in his brother's shadow?

Perhaps that was why he had chosen to set his feet upon warrior's road.

"Chosen?" Younger Wolf asked, shaking his head as he gazed at the brightly painted pipe resting lightly in his hands. "No, you were right, Nam shim'. I did no choosing."

Even as a slight-shouldered youth, war had stalked Younger Wolf. While others organized horse raids or formed parties to whip the Crow and Snake, it was usually Younger Wolf who struck the enemy first, who stood and turned the enemy charges or rescued the helpless.

"It's good to be brave," Younger Wolf advised his nephews. "But don't be foolish. A brave man is sometimes the easiest to kill. One who's careful makes a deadlier enemy."

"Yes, but our uncle would always ride to save us," Arrow Dancer boasted as boys of ten did.

"He's right, See' was' sin mit," Stone Wolf had added. "It's the fate of a man of the People. Didn't our own father die trying to save a party of fools from the enemy?"

Those words brought a weight to Younger Wolf's chest as he smoked. He rarely climbed the hills alone anymore to make the morning prayers, but he had found solitude a healing cure for his tormented soul. Even cedar smoke and sacred tobacco brought no comfort that morning, though. A handful of young Fox warriors had vowed to raid a nearby Crow camp, and Younger Wolf felt the obligation to lead them.

"Grandfather, you make my road a hard one," the Wolf spoke to the rising sun. "Sharp stones torture my feet, and fallen trees threaten to lame my pony. Give me a strong heart and far-seeing eyes to find the enemy."

His only answer was a stirring of the wind. He smoked and prayed and reflected on his past triumphs. What was it the Lakotas said? "It is a good day to die!" It was a call to drive the young men on, but not a cheering thought for those left behind to mourn. This Crow fight would bring few honors and little profit. The camp was poor, and the few guards were just skinny boys.

"Brothers, it will be easy," young Fire Hawk had insisted, pulling his arms back so that his chest appeared larger. The Hawk was still more boy than warrior, Younger Wolf noted. Words were easy enough to throw, but often as deadly as a lance. A man learned that if he was fortunate to live long enough. Fire Hawk's eyes burned with a hunger to avenge his slain father, struck down by the Crow three summers past, and the young man had no patience for the cautious admonitions of his elders.

"Our fathers are afraid of these Crows," Fire Hawk had grumbled as the chiefs rejected the pipe he brought to one after another. "Have the Tsis tsis tas become a people with only old women to lead them? Where are the men?"

Fire Hawk had collected his raiding party—mostly boys who had ridden with their fathers to hold the horses on pony raids. There wasn't a one of them who had counted coup on a live enemy.

"You should go and play the hoop game," said Wood Snake, the leader of the Foxes, when he first spied the young band. The chief chastised the foolish boys, but his strong words had only elicited more boasting.

"Watch us, Uncle!" Fire Hawk had shouted. "We'll carry many scalps to the Fox council."

"Crows don't make camp so near the enemy and leave only boys to watch their ponies," Wood Snake had warned. "It will be your hair, and that of your brothers, that will decorate a lance. Boasting won't

8

bring you success. You need power, and who are you to make it? What medicine do you know? You've seen nothing in your dreams and own no charms to blind the enemy."

"It's true," Fire Hawk had admitted. "My heart demands this raid, but I'm no great man. We require a leader. Who will help us onto warrior's road?"

And so Younger Wolf had reluctantly offered his help.

"Ah, it's a good thing," Wood Snake had remarked when Younger Wolf shared his decision. "For them. I fear you'll find your death, though, old friend."

"Already I've lived longer than some," Younger Wolf had answered. "And I leave no wife or son to weep in an empty lodge."

"There are those who will mourn," Wood Snake had insisted. "Make your medicine strong. The Crow know many tricks."

"Yes, we know that well," Younger Wolf had agreed. "I have scars to remind me. But now I carry the Buffalo Shield. Its power will protect us."

"Yes, it's strong medicine, but you won't find pony boys to fight. The Crow will run Fire Hawk, and who will stand with you?"

"Then mine will be a remembered death," Younger Wolf had vowed. "Can a warrior ask for more?" As he stood and prepared to return to the camp, and recalled another of Cloud Dancer's admonitions: "Always place first among all things the welfare of the People."

"Even young fools," the Wolf whispered. He watched Fire Hawk take a spotted pony from one of his younger cousins. What was it that hurried boys to their

9

deaths? "You sound like an old man," he muttered to himself. "And you weren't any different. Can a boy chew roasted buffalo and not long to join the hunt? Can he listen to his uncle's stories and not hunger to count coup on an ancient enemy?"

Slowly, reluctantly, Younger Wolf joined the eager young Fox warriors. Already Arrow Dancer had brought two war ponies out from the herd.

"Uncle, I've brought food, too," the boy said, offering a beaded buckskin bag. "Maybe you will need someone to hold your horse."

"Soon," Younger Wolf said, nodding solemnly as the boy did his best to stretch himself taller. "Now Stone Wolf needs you."

"Fire Hawk says he will take many scalps," Arrow Dancer said, gazing enviously at the young raiders. "He's not so much older."

"Seven summers," Younger Wolf said. "If they had been put to better use, perhaps Fire Hawk would know boasts are better made after a fight."

"You're worried," the boy said, his voice betraying his surprise. "You can't be afraid!"

"Afraid?" Younger Wolf asked, laughing. "A man can't fear something he knows as well as I know war. No, I'm only sad that I must miss my nephews' singing for a time."

"We'll sing when you return," Arrow Dancer said, smiling broadly. "And maybe we'll hunt deer."

"Yes, it's a good thought," Younger Wolf agreed. "One that will hurry me home."

As Younger Wolf took charge of his ponies, Fire Hawk and the other Foxes turned toward him.

"All has been made ready, Uncle," the Hawk said,

using the title out of respect rather than kinship. "The Crow are helpless now, but they won't remain so forever."

"You have scouts watching their camp?" Younger Wolf asked.

"My cousins Red Woodpecker and Spring Hawk are there," Fire Hawk explained.

Younger Wolf scowled. Spring Hawk was scarcely as old as his boastful cousin, and Red Woodpecker was a boy of fifteen.

"We'll make a camp near Crazy Woman's River," Younger Wolf declared. "It's a good place, with plentiful game and no cover to hide an enemy's approach. Send a man to bring in your scouts. We'll smoke and make medicine. Then we'll steal the Crow horses."

"And kill them!" Fire Hawk vowed.

"The Crow have good ponies," Younger Wolf said, gazing forcefully at his young companions. "A man finds honor in taking his enemy's mounts. But killing pony boys will only disturb the harmony of the world. It will kindle the fires of revenge in the Crow, and it will put your brothers in peril. No good will come of such killing."

"A warrior kills his enemy!" Fire Hawk insisted.

"You have seen many fights, of course," Younger Wolf said mockingly. "You ask the protection of my medicine. Don't break its power. We'll make the proper prayers, and we'll fight only if it is necessary. Remember, there's honor in facing equals, not in slaying the defenseless ones."

"They killed my father," Fire Hawk muttered.

Younger Wolf nodded, but he didn't relent. Instead he silently vowed to keep a sharp eye on the young

11

men. They were all of them too eager, and such raiders are easily snared in an enemy trap.

Younger Wolf approached the Arrow Lodge silently, with a grave face and solemn eyes. Nearby stood the original Buffalo Shields, the two crafted by Stone Wolf after he had seen them in a vision.

"Remember, Brother, the shield holds its power only so long as its holder remains true to the sacred path," Stone Wolf had said when he presented the second shield to his brother. "Remain pure of heart, and its protection will spare you from harm."

Even now, many summers afterward, Younger Wolf drew the shield from its buffalo hide cover with great reverence. It was a wonderful sight, round like the circle of life, with a white buffalo skull in the center. Four prowling wolves surrounded the skull, invoking the cardinal directions. Hair cut from enemy scalps decorated the tough outer hide. Other hair, scraped from buffalo hides and cut from the manes and tails of ponies, was stuffed between two hides to add more strength and to invoke additional powers.

"I hope I made it strong enough," Stone Wolf said as he stood beside his younger brother and gazed at the shield.

"It will turn the enemy's arrows from my heart," Younger Wolf declared.

"I saw you make the morning prayers, See' was' sin mit," Stone Wolf added. "I've smoked and prayed, but I can find no good signs. There's danger in this undertaking. Fire Hawk rides with anger, and he'll bring you all to a bad end."

"Ah, I see it, too," Younger Wolf confessed, sighing. "Nah nih, they are Foxes. Our chiefs warn them, but

Fire Hawk has no ears to hear caution. They are other men's sons, but their fathers won't stop them. I am a man of the People. I must see after their welfare."

"They'll hurry your death."

"Perhaps, Nah nih, but I'm not a man easily killed. I have the Buffalo Shield's power and far-seeing eyes. I hope to prevent mistakes and protect these young fools."

"It's a hard road you walk."

"Yes," Younger Wolf agreed. "As is yours. Keep the Arrows safe, Nah nih, and watch my nephews."

Stone Wolf nodded gravely. Younger Wolf then tied the shield to his buffalo rib saddle and climbed atop his white-faced war pony. He drove the second horse along and shouted encouragement to the others. Boys raced out, whooping and waving short bows and bird arrows in the air. Some of the young Foxes blew shrill notes on their eagle bone whistles. Others howled or shouted insults about the Crow.

"Who will stand before us?" Fire Hawk screamed, waving a painted lance at the sky.

"Come, bring your brothers along," Younger Wolf urged as he started toward Crazy Woman's River. "There's much to do."

Crazy Woman's River was half a day's hard riding north of the Tsis tsis tas camp, and Younger Wolf set a brisk pace. He galloped along on one mount, then switched to the spare, pausing but a moment in between. He wanted the horses worked hard, for the return ride might be swift as well, but of more desperate necessity. He also wanted to drive the warriors. Several were mere boys who had seen only fifteen snows. They had hunted elk and buffalo, but their knowledge of war came from stories shared in councils or recalled by grandfathers.

By nightfall three of the younger boys had turned back, forced by lame mounts or fatigue to give up their chance for glory. Fire Hawk taunted the first one, but afterward, when his own weariness tormented him, the Hawk merely nodded and urged the remaining riders onward. When they finally arrived at the river, the young men fell off their horses and collapsed.

"Up!" Younger Wolf shouted angrily. "See to your ponies."

The weary warriors responded reluctantly, but they did as instructed. Afterward, when they had devoured such provisions as they had brought along, Younger Wolf ordered a fire built. They gathered around it as darkness fell, and the scouts shared their news of the Crow camp.

"We'll all be rich in ponies," Red Woodpecker declared. "Three hundred good mounts graze only a short ride from here, and there are only five boys keeping watch. Others guard their mothers in the camp beyond. The men have ridden off to hunt."

"Leaving so many horses?" Younger Wolf asked warily.

"These Crows are rich in horses," Spring Hawk replied. "Rich in women, too. We should take some of them."

"Ah," Red Woodpecker said, grinning. "We should."

"You're too young to have use for one," Fire Hawk barked. "Crows are only good for killing. We should burn the camp."

"No," Younger Wolf argued. "We'll take only horses.

We come to this place as Fox warriors, keeping the old ways, invoking the power of the spirits and making medicine to protect us from harm. If the enemy strikes at us, we will strike back. Anyone may count a coup with the flat of his bow or touch the enemy with a lance. But let none of us strike a fatal blow. That will destroy our medicine and bring the Crow down on us."

"I have no fear of pony boys," Fire Hawk grumbled.

"We've seen no men, Uncle," Spring Hawk pointed out.

"You believe what you see," Younger Wolf answered as he mixed war paint. "I know what I can't see. I look in the fire and see hidden dangers. We'll make prayers that these hidden enemies will be blind to our approach. Later, when it's time, I'll paint your faces and chests. We'll tie up our ponies' tails, and you will tie elk charms in your hair. Now we'll rest."

"When will we strike?" Fire Hawk demanded.

"Tomorrow, after our horses have rested," Younger Wolf explained. "When the sun is eaten by the western hills." *And after I have seen this Crow camp myself,* Younger Wolf thought.

TWO

Younger Wolf fought off his own exhaustion long enough to inspect the camp. He sent two of the young men out to keep watch over the ponies, and he urged all to sleep with their arms close by.

"The Crow know this country, too," he warned his young companions. "One may have crossed our trail or smelled our camp smoke."

"Old man's talk," Fire Hawk muttered.

Younger Wolf didn't argue. He felt like an old man, even if he had seen but thirty snows. The scars of too many skirmishes marked his chest and thighs. Iron Wolf, his father, hadn't been old when death found him. Often his dreams had warned of violent death, and he had no reason to doubt their truth.

After passing a restless night on Crazy Woman's River, Younger Wolf rode out shortly before dawn with Red Woodpecker and Spring Hawk to examine the Crow camp. Actually, there were two camps—a village of women and little ones set between two forks of the river, and a small camp for the pony boys beyond, where the grass was better for grazing horses.

"It's as we said," Spring Hawk declared. "These Crows are making it easy for us to take their ponies."

"Too easy," Younger Wolf observed. "Where are the warriors?"

"Hunting," Red Woodpecker suggested.

"Where?" the Wolf demanded. "Have you seen their trail? Has anyone returned with meat? When did a people send the men off to hunt without women to butcher the meat and work the hides? Men leave a camp only to make war."

"Perhaps they go to raid the Lakotas," Spring Hawk said, nervously eyeing the surrounding country. The pine-covered hills and treacherous ravines could conceal a thousand men, after all.

"Yes," Younger Wolf agreed as he followed the seventeen-year-old's eyes. "They could be there waiting for us. Or hurrying to strike our own people."

"We should hurry homeward," Red Woodpecker said, sighing. "But we can take the ponies with us."

"We can't appear foolish to the others," Spring Hawk added. "To ride so far and return with nothing . . ."

"We'll run the ponies," Younger Wolf agreed. "But we must leave the Crow camp untroubled. The horses are enough to win you honor. Crows on foot won't threaten us."

"And if the warriors are in the hollows, waiting?" Spring Hawk asked.

"We will steal upon their horses and be gone before they can snare us," Younger Wolf explained. "We'll succeed as long as no one breaks away."

The scouts both knew Younger Wolf spoke of their cousin. Fire Hawk's recklessness was the true enemy.

17

Younger Wolf left Spring Hawk and Red Woodpecker to keep watch over the Crow while he returned to the camp downriver. The others had busied themselves readying their ponies and shooting a deer to satisfy their hunger. Younger Wolf joined them as they sat around a low fire, chewing venison and sharing tales of remembered fights.

"You've seen the Crow camp?" Fire Hawk asked. "It's as I said."

"There are many horses," Stone Wolf said, accepting a rib from Broken Bear Tooth, the young nephew of Wood Snake.

"And few guards," Fire Hawk added. "We can run the ponies and burn the camp."

"We will take many horses," Younger Wolf said, staring with grave eyes at Fire Hawk. "If we approach with caution and strike quickly, we will enjoy success. But there are a hundred places to hide men in that country, and there's a smell of deception in the air. The main camp is enclosed by water. A man who charged that place would be exposed to concealed enemies. I haven't come to Crazy Woman's River to lead anyone to his death."

"This is my raid," Fire Hawk argued. "It's for me to decide."

"No, it's for them," Younger Wolf argued, pointing to the others. "As for me, I can only guide you with words. You talk of hard fights, remembering the stories you have heard in our council. But if the enemy appears, who will stand and protect his brothers?"

"I will," Fire Hawk boasted.

"No," Younger Wolf said scornfully. "You will be in

18

the Crow camp, fighting their women. Even a Buffalo Shield won't turn the arrows of the Crow if you ride down the helpless ones. My power will be broken, and death will find us."

"Uncle, you spoke with the Arrow-keeper before leaving," Broken Bear Tooth observed. "What did Stone Wolf tell you?"

"To keep my feet on the sacred road," Younger Wolf answered. "To make strong medicine. You are young, Brothers, and in a fight your blood will be up. Don't let it steal your caution. Do as I warn. Count coup on the pony boys and take the horses. Leave the camp untouched. Those who will honor my admonition can enjoy what protection I offer. I'll help them paint themselves and tie charms in their hair. It's all a simple man can offer."

"Do as Younger Wolf instructs," Dancing Lance urged. "My father has fought with him. Once, when the Pawnee killed Ne' hyo's pony, Younger Wolf rode to the rescue. He killed a Pawnee and struck a second senseless. Then he pulled my father up behind him and rode to safety."

"I, too, heard the story," Broken Bear Tooth added. "Wood Snake has called the Wolf a man of the People. I follow him."

Younger Wolf smiled as others howled their agreement. He gazed at Broken Bear Tooth with a mixture of surprise and appreciation. The boy had spoken more words that day than the Wolf had heard him speak in fourteen summers.

The discussion continued as the sun climbed high in the sky. Fire Hawk continued to argue the merits of striking the Crow camp, but he found few followers.

19

Most of the young Foxes saw the strong medicine of the Buffalo Shield, recalled their fathers' stories of Younger Wolf's exploits, and eagerly accepted their elder's advice and protection. As for the Wolf, he tied elk tooth charms behind ears, tied eagle and owl feathers in hair, and painted wolf and bear claws, lightning bolts, and hailstones on one young man after another.

Stone Wolf himself dressed simply. He carried no trophies of earlier battles, and he wore no scalp shirt. Except for a breechclout of yellow buckskin, he stood naked beside the white-faced pony.

Fire Hawk, in contrast, wore a beaded shirt and an uncle's war bonnet.

"He intends to lead us even now," Dancing Lance grumbled.

"You should wear better clothes," Broken Bear Tooth said to Younger Wolf. "Only two feathers dance in your hair, but you have counted many coups."

"My medicine demands modesty," Younger Wolf explained. "I take no scalps, nor boast of coups. It's enough for me to keep my feet on the sacred path and leave high living to fools."

"The others won't understand," Broken Bear Tooth mumbled. "They'll follow Fire Hawk."

"I've done what I can," Younger Wolf insisted. "They must decide for themselves."

Even so, it was Younger Wolf who formed the band and gave them their instructions. Split into groups of four, they stealthily made their way toward the Crow ponies, using the setting sun and the darkness that followed to mask their movements. Then, when all was ready, Younger Wolf blew on an eagle bone whistle, and the Foxes fell upon the pony boys.

Even though Younger Wolf had suspected a trap, the skillful retreat of the young Crows surprised even him. Yes, the enemy was prepared for them.

"No!" he shouted as Red Woodpecker hurried after a Crow boy. "Run the ponies!"

"Kill him!" Fire Hawk urged instead.

Red Woodpecker swung his horse around to cut off the pony boy's retreat, and in the twilight haze Younger Wolf lost sight of both. Then Red Woodpecker's horse bolted past. Its rider had vanished.

"Hurry the others!" Younger Wolf told Dancing Lance. "Danger's at hand!"

The Wolf then rode past the embers of the pony camp's fire to where Red Woodpecker had charged the Crow guard. A boy of twelve or so lay in the rocks, bleeding from a gash in his side. Nearby two Crows cut the forelock from Red Woodpecker's scalp.

"*Ayyyy!*" Younger Wolf cried, galloping toward the Crows. They fled instantly, but when the Wolf reached Red Woodpecker, it was too late. Even in the dim light Younger Wolf was able to count seven fatal wounds on the boy's bare belly.

"Nothing lives long," Younger Wolf sang as he turned back toward the others. "Only the earth and the mountains."

Elsewhere, confusion reigned. Pony dust mixed with the darkness to conceal wild fighting. Bands of Crows were galloping out of ravines and descending hills, whooping furiously as they fell on startled raiders. Spring Hawk tried to form a line, but was cut down by three arrows. Fire Hawk and three others charged out of the swirling dust and raced toward the Crow camp.

"No!" Younger Wolf howled, raising his shield high and slapping its tough outer hide with a lance. The sound startled the ponies and gave him a path through which to ride. Broken Bear Tooth and Dancing Lance hurried to his side, and the three of them turned the pony herd southward. Other young Foxes galloped over, and Younger Wolf instructed them to drive the horses homeward.

"What of the others?" Weasel Tail cried.

"I'll see to them," Younger Wolf answered as he waved them along. In truth, there was little left to be done, though. Screams from the banks of the river attested to Fire Hawk's failure, and a Crow chief climbed a nearby ridge and waved one of Spring Hawk's dismembered legs defiantly.

"We can't leave our dead to be mutilated," Dancing Lance cried.

"The dead aren't our concern," Younger Wolf argued. "We must aid the living."

With a heavy heart the Wolf sang a warrior prayer and nudged his horse toward the Crow camp. If ever a man had earned death, Fire Hawk had. But if the young man remained alive, Younger Wolf intended to spare him his cousins' fate.

The Crow camp was alive with activity. Torch-waving boys prowled the banks of the river, searching for fallen enemies to finish or wounded comrades to help. Bands of warriors rode in to boast of their triumphs while others formed to pursue the stolen ponies. In the shallows of the river, three young Tsis tsis tas warriors fended off the lance points of ten taunting Crows. Fire Hawk's disdain for the enemy had left his eyes. As he repelled blows with a stringless bow, he screamed skyward for help. His companions, their quivers also empty, chanted their death songs.

"Courage!" Younger Wolf shouted as he slapped his pony into a gallop. "We're Foxes! Always we run our enemies! We're Foxes! We ask the difficult things to do!"

"We're Foxes!" Broken Bear Tooth and Dancing Lance echoed.

The three horsemen took the Crow by surprise. Dismounted, hindered by waist-deep water, they had little choice but to flee. Dancing Lance struck one across the forehead with his bow, and Broken Bear Tooth slapped another with his bare hand, but it was the violence and the shrill scream of Younger Wolf that drove the enemy through the river to the far bank.

"Get them to safety!" the Wolf shouted as he halted his horse between the startled Crows and the shivering Fire Hawk.

"Come!" Dancing Lance urged as he pointed to several abandoned ponies. "Run, Brothers!"

Fire Hawk's companions took flight, splashing out of the river and hurrying along. Dancing Lance rode along behind to shield them from attack. Then the three young Foxes galloped off south after the pony herd.

Fire Hawk grabbed a discarded lance and charged the bewildered Crows across the river.

"He's learned nothing!" Younger Wolf cried in dismay as the Hawk plunged the lance into the side of a Crow and drew his knife.

"I was first!" he shouted as he cut the forelock from the dying Crow.

As the Crows recovered their wits and descended on their lone enemy, Broken Bear Tooth notched an arrow and shot a long-nosed Crow in the throat.

"Ayyyy!" Younger Wolf shouted as he whipped his horse into the river and covered Fire Hawk's withdrawal.

"See how I've run the enemy!" Fire Hawk exclaimed, waving the bloody scalp in the air.

"Yes, I see," Younger Wolf said, fighting off the memory of Red Woodpecker's slashed corpse.

"I've avenged my father," Fire Hawk cried. "Follow me, and we'll kill them all."

"You've killed enough," Younger Wolf growled, knocking the scalp from the young man's hand.

"Hurry him!" Broken Bear Tooth cried as he shot arrows into a line of Crow forming at the edge of the camp.

Fire Hawk was searching the shallows for the scalp and muttering to himself. Younger Wolf grabbed the Hawk's shoulder, clubbed him across the forehead with the Buffalo Shield, and pulled him up onto the horse.

"Ride!" Younger Wolf shouted, and Broken Bear Tooth slapped his pony into motion. Younger Wolf galloped after him.

They rode from Crazy Woman's River as if chased by demons. Only after joining the other Foxes did Younger Wolf release his reluctant companion to climb from the back of the white-faced pony.

"I would have run them all," Fire Hawk grumbled as he mounted a restless mare.

"You would be dead," Broken Bear Tooth insisted. "We saved you."

"Should I be grateful that my brothers fled from the enemy?" the Hawk cried.

"Look around you," Dancing Lance said, joining them. "How many of us are bleeding? You sat in council with us, listening to Younger Wolf's warnings, but you struck the Crow camp. You broke the power of his medicine, but he rode to rescue you anyway. Now you cry like a boy who wets himself. I hear no gratitude. I hear no mourning wail for the dead. Where are your cousins?"

"They ran the pony boys!" Fire Hawk boasted. "They will return with scalps to show their father."

"They are dead," Dancing Lance muttered bitterly. "Spring Hawk, who rode to the buffalo hunt at my side. Red Woodpecker, who was to walk the river with my sister when we returned."

"No!" Fire Hawk screamed.

"Yes," Broken Bear Tooth said, dropping his gaze. "I saw his body near the pony boys' camp."

"Spring Hawk?" Fire Hawk asked.

"Struck down by arrows," Dancing Lance explained. "The Crow tore him apart. When we meet again in council, tell his father how his bones lie scattered in Crow country because you had no eyes to see the truth of Younger Wolf's warning."

"It was the Crow," Fire Hawk insisted.

"They did the killing, but who brought us to them?" Dancing Lance asked. "You may lead other bands, but I will never follow. The Tsis tsis tas have enemies enough without our young men leading us to such misfortune."

"And what of the horses?" Fire Hawk asked.

"We should have taken them all," Broken Bear Tooth grumbled. "Three hundred. I count sixty that remain, and the Crow may yet catch us. We're weary, and some of us are hurt. They may kill us all."

"No, there's been enough dying," Younger Wolf declared. "The wounded can continue homeward. I will stay behind to meet the Crow."

"Alone?" Fire Hawk asked. "And you called me a fool."

"It's an obligation," Younger Wolf stated, contempt in his voice. "A shield carrier is bound to protect the helpless ones."

"I'm unhurt," Dancing Lance said. "I'll stay, too."

Others also insisted on remaining behind, but Younger Wolf sent most of them to help the wounded or to escort the captured ponies to Stone Wolf's camp. Only Dancing Lance and Weasel Tail were to stay, but Broken Bear Tooth lingered as well.

"Wood Snake would remain," the Tooth explained. "I have arrows again, and my aim is good."

Younger Wolf would have ordered the boy home, but Broken Bear Tooth folded his arms as his uncle was fond of doing. It was a sign that thereafter words were pointless. Instead the four Foxes made camp atop a low ridge overlooking the river and waited for the enemy. They slept in turns, allowing the quiet night to restore their strength.

The sun found them weary but alert. Younger Wolf was surprised the Crow hadn't arrived, but upon considering it, he realized the advantage the enemy had in striking by daylight. He hoped they might even have been satisfied with rounding up their ponies. But blood had been shed, and there were men bound to cry for vengeance.

The Crow appeared late that morning. They rode in a single file, thirty of them, brandishing lances and bows. Their leader was a tall, bent-nosed young man, painted yellow with black streaks across his chest. He approached the ridge with caution, then halted and shouted taunts at the four Foxes standing beside their ponies. Younger Wolf made nothing of the words, but the gestures that followed were clear. The Crow was challenging the enemy.

"I can kill him," Broken Bear Tooth said, notching an arrow.

"Then they will all fall upon us," Younger Wolf said, waving for the boy to put aside his bow. "No, it's for me to meet this yellow face."

Younger Wolf then mounted his pony, fixed the Buffalo Shield on his left arm, and balanced a lance in his right.

"Ayyyy!" he howled at the Crow. "I'm a Fox. It's for me to do the difficult things. Run, dogs, before my power!" He urged his pony forward.

The Crow leader stood his ground, but the others retreated to let the two fighters have room. They circled each other, exchanging insults, but neither made an aggressive move. The Crow finally raised his lance and made a rush forward, but Younger Wolf nudged his pony to the left, allowing the blazing sun to reflect off the Buffalo Shield. For a moment the Crow tried to blink away the glare, but his horse grew unsettled. Younger Wolf lifted his own lance and parried the enemy's blow easily. Then, with a terrible shout, he struck the yellow-faced Crow across the chest, knock-

27

ing him to the earth.

"*Ayyyy!*" Younger Wolf howled, dismounting and touching the tip of his lance to the shaken enemy's forehead. "I'm first!"

The stricken warrior gazed up in surprise, then froze as Younger Wolf remounted his pony and rejoined his companions atop the ridge. The Crow raised a howl of their own and raised lances and bows. But when their fallen chief regained his feet, he offered no second challenge. Instead he limped to his pony, mounted, and rode away. The others followed.

Three

Trailing behind the others, as was his custom, Younger Wolf arrived at Stone Wolf's camp long after the other raiders. Sad and weary, he was ill-prepared for the stir his return brought to the camp. Men howled and slapped their lodge skins with bows, and boys ran alongside his horse, whooping and singing brave heart songs.

How can it be? he asked himself. Didn't they know of the brave ones left dead at Crazy Woman's River? Doesn't the smell of blood foul the air even now?

"Uncle is back!" Arrow Dancer shouted.

"Yes," others agreed. "Younger Wolf has returned. He's counted coup and rescued the helpless ones!"

As he dismounted, Younger Wolf was half crushed by his admirers. Young men touched his wounds or gazed in awe at the Buffalo Shield. Older men whispered their gratitude for the safe return of a son or nephew.

"Give me your horse, Uncle," Arrow Dancer urged as he fought his way to Younger Wolf's side. "You're tired, and your wounds need attention. Ne' hyo is waiting."

Younger Wolf eagerly passed the exhausted pony into his nephew's care, pausing only long enough to take the Buffalo Shield from its perch behind his horn saddle.

"Tell us of the battle," boys pleaded as the Wolf turned toward the sacred Arrow Lodge.

"Yes, tell us!" others called.

"I must honor the shield," Younger Wolf insisted. "And rest. Later I'll speak, in the council."

The younger boys sighed with disappointment, knowing they would have to wait for the older boys to pass on the tale. One or two argued their cause, but now the Foxes had arrived, and they chased the children away.

"Ah, it's a good day," Wood Snake declared, clasping Younger Wolf's arms. "My nephew has recounted your coups. We're rich in horses! You've run the Crow."

"No, I've survived them," Younger Wolf grumbled. "We have brothers to mourn. I couldn't save them all."

"Few fights are won without cost," the Snake replied. "And the loss might have been greater. Tonight we'll dance and feast and speak of brave heart deeds."

"Not tonight," Younger Wolf said, sighing. "Three days hence, after the mourning is finished."

"The mourning is well begun already," Wood Snake argued. "The mother of the dead boys has taken the necessary steps."

"Perhaps her heart is whole then," Younger Wolf said, staring at his feet. "I haven't yet mourned them, and my wounds merit attention. Later, when I have bled for the dead and had a sweat, call the council."

"Yes, mourn them, Brother," Wood Snake agreed. "Rest. Restore yourself. It's only proper. There will be time for celebrating later."

Younger Wolf nodded to his comrades, then stepped past them toward the Arrow Lodge. He took great care to return the Buffalo Shield to its stand. Then he built a small fire, filled a pipe, and invoked the favors of the spirits. After smoking, Younger Wolf whispered the required medicine prayers, reviving the expended powers of the shield. He then added an apology for the disharmony his actions had brought to the orderly world.

"Heammawihio, we are but foolish children," he said, gazing past the brightly painted shield at the midmorning sky. "You give us Bull Buffalo to feed and clothe us, Sun to warm us and light our path, and sleep to restore our energy. Even so, we war among ourselves and reach out with greedy hearts for the possessions of others. Forgive us. Be patient."

It was an old prayer, one he had learned from Cloud Dancer as a boy. Then it had been hard to understand how a weathered old man such as his grandfather could be a child. Now, having walked man's road himself, the Wolf knew the meaning of the words only too well.

Stone Wolf completed his meditation, emptied the pipe, and extinguished the fire.

"You've returned from yet another trial," Stone Wolf observed, stepping to his brother's side. "Come, I'll treat your wounds."

"They're nothing compared to the hurt inside," Younger Wolf confessed.

31

"Yes," Stone Wolf said, nodding.

"Nah nih, why is it always the same?" Younger Wolf asked. "How many times will we allow these loud talkers to lead our young men to their deaths? Once the Tsis tsis tas had great power, but we allowed a rash young man to carry it into battle."

"Bull," Stone Wolf muttered bitterly. "I warned him, but he lost Mahuts, the sacred Arrows. The People suffered for his foolishness."

"How many brave men have died because their leaders failed to heed your warnings or prepare strong medicine?"

"See' was' sin mit, you now stand high in the eyes of the young men. It's for you to direct their path."

"Not me," Younger Wolf declared, closing his eyes and fighting off the challenge of his brother's words. "I have no dreams to show me the way. I'm an ordinary man with no great power to break another's will."

"You have courage," Stone Wolf argued. "The others respect you. Where you set your feet, they will follow. It's always been that way, even when we were boys. Look how my sons drink in your every word. It's time you joined the council of forty-four."

"Became a chief?"

"Led our People. I know once you dreamed of keeping the Arrows as our grandfather did. Your destiny took you to another path. Spotted Horse has died, and a man must be chosen to take his place. Many have spoken your name, even before you brought the young men back from the Crow camp. Few will oppose you now."

"I'm no old man to wrap myself in an elk hide and remember my past days," Younger Wolf declared.

"Others would be better choices."

Stone Wolf laughed and slapped his brother's back.

"I told them you would hesitate," Stone Wolf said. "It's right. A man who would eagerly don a chief's bonnet is one to watch carefully. You'll bear the burden well, See' was' sin mit, and the People will be glad of the choice."

"When will they ask me?" Younger Wolf inquired.

"After the Foxes gather," Stone Wolf explained. "When the People are hot with stories of your brave heart deeds."

"A chief's burdens are great, Nah nih."

"You'll have less time for the children," Stone Wolf noted. "It's time I was a father to them more."

"I'll miss their company."

"It's time you found a wife to warm your lodge," Stone Wolf suggested. "You should have sons of your own."

"They're mostly trouble," Younger Wolf declared, eyeing the shy approach of Arrow Dancer. Little Crow Boy and Porcupine peered out from behind the shield stand.

"But of some use," Stone Wolf argued. "Come now. We must treat your wounds."

"And ready the sweat lodge," Younger Wolf said, following his brother toward the Arrow Lodge. "I need to rid myself of death and anger."

"I'll send the boys to collect wood," Stone Wolf said, waving the young ones close. "Maybe we'll share a sweat with them this time. *Ayyyy!* That would be a good notion."

"Yes," Younger Wolf agreed. "They're old enough."

And, he thought, *I may have little time for them in the*

days to come.

Younger Wolf passed those next three days in quiet contemplation of the challenges which would follow. Even while Stone Wolf and his new wife, Dove Woman, painted his torn flesh with healing herb pastes and shook the medicine rattles, Younger Wolf imagined the other wounds his body would bear when the heavy responsibilities of a chief were placed on his shoulders.

There can be no refusing, though, he told himself. *Cloud Dancer spoke of this day. Stone Wolf, too, predicted it. I must accept.*

Younger Wolf cut his hair and bled himself in recognition of his dead comrades. Then he shared a sweat with Stone Wolf and his three eldest sons. It was a quiet moment, but afterward, sitting around the cook fire with Arrow Dancer at one elbow and the smaller boys, Crow Boy and Porcupine, on the other, he shared the tale of his first buffalo hunt and watched the eyes of the young ones brighten with the fires of adventure.

"I'll soon ride with the young men," Arrow Dancer boasted.

"We, too, will go, Uncle," Crow Boy added.

"Yes," Younger Wolf told them. "All boys hunger to set their feet on man's road." It was only afterward that they appreciated the days left behind.

The Foxes gathered at last to celebrate the horse raid, and the many coups were recounted for all to cheer. Younger Wolf fought back an urge to strike when Fire Hawk boasted of the Crow he'd killed and lamented the scalp lost when Younger Wolf hurried him from the river.

"Better that hair was lost than your own," Broken Bear Tooth nevertheless suggested. "Some haven't forgotten how you ignored the admonition to strike the Crow camp."

"Many," Dancing Lance added.

"We've come here to restore the harmony of our society," Wood Snake insisted, and the young men grew silent. "Also, men have come from the chief's society to speak with one of our brothers."

"Younger Wolf," the younger ones whispered.

"*Ayyyy!*" Weasel Tail whooped.

Now it was Fire Hawk who glared.

The Hev a tan iu, or Rope Men, as the band was known, had long been led by good men. South Wind, a hard fighter who was also looked upon as a leader by the Crazy Dog warriors, was a man of forty summers and many coups. He now entered the Fox council with Tall on the Mountain, a white-haired man highly regarded for mediating disputes and providing for the helpless. Wood Snake rose to greet them, for he also was one of the band's four chiefs. The other had been Spotted Horse, who had died of fever after only a brief time in the chief's council.

"Younger Wolf, we have come to invite you to join the chiefs," South Wind announced. As the youngest, he was expected to carry all messages.

"Brother, you are needed," Wood Snake added. "Spotted Horse has no son to walk his father's path, and his grandsons are small. You have so often shown us the way. A chief should be a man of the People. Your generous heart is well known."

"*Ayyyy!*" the Foxes howled.

"Often, you have led us in war," Tall on the Mountain said, "but your voice has never been eager for killing. Many coups honor your name, but you ride modestly to war and make no boasts. Mahuts knows your heart, and the young follow your example. Many find the road a chief walks to be a difficult one, but you, my friend, walk it already."

"Join us," Wood Snake urged.

"*Ayyyy!*" the Foxes howled again.

"It's a difficult road, yes," Younger Wolf agreed as he searched the faces of his comrades. "But I am a Fox. It's for me to do the difficult things."

"*Ayyyy!*" the Foxes screamed even louder.

"You are one of us then," Tall on the Mountain declared, driving a brightly painted stake into the earth beside Younger Wolf's feet. South Wind then produced a pipe, and the good will of the earth, sky, and cardinal directions were invoked. Afterward the Wind tied two eagle feathers, the symbols of the Chiefs Society, in Younger Wolf's shortened hair.

"Once, long ago, Sweet Medicine brought great power down from Noahvose, the sacred heart of the world," Tall on the Mountain explained. "He admonished those who would lead to be foremost men of the People. Where there is need, a chief must address that need. If a boy is naked, he must be clothed. If a woman is hungry, she must be fed. If a family has lost its horses, a chief must give up his own."

"A chief must show patience and practice wisdom," Wood Snake added. "He must never strike another

Tsis tsis tas. If others quarrel, he should try to restore the harmony of the band."

"His burdens are great," South Wind noted, "and so Sweet Medicine brought us the power of Eagle. You will rely on Eagle's strength to find the sacred path. You will guide the People and insure harmony."

"*Ayyyy!*" the others shouted when Younger Wolf stood. The eagle feathers danced in his hair, falling lightly on his neck, and the young men blew eagle bone whistles and took up a dance.

"Difficult days lay ahead," Wood Snake whispered gravely, and Younger Wolf nodded his agreement. "It's good we have your strength with us," the Snake added.

Will it be enough? Younger Wolf wondered.

Life was nothing if it wasn't change, and Younger Wolf had never questioned the destiny ordained for himself. As he accepted his new responsibilities, he quickly established a reputation for fairness. As the captured Crow ponies were divided among the raiders, Fire Hawk insisted on taking a greater share.

"I led the way," he argued. "It's for me to choose the best animals."

"Another might be generous with those who saved him from the enemy," Broken Bear Tooth grumbled.

"You brought no ponies away at all," Weasel Tail spoke up. "You had no eyes for horses. Only killing. No ponies grazed in the Crow village. Take your life away, Fire Hawk, and consider your brothers generous."

There were loud cries of agreement, and the Hawk

searched for supporters. The cousins who might have argued his claim were dead, and men with little patience for greed found no time for Fire Hawk's demands.

"Am I to be forgotten?" the Hawk screamed in outrage. "Are my wounds to be ignored?" he asked, tearing open his shirt so that the marks left by Crow quirts and lances could be seen.

"There are few marks on his chest," Dancing Lance observed. "Most are on the flanks or back. Not earned by a brave heart."

"Given by coward Crows!" Fire Hawk insisted.

When the discord grew loudest, Wood Snake ordered silence.

"Nephew, what brings such disharmony to our circle?" the chief asked Broken Bear Tooth.

"Fire Hawk's greed," the young man answered. "It's good you've come, Uncle. Chiefs should settle disputes."

"Yes," the Snake agreed, and the quarrel was set before the four headmen. Tall on the Mountain asked many questions, and men voiced their opinions.

"All men should share in a raid's success," South Wind suggested, "but a man who would take an undeserved share should be punished."

"That's for the Foxes to do," Wood Snake declared. "They say the horses which would have been given to Fire Hawk should be awarded the families of the dead ones."

"That's fair," Tall on the Mountain said, nodding. "In such a way, Fire Hawk may earn back the honor lost in quarreling."

"Perhaps," Younger Wolf said, frowning. "But it will

darken Fire Hawk's heart. Read his eyes, Brothers. Our duty is to restore *his* harmony, too. Do as the Foxes have suggested, but give Fire Hawk his choice of two ponies."

"He hasn't earned them," Dancing Lance complained.

"It's not for you to say," Wood Snake admonished the young man. "Would any dispute Younger Wolf's right to cut two ponies from the herd?"

"No," the Foxes murmured.

"These two will be my gift," Younger Wolf said, nodding to Wood Snake. "As my share. Divide the others among you, Brothers."

The young raiders sat, perplexed, for several moments.

"But you above all others merit a share, Uncle," Weasel Tail argued.

"Are horses so important?" the Wolf asked. "It's a small gift if it makes good your hearts and restores the harmony of our camp."

"Yes," Tall on the Mountain agreed.

The Foxes dropped their eyes solemnly, knowing they had been chided for their greed. When they next met in council, each raider offered a pony to a poor family or some boy needing a good mount to carry him on the buffalo hunt.

"I give this horse in honor of my chief, Younger Wolf," each said in turn.

"He is an example to us all," Broken Bear Tooth spoke. "We are small in his shadow."

"We chose well," Tall on the Mountain told the Wolf as they stood beside the river, watching the pony boys keep watch.

"Our young men want only a good path to walk," Younger Wolf declared. "And men to lead them."

"Now they have both," Tall on the Mountain declared.

Four

When the many bands gathered that summer to make the New Life Lodge and plan the buffalo hunt, the four chiefs of each of the ten bands met with the head chiefs of the People. Around a blazing council fire, the forty-four headmen sat and considered the future. When Younger Wolf took his place before the painted stick signifying his office, he felt strangely small. Most of the other men were older. Some already crafted bows for grandsons, and many recalled old Cloud Dancer and the better times before the pale people rode Shell River.

They were an odd mix, the forty-four. Some men sat in fine elk robes, wearing beaded bonnets decorated with buffalo horns or fox heads. Many wore eagle feathers in their hair. Younger Wolf appeared in a painted buckskin shirt, beaded moccasins, and simple breechclout. Except for the two feathers tied in his hair, he wore nothing to mark him as a great man.

"Why should he?" one boy asked. "He's Younger Wolf. All know him."

"His power comes from the Buffalo Shield," another noted. "It grows when he observes modest manners."

Others thought it strange the new chief should be such an ordinary man, but as the Rope Men spoke of their young chief's coups, few questioned Younger Wolf's right to sit in the council.

Younger Wolf remained quiet while the Council of Chiefs considered what troubles afflicted the Tsis tsis tas. The chiefs spoke of many things, but they made few decisions. The authority rested with the People themselves, and chiefs could do little more than offer guidance. Mostly they heard disputes and offered solutions.

"Our intent is not to punish," Tall on the Mountain told a man of the Rope Men, Mud Turtle, who was summoned before the council. "Your anger brings strife among the People. We wish to restore the harmony."

"You can't mend a broken sparrow's egg!" Mud Turtle raged. "How can you restore my wife's faithfulness? She's been with the traders and is lost to me."

"It's a sad thing, yes," South Wind agreed. "She must go to her father."

"I've sent her already. And my sons?" the Turtle asked. "They share her tainted blood."

"What wrong have they done you?" Younger Wolf asked. "I know Weasel Tail well. He's a fine rider and good hunter. How can you dishonor him?"

"It's wrong you should do so," Wood Snake declared. "Once they were close to your heart. Don't

42

pluck them like chin hairs! They, too, feel the loss of their mother. Find comfort in them."

"I wish them gone," Mud Turtle demanded.

"Have they uncles?" Otter Skin, a chief of one of the northern bands, asked.

"Only a grandfather," Wood Snake answered.

"The oldest already rides with the Fox warriors," Wood Snake explained. "Another will ride to the buffalo hunt this summer. Only one remains small, and he would be welcome in my lodge. I have young nephews there."

"They'll leave then," Mud Turtle said, calming.

"They should take two good horses and what possessions they desire," Younger Wolf suggested.

"I have few horses," Mud Turtle muttered.

"Weasel Tail brought twelve from the Crow herd," Younger Wolf pointed out. "We would leave you half of them."

"Yes, I'd forgotten," the Turtle mumbled. "They can have the horses."

"You should undertake a healing cure to cast off the anger in your heart," Tall on the Mountain then advised. "Afterward you will take your lodge from the Rope Men and return to your relatives among the Windpipe People."

"I'm cast out?" Mud Turtle cried.

"You cast yourself from us," Wood Snake explained. "Go elsewhere and forget. Maybe your sons will forget, too."

Yes, Younger Wolf thought. *To have a faithless mother is hard. To have a heartless father, too, is more than many could bear.*

43

Fortunately such grave matters were rare. More often the council considered lesser quarrels. Sometimes a woman and her husband would present themselves, but more often a woman returned to her father or placed her husband's belongings outside the lodge, breaking apart their marriage.

Most wrongs brought to the council were made right by the performance of small services or gifts of horses or buffalo robes. Only when a grudge remained was a man admonished, and if it continued, he would be sent from the People.

"To be cut off from the People would be hard," Arrow Dancer noted when he brought Younger Wolf food following the conclusion of the council.

"Not so bad as dying," Porcupine argued. "The white men kill those who steal or kill other white men."

"They must kill many," Younger Wolf said, grinning. "I have watched the pale ones, and they are all thieves. They come to steal the rivers and the hills. They would take Bull Buffalo if we allowed it. As to dying, there are many deaths. To breathe—alone, unloved and unwanted—is a slow death. I wouldn't welcome it. Better a sharp arrow in the heart!"

"Soon we'll be older, Uncle," Crow Boy observed. "Who will keep you from such a fate then?"

"You should take a wife, as Ne' hyo has," Arrow Dancer suggested. "Dove Woman is a good mother to us, and she's brought us our brother, Porcupine, and little Dreamer."

"Maybe she has a sister," Younger Wolf said, laughing.

"All are married," Porcupine muttered. "But I'll find a good wife for you, Uncle."

"I'll look, too," Arrow Dancer promised. "Porcupine is a good swimmer, but he likes fat girls. I'll find you one with a pretty face."

Younger Wolf laughed at the notion of the children roaming the camps, seeking out a wife for him. It grew less humorous when maidens began following him along the river. Many young men presented their sisters, and some of the older ones spoke glowingly of daughters or nieces.

"It's the boys," Stone Wolf explained. "They tell everyone Younger Wolf is seeking a wife."

"Everyone?" Younger Wolf asked.

"I will make them stop," Stone Wolf declared, "before the Arapahoes and Lakotas arrive with girls for you to see."

Younger Wolf laughed at the notion.

While Stone Wolf busied himself with preparations for the New Life Lodge ceremony, Younger Wolf took his nephews in hand. They scoured the thickets for rabbits one day and crafted bird arrows the next. The sharing of those days warmed Younger Wolf. Peace settled over the ten bands, and it seemed that, indeed, the world was being reborn.

It was at the great feasting after the conclusion of the ceremonies that Otter Skin, the Windpipe chief, introduced Younger Wolf to his sister, Hoop Woman.

"She's heard many good words about you," Otter Skin explained. "I think she would walk the water path with you."

Younger Wolf smiled to himself. His nephews were still at work. When he glanced at Hoop Woman, he expected to see an older woman, even perhaps a widow. Instead he saw a delicate girl of sixteen summers. Her bright smile and admiring eyes froze him for a moment.

"Go, walk with her," Otter Skin urged.

"She's just a child," Younger Wolf objected.

"Old enough to take a husband," her brother insisted. "Already I've refused three offers."

"I have responsibilities."

"None you can't carry better with a good woman at your side," Otter Skin argued. "We're making no bargain now. She has asked to meet you, and I am honoring a promise. Come. Speak with her. You undertake no obligation."

Younger Wolf thought to decline, but the girl's eyes drew him to her. An unspoken plea flooded her face, and he couldn't turn away from it.

"Sister, this is Younger Wolf," the Windpipe chief said, nudging his companion forward.

"I hoped to meet you," she said, shyly avoiding Younger Wolf's eyes. "I've heard much."

Younger Wolf stood in awkward silence. He couldn't form a reply on his tongue.

"Maybe you would walk?" Otter Skin suggested.

When Younger Wolf didn't answer, Otter Skin nodded to his sister and returned to the feast.

"It's a fine day for a walk," Hoop Woman observed as she touched Younger Wolf's elbow. "Was the sky ever so blue?"

"Maybe . . . not," Younger Wolf managed to reply.

46

"The grass is good here, and the river flows swiftly. Stone Wolf has remade the world well. We'll enjoy prosperity."

Younger Wolf nodded. They walked along the river for some time before reaching a deep pool where children were swimming away the afternoon. A band of boys tossed pebbles at some gawking girls to drive them away, and Hoop Woman laughed.

"My nephews," she said, pointing to a pair of swimmers.

"Rabbit Foot and Sandpiper," Younger Wolf noted. "I know them both. The one beyond is my own nephew, Arrow Dancer."

"So our families are already acquainted," she observed. "You sit with Otter Skin in the council."

"As do others," he pointed out.

"Why haven't you taken a wife?" she asked bluntly. When he stepped away, she covered her face. "Pardon my directness. I had to ask. There are those who say your medicine is marred by contact with women, and I wouldn't bring you harm."

"It's not so," he told her.

"Then why?"

"I'm a man of many burdens," he explained. "My brother is the Arrow-keeper, and he has always needed protection. I have nephews to help onto man's road."

"A man needs sons, too," she argued. "And no one who walks the world alone is complete."

"Many have," he objected. "Old Touches the Sky, who kept the Arrows, was such."

"The People were strong then, but now our numbers thin. We have need of strong sons."

"Hoop Woman," Younger Wolf said, turning so as to face her, "I have no need of a wife. Otter Skin speaks of the many who would open their hearts to you. Some are young and more fit to be your husband. You would find me a scarred old man who is too often in the hills, hunting game."

"My brothers have told me how you teach them to craft arrows," she said, gazing at the splashing boys. "Often I've seen you gathering the young men so you could tell of some remembered time. Sometimes, when no one is watching, I've crept close to listen to your words. You've filled your life with honorable actions, but I've read the hollowness in your eyes. You need a woman to warm you when winter's chill brings out the aches left by old wounds. You need someone to cook and make clothes. There are many older you could choose, widows with sons to walk the war road with you. None would come to you fresh, with eyes eager to see what you would show them."

"I don't know you," Younger Wolf complained.

"Ah, I hurry you," she said, laughing. "My brothers tell me to be patient, but soon you'll ride to the buffalo hunt, and who knows what will happen afterward? I must seize my chance."

"I'm much older," Younger Wolf argued. "Twice as old."

"There are fewer years between us than separate my father and mother," she explained. "I won't hurry you, though. I will wait at my father's lodge each evening, hoping you will bring a blanket for us to share. You have a courting flute?"

"Yes," he confessed. "Rarely used."

"I will wait for it to sing," she promised. "I respect your wisdom and know you will do what is best for all. But I hope you will bring the blanket and the flute. I would enjoy your company."

When she turned to go, Younger Wolf almost reached out to hold her. He didn't, though. Instead he stepped to the river, stripped himself, and joined the swimmers.

Younger Wolf devoted his days to making ready for the buffalo hunt. He crafted a good elk rib saddle for Arrow Dancer, who would come along to hold horses, and he showed other young men how to mark their arrows or identify sign. But in the evening, when the sun hung low in the western sky, his eyes drifted across the camp to Marsh Frog's lodge. Soon they settled on Hoop Woman, sitting by her father's cook fire, waiting.

"Go to her," Otter Skin urged. "You would be welcome."

"She's pretty," Arrow Dancer argued. "She would be a good wife."

"See how she watches you," Stone Wolf said. "Her heart is full of affection and respect for you. A husband can ask for nothing more."

"She's a girl," Younger Wolf insisted. "Little older than your son."

"She'll marry soon," Stone Wolf said, studying his brother's eyes. "Her father's a poor man with too many children. He needs a son-in-law's help. Long I walked the world without a woman's softness beside me. Now I've brought Dove Woman to my lodge, and the world is warmer. I am reborn. It's time you tasted such sweetness, See' was' sin mit."

"Ah, but Dove Woman was older, with a son half grown. Once you took a young woman to your lodge, and she brought only death and sadness to you."

"She bore me sons," Stone Wolf argued.

"And brought disgrace. This girl would be drawn to younger men, and my brothers would see me for the old fool I have become. When my hair is white, and my legs are bent with old age, she'll be young yet."

"Don't judge all women by Star Eyes," Stone Wolf said, referring to the wife who had deserted him for a white trader. "I've heard of how you scolded Mud Turtle in the council. As you warned him not to see their mother's faithlessness in her sons, don't see Star Eyes in every girl. Hoop Woman was reared among the People, and her family has a good reputation. Her own mother was a young girl when Marsh Frog took her to his lodge. You must make the choice, See' was' sin mit, but what harm can it bring you to play a flute and walk the river with a woman?"

"None," Younger Wolf confessed.

"Then instead of gazing across the camp at her, take up the flute and carry a blanket to Marsh Frog's lodge."

Younger Wolf paused to glance at her once more. Hoop Woman's eyes were waiting, and for a moment she fixed him with a pleading gaze.

"Go," Stone Wolf urged.

"What can it hurt?" Arrow Dancer added as he set a buffalo hide at his uncle's feet and passed over a courting flute. "She's pretty. If you don't go soon, I'll take her a flute myself."

Younger Wolf laughed at the twelve-year-old's grin, but he accepted the flute. Slowly, with great uneasiness, the Wolf draped the hide over one shoulder and started across the camp circle. Twice he halted. But an unspoken invitation flowed out of her laughing eyes, and he quickened his pace.

"Ah, it's good you've come," Marsh Frog said when Younger Wolf arrived. "You can sit here, by my good fire. Later you will walk the river?"

"Perhaps," Younger Wolf replied.

"Yes," Hoop Woman assured her father.

Younger Wolf then accepted a cup of sumac tea and took his place beside Hoop Woman. She wrapped the warm hide around them, and Younger Wolf played an old courtship song on his flute.

"I'm glad you came to me," she whispered as she slid closer. "I thought maybe you wouldn't."

"I'm too old for you," he muttered.

"Would you do me the favor of giving me some young fool like Fire Hawk for a husband?" she asked. "It's a great honor to be courted by a proven fighter. You're a chief now. Can I know greater esteem?"

"There are good young men, too," he said, sighing. "Dancing Lance will soon take a wife."

"Ah," she said, laughing. "He's a good fighter, too,

and one day will perhaps be a chief. He's also my cousin."

"Then you must consider another."

"I have," she said, taking his hands in her own. "You suggest others with your words, Younger Wolf, but your eyes grow warm whenever I look at you. Mine also. I don't feel that way when others are near."

"I see admiration in the eyes of your brothers, too," he remarked.

"It's different," she told him. "I long to be with you, to hold myself close, to be part of you. I know you fear I would tire of you, but there is no faithlessness in my family. I would always stay at your side, giving you tall sons to walk the sacred path. You would complete me, and I would want no one else."

"You don't know me," Younger Wolf whispered.

"I think I do," she objected. "Maybe I know you better than you know yourself. Walk the river with me now. There's no need to decide this night."

"No," he agreed. "And a walk would be pleasant."

Five

For the first time Younger Wolf rode to the buffalo hunt as a chief of the People. In addition to his duties as leader of the Fox warriors, he now bore the additional burden of looking after all the Rope Men, especially the young ones who were setting out after Bull Buffalo the first time.

Looking over the hunters, Younger Wolf sighed. So many were young. It seemed the prairie winds hurried them onto man's road. Boys as young as ten carried killing lances where once they would have been content to hold a father's extra pony or assist in the butchering. Disease and battle had taken a toll, for each boy was needed.

"I should go with the hunters, Uncle," Arrow Dancer declared when he gazed at the others. "I can pull a man's bow, and I'm a much better rider than Owl Foot or Rattle Boy. Let them hold the horses."

"Yes, you are growing," Younger Wolf admitted. "It would be a comfort to have you alongside, running Bull Buffalo. There are seasons, though, to a man's life, just as there are in the great hoop that makes up our world. Can you pluck chokecherries under the hard face moon?"

"No," Arrow Dancer answered. "They ripen in summer."

"Exactly so. Each thing must be done in its own time," the Wolf explained. "You'll ride to the hunt soon, but not this summer. Be patient. Watch. Learn. Grow."

"But the others . . ."

"Have no uncle to bring meat to their lodge," Younger Wolf observed. "A grandfather can help with many things, but old men are a hazard on the hunt. Can Running Horse endure such an ordeal? No. So Owl Foot goes in his grandfather's place."

"He has cousins," Arrow Dancer argued.

"Many of them smaller. It's right he should come, even if it's too much to ask a boy so small to make a kill."

"Then will his family go hungry?"

"Not so long as there are chiefs among the Tsis tsis tas," Younger Wolf said, grinning at his nephew. "It's for those who consider themselves men of the People to provide for everyone. You, too, will share your kill when you're older. It's the way of our family to stand tall. We'll always help those who need it."

"She who was once my mother spoke hard against giving up our meat," the boy said, staring sadly at the earth.

"Ah," Younger Wolf whispered, recalling the greedy habits of Star Eyes, Stone Wolf's unfaithful wife. "What does Dove Woman say?"

"She's of the People," Arrow Dancer declared, brightening. "She and Porcupine, my brother, knew hunger. She understands the need to share."

"Man Above provides enough for all," Younger Wolf explained, motioning toward the wide world all around them. "Bull Buffalo gives himself to us that we may grow strong, but the arrows of a greedy man will never find their target. We must walk the sacred path, Nephew, respecting the old ways. So long as we fill our camp with harmony and respect the earth, our needs will be satisfied."

Perhaps Arrow Dancer didn't understand it completely, but he nevertheless nodded his agreement. Others studied their chief with curious smiles as he disdained the fine rifles carried by many and took up instead a weathered bow of green ash blackened in the ashes of a fire. Younger Wolf carried a quiver of stone-pointed arrows, and he had forsaken his finest clothes for the simplest of buckskin breechclouts. Otherwise he was bare.

"It's his medicine," Stone Wolf had told the young men. "There is no hiding what a man is from the Great Mystery. Man Above sees and understands everything."

"But why carry such useless arrows?" a boy had asked.

"These arrows are of the earth," Stone Wolf had explained. "They don't rely on the white man's iron for points. They test the skill of a hunter, but a man with true aim can kill with them. Bull Buffalo accepts the point of a brave heart and gives himself up to us. Many times I've watched a bull hit by many bullets continue to run."

Younger Wolf relied on more than the medicine of his arrows and simple dress to bring success to the Hev a tan iu hunters, though. He insisted the old ceremonies be performed, and that Stone Wolf invoke the aid of the spirits. Even before the first band of scouts departed, the men gathered to make medicine prayers and purify themselves for the sacred undertaking. A sweat lodge was erected, and even the pony boys entered. The dry heat and the ancient purification prayers drove all inharmonious notions from the hunters and allowed them to set out reborn.

As for the hunt itself, the different soldier societies organized themselves in bands and scoured the country in search of sign. Each band chose young men to ride ahead in search of Bull Buffalo, and once the first animals were located, other riders set off to collect the other hunters.

That summer it was Weasel Tail who found the herd. The boy had ridden out with a heavy heart, feeling the weight of his mother's dishonor and his father's abandonment heavy on his shoulders. When he and Broken Bear Tooth raced their ponies to where Wood Snake and Younger Wolf rode at the head of the main band, it was the first time in many days the Tail's face was lit with a smile.

In his excitement, Weasel Tail stammered out a torrent of words, but Younger Wolf made no sense of them. The boy gazed at Broken Bear Tooth with pleading eyes, and the Tooth laughed.

"Uncle, we've found Bull Buffalo," Broken Bear Tooth announced. "It was Weasel Tail who spotted them. He raced his pony toward the trailing bull and counted coup on it with his bow. *Ayyyy!* My brother was first!"

The men howled wildly, and Weasel Tail glowed.

"Where are the buffalo?" Younger Wolf asked.

Again Weasel Tail turned to his companion, and Broken Bear Tooth answered, "On Shell River, near Turkey Wing Butte."

"It's a good place," Wood Snake observed, "but the Crow have camps nearby. We'll send young men to gather the bands."

"We'll send out watchers to warn us if the Crow approach," Younger Wolf added.

"Yes," Wood Snake agreed. "We've had enough trouble with them already."

Younger Wolf then counted off young men to ride in pairs to locate the other bands. He sent ten others to nearby hills where they could watch for approaching enemies. Finally, Younger Wolf led his companions to a rocky slope overlooking the Shell River. There the Foxes made their camp and waited for the rest of the Hev a tan iu to arrive.

It took two days for the young riders to escort the far-flung bands to the Fox camp. Younger Wolf devoted that time to instructing the younger hunters, teaching them the medicine prayers, and admonishing them against rushing ahead of their elders and endangering themselves or others. In the evenings he sat on the ridge with Arrow Dancer, sharing stories or explaining how the hunt would be carried out. Later he chased the boy to the river, and they swam away their weariness in the cooling waters.

Others found the waiting difficult. Fire Hawk, having fallen out of favor with his age-mates, stirred the younger ones with his bold words. He boasted of past exploits and argued that it was time to strike the herd.

"These old men will wait until Bull Buffalo dies from age," Fire Hawk complained.

"We must perform the ceremonies first," Wood Snake insisted.

"We know the prayers," Fire Hawk snapped. "You only mean to hold us back."

There were murmurs of agreement among the boys, and Fire Hawk grew bolder.

"I remember how you led the young men against the Crow," Broken Bear Tooth said, stepping closer until his nose touched Fire Hawk's chin. "Ah, we all thought you a great fighter, but you only ran after your own glory. Where are your cousins? Dead. You yourself would lie in Crazy Woman's River if we hadn't rescued you."

"Yes," others grumbled, pulling out their quirts. "Be silent or we'll whip you from our camp."

"I would be followed!" Fire Hawk insisted.

"Only by pony boys," Weasel Tail shouted. "And they would soon learn their mistake."

Weasel Tail was a full head shorter than the Hawk, and thin even before his mother had left. Fire Hawk shoved him away, then further enraged the boy by muttering a remark about his mother.

"*Ayyyy!*" Weasel Tail shouted as he sailed through the air. He fell on Fire Hawk like a thunderbolt and rolled him to the edge of a cook fire, pounding him severely about the head and shoulders. It required three men to pry the Tail from his tormenter.

"Enough!" Younger Wolf said, stepping between the two. "Don't anger Bull Buffalo by disturbing the harmony of our camp. Are we quarrelsome old women? No, we're Foxes. You two must take a sweat and cast off your anger."

"Yes, Uncle," Weasel Tail said, respectfully dropping his head.

"I will walk my own path, old man," Fire Hawk muttered. He turned and headed for the horses, glancing back from time to time at those he expected to follow. None did.

"He's a good rider, and a fine rifle shot," Owl Foot observed. "We should call him back."

"He says he struck down four bulls last summer," Rattle Boy added.

"He hit four, but he killed only one," Dancing Lance explained. "He is never more than half of what he boasts, Brother, and often less."

"He would lead you to a bad end," Weasel Tail declared.

"Enough," Younger Wolf said sternly.

The young men grew quiet. For a moment Younger Wolf thought Fire Hawk might abandon his threat and return. Clearly the notion of turning away from the People was a hard one. But the Hawk had more pride than reason, and he stomped off down the hillside, located his horse, and readied it for a long ride. A bit later the sounds of a pony splashing into the river marked Fire Hawk's departure.

Younger Wolf devoted little thought to Fire Hawk. The other warriors began arriving the following morning, and there was too much to do. Ceremonies and prayers were begun, and warriors engaged in the buffalo dance to brave themselves for the hunt. Afterward the chiefs met, split the hunters into smaller bands, and sent criers out to explain their decisions to the others. At the first trace of dawn young men charged from their prepared places on the flanks of the buffalo herd, striking down a few animals and setting the rest rumbling along the river.

"Ayyyy!" one hunter after another screamed as he touched a stricken animal with bow or lance. "I am first."

Others fired rifles or iron-tipped arrows, but Younger Wolf notched a stone-tipped arrow, raced alongside some lumbering bull, and drove the flint point deep under the shoulder and into the bull's vitals. Three times the Wolf shot arrows, and three times a bull fell.

Not everyone met with equal success. Little Owl Foot, who was warned to ride with Thunder Coat, a young man of twenty-five summers, broke away and threw his horse against the side of a wounded bull. The buffalo turned suddenly, goring the horse and gashing Owl Foot's left leg.

"Help me!" the boy screamed as his horse fell,

head forward, and rolled over him. In the dust stirred by two hundred stampeding buffalo, Owl Foot simply disappeared.

"*Ayyyy!*" Younger Wolf shouted. "I'm a Fox. It's the difficult things I must do!" He turned his white-faced pony into the dust and skillfully maneuvered past the charging creatures to where Owl Foot lay struggling to free himself from the body of his slain pony.

"Hurry!" Younger Wolf urged as he fought to keep his own horse under control. All around them buffalo surged. They had begun to circle, and there was little time.

"My leg's caught," Owl Foot explained as he struggled to stand on his other leg. He reached a thin arm up toward his rescuer.

"I have you," Younger Wolf said as he closed his fingers around the boy's wrist. "I'll pull you up." Younger Wolf gave a mighty pull and the boy gave a yelp as his leg tore its way free.

"Wrap your arms around my waist and hold on," Younger Wolf rasped as he kicked his pony into a gallop. From out of the dust and confusion the chief emerged like a phantom, howling and waving his bow in triumph.

"It's a good day for the Foxes!" Wood Snake proclaimed as he hurried his horse alongside. "We thought to have lost a chief, but instead we've regained a brave heart."

"A foolish one, but a brave heart," Younger Wolf agreed, prying the frightened boy's fingers from his back and gazing at a dust-coated face smudged with tears.

"I owe you my life, Uncle," Owl Foot managed to say between shudders. "I was wrong to go ahead."

"You're fortunate," Wood Snake told the youngster. "Many never survive to learn from such a mistake. Instead you will be part of a remembered tale."

"Ah, but there are enough tales already of Younger Wolf's rescues," Broken Bear Tooth argued as he joined them.

"This one is different," Wood Snake said, laughing. "It's not often a hunter rides out to skin Bull Buffalo and instead is peeled himself." Laughter broke out among the braves.

"What?" Owl Foot cried. Only then did he realize that in his struggle to squirm from under his mount he had managed to pull his breechclout free of his belt. Other riders now surrounded the rescued boy, grinning and laughing at the unfortunate one.

"Here," Broken Bear Tooth said, passing over a blanket. "Cover yourself. We'll find you a horse before these old men choke themselves."

"This one's won himself a new name, hasn't he?" Wood Snake cried. "Bare Bottom Boy."

"*Ayyyy!*" the others howled.

Owl Foot hung his head and gladly accepted the pony brought out by Arrow Dancer.

"I told you," the boy whispered to Younger Wolf. "I could ride better."

"He, too, should have stayed with the horses," Younger Wolf declared. "But boys have no patience."

"I can ride with you for a time?" Arrow Dancer asked, grinning with anticipation.

"Yes, but if you charge ahead, Owl Foot won't be the only limping boy in our camp."

The Dancer nodded and nudged his horse alongside that of his uncle. *He is growing taller,* Younger Wolf noted as he rode past the slain bulls. Already the women were busy with the skinning. *There will be no holding him back next summer.*

Well, that was only natural. As a man made his way along man's road, he grew older, and the little ones rose to take his place.

Once the hunt concluded, and the main camp spread out along Shell River, the air filled with the wonderful aroma of smoking meat and sizzling buffalo steaks. Younger Wolf sat beside his brother's cook fire, watching Arrow Dancer boast of his exploits. Porcupine and Crow Boy drank in every word, and their eyes blazed with imagined adventures of their own. Even tiny Dreamer wrapped pudgy arms around the Dancer's leg and cackled a remark.

"He's grown tall riding at your side, See' was' sin mit," Stone Wolf observed.

"It was a comfort, having him so near, Nah nih," Younger Wolf replied.

"The People did well choosing you their chief," Stone Wolf added. "I watched as you brought meat to the old ones. Red Bark Woman brought you a fine shirt as payment for her son's life."

"It's a young man's shirt," Younger Wolf observed. "Arrow Dancer might like it."

"When he's older, Brother. Already he considers himself a blooded warrior, and he's done little other than watch the ponies. A war shirt should be earned."

Younger Wolf nodded. As always, Stone Wolf's judgment was sound. The shirt would wait.

"Uncle, see how well I've put the points on my arrows?" Crow Boy called and Younger Wolf stepped over and sat among the boys. The arrow was quite good, especially for one crafted by a boy of only seven summers. But even as Younger Wolf praised his nephew's craftsmanship, his eyes drifted past the fire to where Hoop Woman stood, holding an elk robe and smiling brightly.

"Go," Dove Woman urged, poking his ribs. "The boys will wait."

"She won't," Arrow Dancer whispered. "Nah' koa's right. Go."

Younger Wolf glanced around as if seeking refuge, but his eyes only met with knowing grins.

"Come along," Hoop Woman finally said. "Bring your flute."

"Here it is," Porcupine said, passing it into Younger Wolf's trembling fingers.

Younger Wolf accepted the flute, and he managed to walk with Hoop Woman to the river in spite of his nephews' giggles.

"I've missed you," she whispered. "My nights have

been long and empty."

"Mine haven't," he answered. "A chief has responsibilities. There's little time for a woman."

"But there's need," she argued. "A man of the People provides for those who are hungry."

"Yes," Younger Wolf agreed. "I've fed many empty bellies."

"There are other hungers," she whispered. "My belly is full, but my heart is in terrible need. As yours is."

"Yes," he confessed, pulling her close. She eased the robe around his shoulders, then slid over beside him. They sat by the river, covered by the robe, for a long time, allowing the silence of the evening to envelop them.

"It wouldn't be the best bargain a woman ever made," Younger Wolf finally said.

"My father will expect four good ponies."

"Then your father would have satisfaction. But you, Hoop Woman, would know mostly sacrifice. The needs of the People would always come first."

"True, but there would be much of you remaining."

"Enough?"

"It will have to be," she said, resting her head on his shoulder. "I've given myself up to you. You'll be my husband, or there will be no one."

He took up the flute and blew a soft melody, and she smiled.

"I can tell my father to expect you?"

"Yes, but four ponies is an unsatisfactory price," he stated flatly.

"You mean to bargain with him?" A pained expression crossed her delicate features.

"I certainly won't have my wife valued so little," he declared. "It must be six at least."

"Younger Wolf, you would have me believe you an old man," she said, laughing. "You're nothing but a boy wearing a chief's feathers. We'll craft a good life, you and I."

"Yes," he agreed. "A better one than I imagined."

Six

Among the Tsis tsis tas, courtships often lasted years. A man would send presents to his prospective wife's family, and the girl's family would then respond in similar fashion. Death and sickness had greatly reduced the bands, though, and a new urgency brought about many marriages with a haste previously unknown.

Younger Wolf felt this new urgency, but he also knew the value of respecting the old ways.

"I have no grandfather or uncle to send to Hoop Woman's family," Younger Wolf told his brother.

"I'll go," Stone Wolf volunteered. "Arrow Dancer can gather the horses."

"Speak to Otter Skin, her brother," Younger Wolf suggested. "Choose six good ponies."

"Six?" Stone Wolf asked, his eyes widening. "Six? For a man who has so long forsworn women, See' was' sin mit, you're certainly valuing this one highly."

"I can't insult a chief's relations," Younger Wolf said, turning his head to avoid his brother's probing eyes.

"Otter Skin will respond to these generous gifts," Stone Wolf noted. "Ah, many a horseless boy will soon be riding. And the feasting! It's good we're hunting Bull Buffalo. We'll all be too fat later."

Indeed, the exchanges of gifts were as Stone Wolf predicted. Rabbit Foot and Sandpiper arrived at the Arrow-keeper's lodge with four good horses and wonderful elk robes. Hoop Woman herself carried a fine war shirt decorated with wonderful bead work.

"My father values his new relations," Rabbit Foot spoke boldly. He was slight of stature, and his voice held no man's sounds, but he stood before the Buffalo Shield with the poise of a blooded warrior.

"I, too," Younger Wolf said as he accepted the shirt.

"It will be good to have an uncle," Sandpiper added.

"As it will be to have more nephews," Younger Wolf agreed.

"Soon we'll have cousins, too," Rabbit Foot whispered.

"Many," Sandpiper agreed, laughing.

Younger Wolf gave the robes to his nephews and offered the horses to those in need.

"You should have kept some," Arrow Dancer declared. "Our herd has grown small, Uncle."

"We should ride north then," Younger Wolf suggested. "If we don't have ponies enough to give away, the Crow will happily provide them."

"It's no time to ride to war," Stone Wolf argued. "Our camp is busy with the butchering, and we can't move fast. The Crow may strike us if angered."

"I'm not Fire Hawk," Younger Wolf replied. "I'll bring no war to our camp. We'll only take a few horses, and we'll strike no pony boys. It's an old game we play with the Crow. They'll take a few of ours, or else rob the Lakotas."

"You'll take me along, won't you?" Arrow Dancer cried eagerly.

"I'll need someone to help with the ponies," Younger Wolf said, nodding. "Rabbit Foot can come, also."

"Two boys?" Stone Wolf asked. "You'll need a reliable man or two."

"Broken Bear Tooth will ride along, and I'll invite Weasel Tail. He could use a good pony."

"Be careful they don't collect too many ponies," Stone Wolf said, laughing. "They may steal your wife."

"She'd be better suited to one of them," Younger Wolf admitted. "But she's chosen me."

"And you, Brother?"

"I've played the flute for her, Nah nih. I'm acting as foolish as a pony boy."

"You've been serious long enough," Stone Wolf declared. "And alone far too long."

"Yes," Younger Wolf agreed. *But that's in the past,* he told himself.

That same evening he carried a pipe to Wood Snake's lodge and invited the chief's nephew and adopted son to follow him to the Crow camps.

"I'll call the Foxes," Wood Snake offered. "Many would follow you."

"I don't intend to make another raid on a Crow

camp," Younger Wolf answered. "No, I'll only run a few ponies. I don't want some big talker racing in to count coup and bring the enemy down on us."

"Then you've chosen well," Wood Snake noted. "Weasel Tail and Broken Bear Tooth will follow your instructions. It will bring them honor."

The two chiefs watched Weasel Tail's eyes glow. That young man needed to feel the esteem of the camp.

"Come," Younger Wolf told the two. "We should smoke and consider our plan."

Both quickly agreed, though when the pipe was lit, they touched their lips to the stem and inhaled very little of the smoke.

"Once before I took it in," Weasel Tail explained afterward. "More than the smoke came out of me."

Broken Bear Tooth laughed at his friend's embarrassment, but admitted he, too, had suffered a similar misfortune.

"You shouldn't swallow the smoke," Younger Wolf advised.

"Ah, you tell us now," Broken Bear Tooth complained. "No one warned us before."

"Some things are best discovered by a man himself," Younger Wolf explained, and then confessed he, too, had undergone an unfortunate encounter with the pipe.

They enjoyed greater success on their ride northward. Only two days passed before Younger Wolf struck the Crow trail, and that same night they drove thirty ponies from the enemy herd. Two startled Crow boys chased them for a time, but they turned back when Younger Wolf made a charge at them, waving his bow and howling out a challenge.

Two wolves echoed the challenge eerily from the nearby ridge, and the stolen horses grew uneasy.

"See how they answer their brother," Broken Bear Tooth told his companions. "It's the wolf medicine that protects us."

"*Ayyyy!*" the boys shouted. "It's good we're led by a man of such power."

Younger Wolf motioned them along. He didn't tell them wolves were prone to howling at the rising moon.

Arrow Dancer led four of the Crow ponies to Marsh Frog's lodge, where Otter Skin accepted them in his father's behalf.

"Enemy horses," the Frog noted. "Your uncle honors my daughter. It's time you summoned your relatives, and we gathered ours. We must feast and dance. I would welcome my new son."

"I'll tell him," Arrow Dancer replied. "It's good he'll have a wife."

But when the boy shared his news, Younger Wolf noticed an unspoken sadness, too.

"My brother knows you'll soon have your own lodge, Uncle," Crow Boy explained. "Soon there will be sons of your own to hunt with. Who then will inspect our arrows?"

"You'll be tall yourselves then," Younger Wolf told them. "My sons will go to their cousins to learn the calls of the birds, the old manners of crafting a bow.

You'll lead them to the river for the morning swims, and they'll hold your ponies when you go to strike the Crow pony herd."

"And who will tell us stories when the winter snows come?" Porcupine asked.

"You'll come to my lodge to hear them," Younger Wolf insisted. "I'm not cut off from you. We'll ride man's road together, hunt Bull Buffalo, and I'll watch you grow tall."

They brightened, but Younger Wolf knew they understood he would no longer be with them in their father's lodge.

"Nothing lasts long," he explained. "As we walk the sacred hoop that is life, we learn many new things. A river that doesn't flow grows foul and dies. Open your eyes and your hearts to see what good will come from this match. You yourselves encouraged it. Hoop Woman is fond of you, and you will be welcome at our fire."

They nodded. Later, when they helped him dress for the wedding feast, he saw they were glad for him, even if their faces betrayed a tinge of personal regret.

The marriage feast was a remembered event. Marsh Frog's many relations came, bringing kettles and clay pots, woven bed mats and good blankets, good pine poles for the brightly-painted lodge erected at an honored place in the camp circle.

Younger Wolf's uncle, Gray Wolf, came with many Lakota relatives. They, too, provided generous gifts to the bride and her family. Men gave away horses and fine clothes to any who needed them, and women brought more and more food until the hungriest child was satisfied.

"It's a wonderful thing, this linking of our families," Gray Wolf observed. His hair was white, and his skin wrinkled. Still, his eyes betrayed memories of his own mating, and his many sons and their wives began the singing. A drummer struck up the beat, and soon the camp reverberated with the wild pounding of dancing feet.

Only then did Younger Wolf have the opportunity to draw Hoop Woman close.

"We should dance," he whispered.

"But not long, Husband," she replied. "I'm eager to share our lodge."

Younger Wolf felt the warmth flow from her into his chest, and he helped her rise. They stood together a moment before separating into the different dancing circles. The Wolf enjoyed the congratulations of his cousins, and he grinned at the younger ones' encouragement.

"She still wears the maiden's belt," Running Antelope noted. "Remember, she must take it off soon."

"Ah, she won't keep you waiting long," Rabbit Foot declared. "She talks of nothing but Younger Wolf. It's you, Cousin, who will be hurried."

"No, it's not something to be rushed like a charging horse," Younger Wolf chided them. "Our hearts are one, and so are our minds. We're truly whole. Our joining will be a consented one."

The younger men scoffed, but their elders nodded. Afterward Younger Wolf received all manner of suggestions, but he simply nodded and walked on. Only Dove Woman's words held any value.

"Follow your heart, Brother," she whispered. "It will tell you what to do. As will her eyes."

Hoop Woman entered the painted lodge while the singing was still loud and strong. Younger Wolf allowed her time to settle herself before following. When he entered, he stood for a time, watching the glow of a small fire dance across her fine features. She sat on an elk robe, bare except for a deerskin dress. The maiden's belt, too, remained.

"I'll remove it," she offered as he sat beside her.

"I won't hurry you," he promised. "I want nothing you can't give with your full heart. Maybe we should lie beside each other and grow comfortable first."

"Some do," she admitted as she loosened the knot and removed the belt. "I'm comfortable enough."

"It wouldn't be truthful to say I didn't hunger for you," he said as he slipped the beaded shirt from his shoulders. He next removed his moccasins and leggings. Finally, as she shyly removed her dress, he bared himself.

"There are so many scars," she whispered as she traced them with her fingers across his bronze chest and leathery flanks.

"You've made no great bargain," he observed. "I have an old man's wounds."

"And a young man's heart."

"Yes," he agreed, grinning as she pulled him closer. "So many nights I've walked alone, imagining how it

74

might be to share myself totally, completely, with a woman. But I've spoken to Dove Woman and others. They warned me to show patience."

"Thirty summers you've walked the earth," she said solemnly. "Isn't that waiting enough?"

"But you're young."

"I'm a woman," she insisted. "And a wife. I will be a good one, Younger Wolf. When my husband needs me, I'll be there."

"And I will always have food for you to eat and good ponies to carry you across the country."

"Will you hold me?" she asked, holding open her arms.

He drew her against him, and they glowed warm, one against the other. Younger Wolf felt the old hollowness flow out of him as he fell back against the soft elk robe. She was atop him, overwhelming him. They rolled to the side, and the drumming and singing outside was forgotten. They were somewhere else, in a world of their own making.

Often before, Younger Wolf had spoken of the wholeness man must know to walk the sacred path. It had been the talking of an ignorant man, he realized. The joy he discovered as he shared that first winter with Hoop Woman was more than he dared to imagine. Afterward he walked with a bolder step, and he rode with new abandon.

"Look how our chief stands tall in the council of forty-four," Wood Snake observed when the bands met following the autumn buffalo hunt.

"Yes," Weasel Tail agreed. "It's more than his

words that carry weight."

Stone Wolf said it best.

"See' was' sin mit," the Arrow-keeper declared, "contentment lends power to your words. Hoop Woman's charms enhance your medicine, and your pony raids make our People rich. Your shield keeps peril from our camp, and your wisdom leads us to put our feet on the sacred path that will bring us bounty."

Even so, Younger Wolf was not Hoop Woman's alone. When he walked through the camp, he was a man of the People, a chief pledged to oversee the welfare of all. If a boy had no arrows, the Wolf crafted some for him. If a woman's husband returned with no meat for her family, Younger Wolf gave her a hump roast or an elk leg.

Often he would sit beside the fire, sharing tales with the young men or preparing them for some undertaking. Younger Wolf devoted long hours to the old and the weak, helping Stone Wolf make medicine cures or bringing warm clothes and hot food.

"We ask much of you," Younger Wolf told his young wife. "You cook and work hides so that I may feed the hungry and clothe the bare. It's hard for a man of the People to grow rich."

"I'm wealthy because I stand tall in your eyes," she declared. "All the other women envy me."

"Do they?" he asked. "Only because they don't see the weariness that torments you. Are you still certain you didn't make a bad bargain?"

"I only regret you're not with me more," she confessed.

He nodded his understanding, and he tried to find more time to pass with her alone. All too often Arrow Dancer, Crow Boy, and Porcupine would appear, though, and their uncle would gather them beside the fire and listen to their stories of hunting rabbits or inspect their arrows.

"You didn't need to send them away," Hoop Woman announced when he ran them to their father's lodge one night that winter.

"They're here too often," he said, sighing. "I know it troubles you. We have so little time without company."

"Maybe," she admitted. "It's wonderful for a man to have nephews, though."

"They're good company."

"Still, a chief must have sons to ride at his side."

"It's a fine thing for him to pass his responsibilities on to one of his blood and temperament. My brother's sons are mine also."

"But the one I'm bringing you will be different." She smiled and held his gaze.

"You're with child?" he cried.

"I've suspected it before, but the grandmothers are certain now. The old ones have touched my belly, and they say it will be a boy."

"Ayyyy!" Younger Wolf howled. "It's a good day for the Rope Men! A brave heart is growing inside Hoop Woman!"

"Younger Wolf will have a son to walk with him along man's road," she said as he held her. "Yes, it's a good day for us."

Seven

The hard-face moons of winter tormented the land that year. Young and old alike suffered from the biting wind and numbing cold. Stone Wolf kept busy making the healing cures, and so Younger Wolf often had charge of his nephews.

Hoop Woman had grown accustomed to the boys, and her own young cousins often visited the painted lodge as well. Dreamer, who was only two, sat at her side and gestured playfully at the older boys.

"Uncle, he's reaching for your bow," Porcupine declared. "He'll be a great hunter like his cousins."

"Oh?" Hoop Woman replied. "What great hunters are these? Surely not the lazy boys who sit around my cook fire and warm themselves. Where are your fathers? Lying about? No, they've gone to find a deer in the thickets."

"More likely telling old men's stories," Rabbit Foot said, grinning.

"Tales of Arapaho women," Sandpiper added, hiding his face.

"We've heard some of them," Rabbit Foot confessed, "but not the best ones."

"I heard that Arapaho women . . ." Arrow Dancer began. Hoop Woman splashed his arm with hot soup, and the boy yelped and hopped away.

"This is no hunter's camp," she scolded them. "Be respectful here."

The boys hung their heads and spoke no more of Arapaho women — at least, not in Hoop Woman's presence.

As for Younger Wolf, he was, indeed, hunting. He was rarely elsewhere. The buffalo hunt had been bountiful, but deep snows had brought many unexpected relatives to the Hev a tan iu camp, and some were in desperate need. Each morning Younger Wolf and Wood Snake led a small band of hunters into the thickets or off into the nearby hills, and most days they returned with a deer or elk. Once they broke apart the ice on Shell River and caught fish in their basket traps.

It was also Younger Wolf's responsibility to maintain harmony in the camp, and so he sometimes spoke with an angry husband or settled a quarrel between young men. Most disputes were easily set aside once food was made available, for hunger fed the fires of anger and envy. The snows also confined the young men and gave them time to make mischief, but Wood Snake dealt with those culprits.

"I warned you my burdens were many," Younger Wolf told Hoop Woman on one of the few occasions they sat alone by the fire.

"My brother, also, is a chief," she noted. "You carry the weight of it more."

"You knew I would," he argued.

"Yes," she agreed. "It's what attracted me. You think of the lonely times I endure, but I obtain satisfaction from my labors as few others do, knowing they allow you to devote yourself to the welfare of the helpless ones."

"Soon you will have other concerns," he said, rubbing her growing belly. "Ah, that will be a day to remember."

"Yes," she agreed. "I think of your son often, especially when Dreamer is in our lodge. I imagine how it will be when our own little one is walking, talking, hunting. He will grow from our love into a man to stand tall among the People, a man like his father."

"I hope he doesn't resemble his father in too many ways," Younger Wolf lamented. "He could be more pleasant to look at and still have courage."

She laughed at the face he made, and they drew closer together.

When the greening moons of spring smiled on the land, Hoop Woman's time was near. Already she was attended by her mother and aunt. Younger Wolf was exiled to the young men's lodge, where he made a poor companion.

"You aren't hatching the child," Broken Bear Tooth complained as Younger Wolf ruined a stone point he was crafting for an arrow. "Calm yourself. Women do this often, and Hoop Woman's well looked after."

"We've made medicine prayers," Weasel Tail added. "Soon you'll climb the hills and invite a dream.

When you return, the little one will already be shattering the night with his birthing cries."

"You're not the first to father a child, after all," Yellow Hand Pony, Wood Snake's younger son, pointed out. "I've got many cousins, and each time an uncle waits on the first one, he goes crazy. If stallions acted as foolishly, we'd tie their feet and drive the madness from them with chanting."

"Maybe we should try that on men," Broken Bear Tooth suggested.

"Not on this one," Weasel Tail advised. "I've seen him fight. We're no match for him."

They laughed and continued their jesting. Younger Wolf retired to his place by the door and tried to concentrate on the arrow. It was hopeless, though. His heart was with Hoop Woman, as were his thoughts.

It wasn't long thereafter that Arrow Dancer appeared with the white-faced stallion.

"Uncle, Ne' hyo is waiting for us," the boy explained. "He's gone to make the birth prayers, and he's sent me to bring you along."

"It's nearly time then," Younger Wolf observed. "My brother went ahead?"

"He wished to seek his own dream," Arrow Dancer explained nervously. "His sleep has been troubled."

"How so?"

"He wakes, crying," Arrow Dancer explained. "He hasn't spoken of it, not even to Nah' koa, but he decided to invite a dream."

81

"It's for a father to do that," Younger Wolf growled. "He was to come and assist me."

"I'll tend you both," the Dancer boasted.

"You're young to watch," Younger Wolf objected.

"Dancing Lance will guard us," the boy explained. "I'm only going to tend the horses, feed the fire, and provide food if it's desired."

Younger Wolf nodded. He understood all but the need of his brother to seek a dream just now. Stone Wolf might consult Mahuts or wait until the child was born. The sudden urgency made Younger Wolf oddly uneasy. There was nothing to be done about it, though. He mounted the horse and followed his nephew along the Shell River to a low ridge. Smoke curled from the slope above, and the two riders directed their horses there.

When they arrived, Younger Wolf discovered Stone Wolf sitting on a buffalo hide, painting his face and chest. For the first time since Mahuts were lost to the Pawnee four long years before, Stone Wolf was dabbing his chest with white horn powder.

"Something is wrong," Younger Wolf said as he dismounted.

"Perhaps," Stone Wolf confessed. "Perhaps not. I'll invite a dream and find the answer."

"Is it the child?"

"The dream will tell me," Stone Wolf said solemnly. "It's for me to worry. You must make the prayers, smoke, and find your son a name. Ah, he'll be a brave heart!"

"Yes," Younger Wolf agreed, calmed by his brother's confident manner. "I've envied you, Nah nih, your four sons."

"They're my heart," Stone Wolf said, smiling toward Arrow Dancer. "But they're your sons, too, See' was' sin mit. You've helped to shape them."

"It's true," Arrow Dancer agreed. "Now, Uncle, I'll build up the fire and prepare the pipe."

He's learned from his father, too, Younger Wolf thought as he watched the boy draw tobacco from a pouch and stuff the bowl of a delicately carved pipe. *Strange he should help me with the birthing dream. I aided his father the night he came into the world. The sacred hoop of life truly continues.*

Younger Wolf performed the pipe ceremony, invoking the attentions of the spirits of earth, sky, and the cardinal directions. Afterward he made the required prayers, stripped himself, and danced beside the fire. As his brother had shown him many times, Younger Wolf cut the flesh of his chest and arms, allowing the blood to flow warmly across his flesh. But as he danced and sang, he grew only weary. No image flooded his mind. Even when he collapsed in a fever, he saw only the painted lodge, Hoop Woman, and other familiar things.

He awoke in a sweat. Arrow Dancer was beside him, draping an elk robe over his uncle's shivering shoulders. Across the fire Broken Bear Tooth stood solemnly, holding a horse ready.

"What's happened?" Younger Wolf cried. "Where's my brother?"

"Gone to the camp already," Arrow Dancer explained. "Uncle, Hoop Woman's time has come. You should go."

83

"I must dance more," Younger Wolf argued. "I've had no dream. My son needs a name."

"You must come now," Broken Bear Tooth demanded. "You're needed."

"Here!" Younger Wolf insisted.

"Does a chief deny the needs of his People, then?" the Tooth asked.

"No," Younger Wolf answered. A frown filled his face, and a hollowness spread within himself. Nevertheless he dressed himself and accompanied Broken Bear Tooth to the camp. Younger Wolf inquired three times concerning the crisis making necessary his return, but Broken Bear Tooth refused to reply.

"It's for others to say," the young man explained. "My uncle is waiting for us."

In truth, most of the camp was waiting. Younger Wolf read their grave faces and grew cold.

"Stone Wolf?" he asked. "My brother is well?"

"He is," Stone Wolf answered, breaking apart the crowd and motioning his brother off the horse. "Come, we must walk."

"Should we mount a guard first?" Younger Wolf cried. "Wood Snake?"

"I'll watch the camp," the Snake promised.

"Your dream was answered," Younger Wolf observed. "You saw something?"

"And you didn't," Stone Wolf muttered. "I'm right?"

"Yes," Younger Wolf admitted. "What does it mean, *Nah nih?* What's happened?"

"Great misfortune," Stone Wolf said, gripping his brother's arms. "Terrible calamity."

"Death?"

"Yes," Stone Wolf said, shuddering.

"It must be a great man to have the camp so alarmed!"

"No, a great hope, See' was' sin mit," Stone Wolf replied. "You wonder why no name came to you. It's because you had no need. The son who would have ridden at your side is dead."

"No!" Younger Wolf screamed.

"He was small to come into the light," Stone Wolf said, swallowing hard. "He appeared to look around, breathed once, and then closed his eyes and began the long climb up Hanging Road. I made the proper prayers."

"Ayyyy!" Younger Wolf screamed, tearing his shirt. "My son is dead."

"The whole camp mourns him already. It's hard news, but you are young."

"Am I?" Younger Wolf asked. "I feel old."

"It will pass. I lost my daughter. It's hard, giving up one's heart, but I pray Dawn Dancer waits to help the little one make his hard climb."

"They'll keep each other warm," Younger Wolf said, breaking loose from his brother and dropping his face into his trembling hands. "And Hoop Woman? Is she bleeding?"

"She's well," Stone Wolf assured his brother. "Young and strong. She'll give you other children."

"Her heart must be broken."

"Yes, but she is even sadder for you. Be strong, Brother. Help her put the sadness behind her."

"Is such a thing possible?"

"If it is, my brother will do it," Stone Wolf declared. "He's always done the difficult things."

"Yes," Younger Wolf agreed. But he doubted any had been as hard as the task before him.

He made his way slowly through the camp, nodding as men and women offered words of comfort and consolation. He found Arrow Dancer watching his younger brothers. The three older boys reached out to touch their uncle's hand as he passed.

"Courage, Uncle," Porcupine whispered.

Younger Wolf noted the boys, too, had torn their clothes, and Arrow Dancer had slashed his chest.

"Nothing lives long," Younger Wolf managed to tell them. The rest he couldn't speak. Even the smallest insect lived more than an instant. He hadn't even seen his son alive.

Hoop Woman lay on a bed of buffalo hides in the brightly painted lodge. Her mother and aunt sat beside her, but when Younger Wolf arrived, they slipped past him and left them alone. Hoop Woman stared up with tear-filled eyes. Her hair was cut short, and anguish shrouded her whole being.

"He was too small," she whispered as Younger Wolf gripped her hands. "In his hurry to be first, he came out too early."

"No, it was I who hurried," Younger Wolf insisted. "You were too young. A thoughtful husband would have been patient."

"I wanted the child as much as you did," she said. "Our People have often known hard times. Well, we have days ahead of us, husband. You'll have your son later."

Younger Wolf sat with her all that night, listening to her sobs and holding her when the shivering was worst. By morning the sadness was beginning to work its way out of them. In its place came the mourning prayers and the burial ceremonies.

Three days all the Rope Men mourned. Many cut off their hair or bled themselves in sympathy. As for the child, he was wrapped in fine elk robes and laid on a rock ledge high above Shell River.

"Our son now walks Hanging Road," Hoop Woman declared when the three days mourning concluded.

"Yes," Younger Wolf agreed, gazing up at the stars sparkling overhead.

"I will want some time to gather strength," she whispered. "But soon we must make another son."

"You're still so young," Younger Wolf pointed out.

"And as impatient as before to be a mother," she declared.

He smiled as the brightness came back to her eyes. And when she was ready, he drew her to him as before.

Many notions tortured Younger Wolf's thoughts in the summer that followed the child's death. Perhaps he was somehow unworthy of Man Above's favor. He was being punished for some shortcoming. If so, he did all that was possible to atone for it. He spoke calmly, considering his words with great care. When among the young men and boys, he practiced new patience. His was a gentle, guiding hand, and he kept his anger in check even when confronted with boasting fools like young Fire Hawk.

"The Crow are everywhere!" Fire Hawk had shouted. "They steal our horses and ruin the buffalo range. *Ayyyy!* Who will ride with me and run them from Shell River?"

Wood Snake and others chided the Hawk, reminding him of his previous failures, but Younger Wolf kept his own council.

"It's not for me to bring disharmony into our camp," he insisted. But when Fire Hawk brought a hundred Crows riding down on the Rope Men, Younger Wolf lifted the Buffalo Shield from its stand and rode out to defend the People.

"Come, brothers," the young men urged. "Follow the Buffalo Shield. Younger Wolf will defend the helpless ones. Who are we to stay behind?"

It was the same story when the People moved south after completing the buffalo hunt. The band moved past Kiowa camps with many good horses, and Younger Wolf organized raiding parties. He himself rode on the wind, darting between enemies, counting coup with his bow and turning the enemy arrows and bullets with his medicine. No name was spoken more often around the soldier fires, and no man was more certain to be consulted when fighting was at hand.

Winter that year, as always, was hard, but Younger Wolf faced it with a new glow in his heart. Hoop Woman's belly was growing again, and the old ones predicted another son.

"This one will be stronger," Hoop Woman vowed.

She allowed others to help her keep the lodge, and she made medicine prayers daily. Younger Wolf prayed and danced and made many giveaways to win the favor of the spirits. And when the time drew near, he again rode with Stone Wolf to the hills and sought a vision.

The dream came this time. Great crowds of dancers encircled a drum, and voices joined in wondrous harmony.

"Here's our young brave heart!" they shouted.

Bull Buffalo and Wolf came to observe. Crane and Eagle flew overhead. All the world seemed eager to celebrate this birth.

When he awoke from his deep sleep, Younger Wolf consulted his brother.

"I saw many creatures, Nah nih," Younger Wolf explained. "What name shall I give my son?"

"What you saw foremost was the dance," Stone Wolf observed. "I saw a similar dream before naming Arrow Dancer. This little one, he should be called Little Dancer."

"It's a good name," Younger Wolf agreed. "We'll give it to him."

When they returned to the camp, Hoop Woman was even then bringing the child into the light.

"You have a son," Marsh Frog informed his son-in-law after receiving the news from his wife.

"*Ayyyy!*" Stone Wolf howled. "It's a good day for the Tsis tsis tas."

Others quickly gathered to celebrate, and Younger Wolf gave many horses away in honor of the newborn. Later, when he held the squirming creature in his arms, he felt himself aglow.

"Look there," Arrow Dancer cried, and all the People gazed in wonder as the heavens were lit by a great fireball.

"Has there ever been such a strong sign?" Stone Wolf asked. "Here's a great man born. A son to my brave heart brother. *Ayyyy!* He'll one day lead the People like his father."

Others echoed the notion, and the boy was held high so all might catch a glimpse of his small, wrinkled face.

"Now I fear it's time I returned him to his mother," Stone Wolf declared. "He remains hers for a time. We others must wait."

The men laughed, and the women nodded their agreement.

"When he's older, we'll teach him to craft arrows the old way," Crow Boy whispered as he accompanied his uncle toward Woman's Lodge. "Even as you showed us, Uncle."

"That would be a good thing," Younger Wolf noted. "It's the way traditions are continued."

The boy grinned, and Younger Wolf lowered the child so his cousin could catch a glimpse.

"He's as ugly as Dreamer," Crow Boy declared, frowning.

"You were much the same," Younger Wolf responded. "Now hurry off and busy yourself elsewhere. I have a son to take to his mother."

Eight

The seasons that followed were good ones for the Tsis tsis tas. In the southern country, where the People had long fought the Kiowas and Snakes, a great council was called by the Apaches. These southern people, who were on good terms with all three tribes, brought a new understanding between the old enemies.

"Other troubles face us," Stone Wolf had argued. "The pale ones are everywhere. We who are similar must forge a new bond."

It was difficult, for many warriors recalled the hard fights made against the Kiowas and Snakes, and there was bad blood on the other side as well. Stone Wolf had a strong vision of peace, though, and the Apaches spoke well. Women, too, saw the peace as a good thing, and although they didn't raise their voices in council, they whispered their wisdom in their own lodges. Finally peace was made, and a great exchange of presents took place. Afterward there was a great deal of intermarriage, making it impossible to rekindle the hot blood.

"I can't strike my relations," many said.

"It's good there's peace in the south," Fire Hawk declared. "The Crow await our attentions in the north country."

Younger Wolf and Hoop Woman also enjoyed those years. They knew great fulfillment as Little Dancer took his first steps and sang his first songs. The boy was a whirlwind, scurrying after his older cousins, eagerly joining in their games and sharing those adventures the older boys would permit. The summer after Little Dancer's birth, Hoop Woman bore a daughter, Red Hoop, and the following summer another girl, Little Hoop, came into the world. The girls seemed to brighten the whole earth, and Stone Wolf was particularly pleased.

"I've missed a daughter's singing," he declared. "And the women will welcome someone to help up woman's road."

As for the boys, they only barely tolerated their sisters' attention. They were always prone to pranks, and once Dreamer and Little Dancer achieved some size, they were regularly caught tormenting any female they could find. And, of course, their sisters were forever at hand.

"Come, walk with me," Younger Wolf finally said after Dreamer and Little Dancer painted the girls with honey and rolled them in a pile of prairie hen feathers. "It's time we put your energies to better purpose."

The boys hung their heads and followed as Younger Wolf led the way past the edge of camp and along to the river. When not listening to Trickster, the coyote-minded devil spirit sure to lead a Tsis tsis tas boy astray, the youngsters were models for their age-mates. But even mischief had its limits.

"I've brought you here to share a tale," Younger Wolf said when he reached a rise overlooking the river. "Sit beside me. Listen."

"We will, Uncle," Dreamer promised.

"Is it a war story, Ne' hyo?" Little Dancer asked.

Younger Wolf examined the excitement suddenly flooding the boys' faces. It was impossible to scold them. They were too dear to his heart. Dreamer was only a boy of eight summers, and his serious days lay across many hills. Little Dancer was but five, and scarcely taller than his sisters. Together they often assailed him, taking his arrows, hiding his moccasins, and earning a measure of retribution.

"You've heard the remembered story of Coyote Smile," Younger Wolf began.

"No," the boys whispered. "Tell us."

"Ah, I understand now," he said, drawing them closer. "I've neglected your education."

"No, Ne' hyo, you've taught us everything," Little Dancer objected. "No one makes better arrows, and . . ."

"Enough," Younger Wolf said, chasing a grin from his face. "Listen, and you'll understand."

"We will," Dreamer promised, putting his hand to his cousin's mouth. "Tell us, Uncle."

"Once, long ago, when there were but a few Tsis tsis tas walking the world, there was a boy who was called Coyote Smile," Younger Wolf told them. "He was a clever one, good at boys' games, and always

93

stirring up trouble. He was a torment to his relatives, and a great trial for his parents. Some suggested sending him from the People, cutting him off, but he was young. 'He'll learn,' his father told the others.

"But years passed, and he only learned better tricks. Once he cut the bowstrings of the hunters so that when they found elk and tried to string their bows, it was impossible. Many went hungry. The games were no longer amusing.

" 'It's unfair to accuse Coyote Smile,' his father insisted when the others came to him. 'He's but a boy.' But Coyote Smile had passed his fourteenth summer, and many expected him to join the men. When he didn't, the headmen of the band met. They sent Coyote Smile and his family away.

"It was a hard thing, being cut off from the People, but Coyote Smile didn't take it to heart. Instead he turned his attentions to his brothers and sisters, tormenting them terribly. One night he spied them alone on a high ridge above a river. Howling like a wolf, he crept toward them. In the darkness, his shape appeared monstrous and menacing.

" 'Man Above, protect us!' his sister pleaded. 'Take us away,' a brother cried. Coyote Smile laughed at their fear and continued his game, but Man Above heard the prayer. With a wave of his hand he sent wind to lift the children from Mother Earth. Eagles flew by and took them high up into the heavens.

" 'Now you're safe, children,' Heammawihio assured them. 'Your brother will trouble you no longer.' He gave them torches to hold so that they

94

might see each other and feel safe in the darkness, and they were glad. Man Above saw that it was well, and he left them there. Even now they play the hoop game at night, where you can see them."

"What happened to Coyote Smile?" Dreamer asked anxiously.

"Ah, his poor mother and father grew sick at heart from the loss of their little ones. They took in no food, and shrank to nothing, leaving Coyote Smile alone. It's said by some he himself became a beast. That's why coyote howls at the sky, pleading with his brothers and sisters to return."

"Is it true?" Little Dancer asked.

"Who can say?" his father answered. "I've seen many strange things. I do know the pain of losing a child, though, and it would be a heavy burden to lose one's whole family."

"Ne' hyo, we've been foolish," Little Dancer said.

"Yes," Dreamer agreed. "We understand why you told us this story. These girl cousins follow us when we go to swim in the river, and they hide our clothes. Sometimes when we set rabbit snares in the thickets, they come along and spring our traps. Ahhh! What's to be done?"

"Perhaps my daughters, too, need to hear the tale," Younger Wolf told them. "Certainly Hoop Woman will give them work to keep them busy when you go to hunt rabbits. Nothing is past solving, you see. Give your ears to your advisors, and don't let Trickster lead you from the sacred path."

"We won't," Dreamer vowed.

"No, Ne' hyo, we won't," Little Dancer agreed.

It was not the end of the mischief, but thereafter the boys saved their pranks for age-mates. Sometimes, when the girls were particularly bothersome, a snake would find its way into Red Hoop's bed, but mostly the children got along.

If harmony was restored to his lodge, it wasn't possible to establish it everywhere. From their camps on Crazy Woman's River the Crow made forays against the Tsis tsis tas bands scattered along Shell River. Mostly young men came to steal horses, but sometimes a woman or child was carried off. If a captive was taken, Younger Wolf would call together the Foxes and form a rescue party. Otherwise he argued against punishing the Crow.

"Better to steal back the horses," he said again and again. But Fire Hawk, who had always been hot for war against the Crow, continued to urge the young men to strike a hard blow against the old enemy.

"The Crow are weak," Fire Hawk argued. "Many Lakotas ride the Big Horn country, and the Blackfeet come south. We no longer need fear the Snakes and Kiowas. The Pawnee are nothing. Follow me! Strike down the enemy!"

Few of the younger men recalled the death of Red Woodpecker and Spring Hawk. Fire Hawk spoke of his cousins as if the three had stood side by side and fought a hundred Crows.

"Can I ever forget the Crow carry my father's hair, too?" the Hawk screamed. "Follow me! Join me in this remembered fight."

The young men howled and danced with excitement. Even the respected words of Wood Snake and Younger Wolf failed to stem it.

"Once again Fire Hawk would lead us to a place of death," Wood Snake said as the chiefs met to consider the proposed raid. "Many lodges will be silent, and others will fill with the mourning cries of mothers and sisters."

Thunder Coat, who had taken the place of his grandfather, Tall on the Mountain, saw it otherwise.

"Many summers our warriors have grown fat on buffalo steaks and easy living," the Coat said. "Who has tested himself in a fight? Very few. We can't leave the welfare of our camp or our People in the hands of old men. It's for the young to fight. Fire Hawk's a poor leader. He's short-sighted, and easily fooled. He's right to speak for war, though. How else can the young ones win honor? How will boys find their names?"

"He's right," South Wind agreed. "If the Foxes hold back, there are many Crazy Dogs eager to strike the Crow."

"Younger Wolf, we've often ridden to war together," Thunder Coat said somberly. "I was there when your nephews won their names. Those were remembered deeds, but they're long past now. It's time the People had other coups to celebrate."

"Your son will one day wish to earn a brave heart name," Wood Snake said, frowning. "As my son does."

Younger Wolf frowned. He recalled well how Arrow Dancer had won his grandfather's name, Iron

Wolf. Crow Boy had become Goes Ahead after counting coup on the buffalo herd. Others envied them. Broken Bear Tooth was a man of twenty-one summers, but he still carried his boy name. As for Weasel Tail, he above all others sought to put away the past and embark on man's road.

"We three are agreed," Thunder Coat said, motioning to his companions. "Will you speak against us?"

"I can't," Younger Wolf told them. "I will never disturb the harmony of our camp. Even so, I warn against imprudence. And I urge you to consult Mahuts."

"It's appropriate we do so," Wood Snake agreed. "I'll carry a pipe to Stone Wolf. We need the medicine of the Arrows to blind the enemy."

Younger Wolf watched the war preparations with foreboding. Too often he'd painted his face and tied his horse's tail.

"Stay behind, husband," Hoop Woman counseled. "You're no longer a young man."

"Thirty-seven summers I've watched come and go," he said, considering the question. "I have a young son and two daughters to look after."

"Yes," Hoop Woman agreed.

"I'm a man of the People, though. A chief."

"And a father to all," she added, sighing. "You must go then. To stay would make you a different man."

"Someone must hold the hot bloods in check."

"And rescue those in peril," she noted. "I know you well, you see. It's for you to take the difficult path."

"Young Iron Wolf and Goes Ahead will be with me," he assured her. "Perhaps it's time they rescue their uncle."

"Otter Skin's sons will ride with you, too. Keep all our nephews safe," she urged. "Our family's known pain enough."

"I'll do what a man's capable of," he vowed.

"And more," she whispered. Her face was painted with the same smile that had first stolen his heart, and he warmed to see it.

"I would rather stay with you," he told her, "than walk on the wind. But I have to go."

She held onto his arm a moment, then passed into his hands the beaded shirt he'd worn at their wedding feast. Both knew he wouldn't wear it, for Younger Wolf's medicine grew from his modest manner. Still, it warmed him to have it along.

Fire Hawk thought to lead the raid, but Thunder Coat and Wood Snake took charge of the Foxes, and South Wind led the Crazy Dogs. They left camp amid a chorus of shouts and boasts, but once they turned north, silence reigned over the broken country. That scarred country concealed a hundred places perfect for ambushing an enemy, and each was known to the Crow.

Younger Wolf trailed along behind in the beginning, as was his custom. He encouraged the younger men by holding the Buffalo Shield up for them to see, and he exchanged jests with the boys. Later, though, he urged the buckskin pony that had replaced the white-faced stallion as his favorite war horse into a gallop. He passed through the main body and joined the scouts.

"It's for us to go ahead, Uncle," Goes Ahead complained when Younger Wolf pulled even with them.

"Did you think you could leave me to chew your dust?" he asked, laughing. "My brother, the Arrow-keeper, warned of danger from a three-pointed lance. You have the energy and keen eyes to see everything, but I have the experience to recognize peril."

"Then ride with us," Broken Bear Tooth called. "Help me win a name."

I will if I can, Younger Wolf promised silently. *If not I'll shield you from harm.*

They were two days riding north before happening upon the tracks of ten unshod ponies in the mud of a river crossing.

"Wild ponies maybe," Goes Ahead observed. "Too few for a war party."

"Hunters perhaps," Younger Wolf said, sliding off his horse and examining the tracks with care. "These here, eight of them, cut deep into the ground. They carried men. Boys maybe. The load wasn't a heavy one. The other two . . . maybe spares. Young men off to hunt or steal horses."

"We'll kill them easily," Fire Hawk boasted.

"You'd find great honor killing them, would you?" Wood Snake growled. "Better to steal their horses and whip them back to their camp."

"A live Crow is a breathing enemy," Fire Hawk

100

argued. "These may be boys, but Younger Wolf could be wrong. Even if he's not, they won't stay young. I was a boy of few summers when the Crow killed my father. They didn't think much of me then, but look now. Before they would have had an easy time. Now they'll suffer greatly at my hands."

"We all recall how you ran the Crow before," Dancing Lance said, laughing. "It's easy to talk. When we face the Crow, we'll see who stands with his brothers and who runs."

"Enough!" Thunder Coat demanded. "We have enemies enough without making new ones among ourselves. Scouts, ride ahead and strike their trail. Tell us what force they have. We'll make camp and paint ourselves."

"Yes," Younger Wolf agreed. "We should dance and pray. Keep only small fires. Remain watchful."

The warriors nodded. Young men nudged their horses into the river and prepared to seek out the Crow. Younger Wolf remained behind now. His help would be of greater use crafting medicine charms and instructing the young ones. Goes Ahead and Iron Wolf could follow a trail well enough, and Broken Bear Tooth would lead them.

Nine

The scouts did not return before nightfall, and many of the younger men gathered beside small fires and stirred each other's courage. Already elk tooth and bear claw charms decorated their hair, and they'd chosen what markings to paint upon their bodies. Now all that remained was the waiting.

Younger Wolf deemed that the hardest part of warrior's road. In all a man's life there were few moments of personal combat, and even fewer tests of his courage. More often he fought off attackers from his camp or charged with the others of his soldier society, shouting and whooping so that the noise drove the fear from a man's heart.

"Men are all fools," he once told young Iron Wolf. "What is there to fear? Death? It's nothing but a long walk to the other side. Old friends wait there to cheer us. We all walk Hanging Road in time. No man chooses the moment. Man Above decides."

Nevertheless he had difficulty finding sleep that night. His dreams were tormented with visions of past battles, and his stomach revolted at the smell of death.

"Uncle, what is it?" Sandpiper asked as he stirred Younger Wolf to consciousness. "What is it you've seen?"

"Death," he whispered, studying the young man's thoughtful eyes. Sandpiper had hunted buffalo and stolen ponies, but he looked far too young to ride to war. Seventeen snows he'd walked the earth.

"Uncle, the scouts have returned," Sandpiper added. "They've discovered a great camp with many good horses to take."

"That's good," Younger Wolf said, shaking off a chill left by the cold ground.

"I'll capture many," Sandpiper boasted. "Then I can win a brave name like my brother, Two Moon, and take a wife."

"I never knew you to take a flute to the river," Younger Wolf said, smiling as he dressed himself.

"Not everyone's content to wait until he's an old man," the boy said, grinning. "Of course, I will have to look hard to find anyone as pretty as Hoop Woman."

"But you've looked?"

"Yes," Sandpiper admitted. "Often."

Younger Wolf laughed to himself as he headed toward a nearby fire. Goes Ahead was gesturing wildly, and although Younger Wolf was too far away to pick out the words, he read enough of the gestures to know the scouts had located the Crow.

"Ah, our brother has joined us," Fire Hawk said sarcastically when Younger Wolf joined Thunder Coat and Wood Snake beside the fire. "He who rides behind can follow us to war."

"It's not war we're talking of," Wood Snake objected. "These ponies will make us all rich. Without them, what harm can the Crow be?"

"We didn't come here to steal horses," Fire Hawk argued. "We have boys among us eager to prove themselves."

"Young fool, sit in silence and listen to your elders," the Snake scolded. "I carried the pipe to Mahuts, and I pledged to keep safe those who followed me. The greatest honor obtained by a war party is the safe return of all to their lodges. The obligation of a leader is to insure no one is placed at risk. You heard the scouts speak of three great camps. Hundreds of warriors. We can't fight so many and remain unhurt."

"Old men's words," Fire Hawk muttered. "Stone Wolf has dreamed of a battle, and so have I. I'll count coup on my old enemies and avenge my father. If you others will not lead, I will. And there are many eager to follow Fire Hawk!"

"Three camps?" Younger Wolf asked. "How many lodges in each?"

"A hundred, maybe more," Goes Ahead explained. "I saw mostly women, little ones in the first."

"What of the others?" Wood Snake asked.

"I counted twenty armed men in the second," Broken Bear Tooth told them. "Each had a good rifle. They would give us a hard fight."

"The third?" Younger Wolf asked. "What did you see there?"

"Many men," Goes Ahead told them. "A tall man dressed in fine clothes, wearing a bonnet of twenty eagle feathers."

"It's the one you fought before," Broken Bear Tooth noted. "When the Crow chased us from Crazy Woman's River."

"I saw him at the fort on Shell River," Weasel Tail said, warming his hands. "Liver Eater, he's called. It's said he eats his enemies."

"I've heard of him," Wood Snake said, frowning. "He ran the Lakotas in the Big Horn country. He carries pieces of those he kills in his medicine bundle. Ears and finger bones."

"We should kill this Crow," Fire Hawk urged.

"Now I understand my dream," Younger Wolf said, glancing away from them.

"What did you see, Uncle?" Goes Ahead asked.

"A bird eating our bones," Younger Wolf replied. "A crow."

"It's a bad sign," Wood Snake lamented. "We should take the ponies and go."

"Run from the enemy?" an outraged Fire Hawk cried.

"Return to the helpless ones," Younger Wolf insisted. "Where are the Crows missing from the first camp? They could be on Shell River even now."

As others awoke and joined the council, those eager to strike the Crow a hard blow were quieted by those urging caution.

"We've ridden too far to return with nothing," South Wind declared. "Many Crazy Dogs stayed behind because they had no mounts. We will carry away the pony herd because we must."

"Those horses we take away won't carry Crows to our camp," Thunder Coat added.

"The horses are too near the camps," Wood Snake said, noting the positions as drawn by the scouts in the ashes beside the fire. "They will strike us hard. Their good guns will kill many."

"We are few," Younger Wolf noted, "but the Crow don't know it. If we prepare ourselves and make strong medicine, we can enjoy success."

"Here's the man who has always spoken against fighting the Crow," Wood Snake muttered.

"I have no appetite for killing the helpless ones," Younger Wolf replied. "Cutting down pony boys brings me no honor," he added, gazing grimly at Fire Hawk. "This must be an honorable fight, for as South Wind says, many are afoot."

"How could it be done, though?" Wood Snake asked. "So many horses and so few men."

"We would be like Bull Buffalo," Younger Wolf explained. "The Crazy Dogs would be one horn, and the Foxes would be the other. The young men would occupy the center. They would have the duty of running the horses."

"I intend to fight," Weasel Tail vowed.

"You must follow your path," Younger Wolf replied. "I spoke for the young ones who can race their swift ponies while we old men hold off the pursuers."

The younger ones laughed at that notion, and many eagerly accepted the challenge of running the ponies south. Others chose to join the soldier bands.

"The important thing's to form a line and stay together," Younger Wolf argued. "Together we're powerful, like the branch of an oak. Cut into little slivers, we're useless to each other and to ourselves."

"It's for the chiefs to keep the bands under control," Broken Bear Tooth declared.

"And for all to do as instructed," Wood Snake added. "Is that understood by all?"

Each man nodded solemnly, but Fire Hawk responded with little enthusiasm.

"You shouldn't expect so much of that one," Wood Snake observed. "He hungers for Crow scalps. Some day he will be killed by the enemy. You won't always be able to rescue him."

No, Younger Wolf thought. *Nor anyone else.*

The fighters scattered to their blankets and sought what rest they could manage. The young ones thrashed about in anticipation, while many of their elders shuddered with nightmare recollections of earlier times. Morning found them all weary, and as they dressed themselves for war and painted their faces, a profound seriousness cloaked the camp.

It was Sandpiper who first noticed Fire Hawk was gone.

"I was to ride with him," the young man cried.

"Perhaps he's with the ponies," Broken Bear Tooth said.

"I've been among the horses," Thunder Coat grumbled. "Only the pony boys are there. No, he's gone."

"And he boasted of striking the enemy," Goes Ahead said sourly. "He's hurried himself home."

"No," Younger Wolf said, frowning. "There's no one waiting to warm him there. He's gone ahead to strike the Crow camps."

"He'll foul the plan," Wood Snake observed.

"And bring down the Crow on us," Thunder Coat declared. "Complete your preparations, Brothers. We must make a count and see how many have followed Fire Hawk."

"Yes," South Wind agreed. As he formed the Crazy

Dogs, Wood Snake and Thunder Coat collected the Foxes. In all, eleven were missing from the two soldier bands—most of them young, untried men.

"What's to be done?" Thunder Coat asked, turning to Younger Wolf.

"We may still succeed," Younger Wolf said, "but we must be prepared for surprises. It's important to run the Crow ponies as before, but now we're certain to have a hard fight."

"How many times must a good plan be ruined by some boy who rushes ahead?" Wood Snake cried.

Or by a man with a heart darkened by hate, Younger Wolf thought.

Some few turned away and rode south, claiming the medicine was spoiled, but most followed their chiefs. Thunder Coat, Wood Snake, and Younger Wolf led the Foxes. Their Buffalo Shields flashed brightly in the morning sunlight, and even the pony boys braved seeing such strong medicine.

As planned, the horns of the buffalo galloped between the horses and the camps, allowing the pony boys to chase the Crow guards and run the horses south. That was all that went as planned. The first Crow camp was already alive with fighting, for Fire Hawk had chosen the nearest and least defended to strike. Nevertheless the Crow had formed a defensive line to allow the helpless ones to escape, and the eleven Tsis tsis tas lacked the weight to break through. Younger Wolf looked on in dismay at the melee. Warriors struck lances against rifles or wrestled in the dust. No one managed much progress.

"Shall we strike the camp?" Wood Snake asked, waving at the Crow's exposed flank.

"We have other perils to attend," Younger Wolf answered, pointing to his right where the Crazy Dogs were struggling to drive a large band of Crows back toward their camp. Another group was assembling at the second camp, and they would fall upon the Crazy Dogs also if not stopped.

"We're too few," Wood Snake lamented.

"My brother rides with Fire Hawk," Thunder Coat said, bitterly eyeing the dust and confusion ahead. "I'll break these Crows and rally our fighters."

"Yes," Younger Wolf agreed. "The Snake and I will stop the enemy from surrounding the Crazy Dogs."

Thunder Coat then counted off ten men and led them to the left. Wood Snake held up his stringless bow and waved the rest toward the second Crow camp.

"*Ayyyy!*" the Snake howled. "We're Foxes!"

"Ours are the difficult tasks!" the others added.

Younger Wolf saw little of the Fire Hawk fight, nor did he note the fierce struggle of the Crazy Dogs on the right. His eyes searched the approaching column of warriors for Liver Eater. He rode third in line, his face painted yellow as before. The bonnet of many feathers crowned his head, and a wolf's foot was painted black where Younger Wolf had struck his chest.

"Courage!" Thunder Coat shouted, and the men beat their bows against their hips. The noise unsettled the approaching enemy and stirred the blood of the Tsis tsis tas.

"Fight in pairs," Wood Snake advised. "Never let your brother be struck unawares."

"We can shoot them with our arrows," Broken Bear

Tooth observed. "Shall we strike them, Uncle?"

"Their rifles would answer," Wood Snake pointed out. "These are Crow warriors. They will fight us man to man as honored enemies."

Thunder Coat then spread the fighters out across the crown of a low ridge. Below, the Crow assembled likewise. Soon each man eyed a particular enemy. Large men confronted large men, and boys faced boys. Younger Wolf studied the furious eyes of Liver Eater, the old enemy.

"Hah!" Liver Eater finally shouted. "Dog people! You came to fight old women and toothless old men. See who's met you!"

The Crow howled, and their emboldened chief rode out, dismounted, and bared his backside at the enemy.

"I wait for you, dog's offspring," Liver Eater screamed. "Fight me or run and hide among your women!"

Younger Wolf laughed. Where had the Eater learned so much of the People's language?

"We fought before," Younger Wolf replied as he nudged the buckskin into a trot. "I see you remember it well."

Liver Eater touched the wolf symbol, then discarded his rifle. In its place he held a war lance.

"Yes, it's good we fight in the old way," Younger Wolf agreed as he dismounted, fixed his shield on his left arm, and took a lance in his right. "It's how wars should be fought."

"All that has changed," Liver Eater growled as they circled each other. The other Crow gazed in wonder at the two chiefs, for few of them understood their leader's words. Now there was no time for others. Liver Eater probed with his lance, but Younger Wolf slapped it away. Next the Wolf tried to strike a blow, but Liver Eater dodged the point and deflected a second blow with his shield.

Strange how similar we are, Younger Wolf thought as he battled the Crow chief. *We could be brothers. Instead one of us will suffer today.*

Younger Wolf dared not let his mind wander, though. Even a slight mistake might leave him exposed to Liver Eater's lance, and the powerful Crow needed but a single thrust to kill any man. Younger Wolf danced away from one blow after another, but he could feel himself weaken. His shield arm felt as if it were made of stone, and the lance was not light and quick as before.

"Yahhh!" Liver Eater screamed as he threw himself at Younger Wolf, but the Tsis tsis tas chief managed to turn and avoid the full force of the blow. Even so, the lance bit the flesh of the Wolf's left shoulder, and a second blow opened a gash in Younger Wolf's left thigh.

"Who counts coup this time?" Liver Eater asked. "I'll cut out your heart and feed my pups!" he boasted. "There will be only pieces of you for your sons to mourn!"

Ah, Yellow Face, Younger Wolf said silently as he found new power. *You've let anger disturb your balance. You are beaten.*

Liver Eater pounced again, but this time Younger Wolf met the blows with his shield. His legs bent, but he held firm. And when the Eater lifted his lance to strike a killing blow, Younger Wolf struck instead. The lance gashed the Crow chief's side, pricked his belly and plunged deeply into his hip.

"Ahhh!" Liver Eater exclaimed as he fought to free himself. "Ahhh!"

Younger Wolf turned his lance and withdrew the point. The yellow-faced warrior fell back, dropped his shield, and tried to stem the blood pouring from a severed artery.

"I am first!" Younger Wolf shouted as he touched the flat of his lance point to the Crow's shoulder.

The Tsis tsis tas line thundered in response, and many encouraged their chief to take the dying Crow's hair.

"I'm a modest man," Younger Wolf said, retiring. "I collect no trophies."

Liver Eater managed to regain his feet and stare defiantly at the enemy. He tried to charge Younger Wolf a final time, but his legs gave way and he collapsed.

"*Ayyyy!*" the Crow shouted. Eight of them charged the slope, and others followed. Fierce fighting followed as Tsis tsis tas met Crow in close combat. Men were struck down on both sides. Wood Snake killed his man and drove another from the hillside. Broken Bear Tooth counted three coups, and Weasel Tail won a name by knocking a young Crow down and taking from him a wonderful silver bracelet. He was known thereafter as Silver Arm.

Among Tsis tsis tas and Crow alike the fight was remembered for the killing of Liver Eater, but many young Foxes counted coups, and they celebrated the fight because they attained their man's name. Broken Bear Tooth, who rode home bleeding, became Four

Wounds while Sandpiper, who anchored the line, was forever called Horned Moon.

The triumph of the Tsis tsis tas was not without a high price, though. Many were hurt and others killed. The Crow broke the Crazy Dogs and recovered most of their ponies. Of the ten who followed Fire Hawk into the Crow camp, only three rode home.

"Fire Hawk?" Wood Snake muttered as he rode alongside Younger Wolf. "Kills His Brothers would be a better name."

Ten

The slaying of Liver Eater established Younger Wolf as a man to follow. Ever afterward his footsteps were trailed by a throng of admiring young men, and the councils often recounted his many coups. Younger Wolf turned away from war, though. Instead he devoted his efforts to hunting, to instructing the young men in man's tasks, and to insuring the welfare of all the People.

"See' was' sin mit, our numbers grow with each dying moon," Stone Wolf observed. "It's your doing."

"And yours, Nah nih," Younger Wolf answered. "It's as our grandfather foresaw. Together we brothers will lead the People out of the old dark days and into new, better times."

More and more, however, Stone Wolf's eyes stared off into a misty future, but his lips never shared what he saw. Younger Wolf nevertheless tried with all his being to believe in the People's prosperity. He refused to consider otherwise as he sat with Hoop Woman and the children or rode the hills with his nephews. Tomorrow, after all, belonged to them. It was their destiny that mattered.

The following summer the Rope Men camped on Shell River, not far from the fort the pale people had built. Many Tsis tsis tas traded hides there for powder and lead for their guns, and a band of Lakotas erected lodges nearby.

"It's as Sweet Medicine warned," Stone Wolf observed. "The pale ones build lodges of stone and stay here even when the snows come. They're strange ones. Sometimes I think they're men without hearts to feel. They use women up and throw them away like shattered arrow shafts. Where are the sons they should help to walk man's road? They don't make the morning prayers, and only a few bathe. You can smell them across the country."

Younger Wolf nodded his agreement, but his thoughts drifted to the young white man who had come into the camp of the Rope Men, lived with them, and shared the hunt.

"Yes, they are odd," Younger Wolf told his brother. "But there are some who watch and learn. Our brother, Corn Hair Freneau, speaks our words and walks the world with reverence."

"He's lived with us, and we've smoked and hunted together, but he's still a strange one," Stone Wolf argued. "Once I thought he would teach us about his people, help us to live with them. But they are men apart."

"The young men have seen Corn Hair in the Lakota camps," Younger Wolf said, eyeing the distant outline of the fort.

"My dreams have told me. He'll visit us soon."

"Then maybe he'll teach us."

"We'll speak," Stone Wolf muttered. "Have you forgotten how his son led the wagon people across our country? It's said another boy rides with the bluecoat soldiers. I fear for us all, Brother. Soon a time is coming when strong words and good hearts won't hold much weight. Already we're feathers in a whirlwind."

"Your power will guide us," Younger Wolf boasted.

"Even Mahuts can't guide people with no ears to hear," Stone Wolf grumbled.

"You've had dreams," Younger Wolf said, his face revealing fresh concern. "You must come to our council and tell the chiefs. We should gather and consider what to do."

"Once we would have done it," Stone Wolf said, sighing. "Once the Arrows would have led us from danger. It's too late now. The storm's coming, and we can't run from it."

"Then we'll stand and fight!" Younger Wolf vowed.

"Fight . . . and die," Stone Wolf added.

"The People must survive, Nah nih," Younger Wolf insisted.

"We should never have permitted the pale ones to come into our country. Sweet Medicine was right to warn us, but we didn't listen. Now it is too late."

Younger Wolf stepped away and watched his brother's chin drop onto his chest. Never had Stone Wolf appeared so dispirited, so downcast and hopeless. Nothing Younger Wolf vowed or said raised even a hint of hope.

Marcel Freneau rode into the Rope Men's camp three days later. The yellow hair that had won him a name was thinning in front, and patches in the back were nearly bare, marking him more than ever as a *wihio* — a white man.

116

"My brothers, I'm glad to see you," Freneau announced as he halted his horse beyond the camp. "I've brought many good presents, and my sons are here to share the summer hunting."

"It's good you've come," Younger Wolf declared as he stepped out to greet the trader. "We've wondered where the wind has carried you, and your children have grown tall since they swam Shell River or hunted Bull Buffalo."

"Yes," Freneau noted as he dismounted. With a wave of his hand, he motioned the three young men behind him to climb down and greet their uncle.

Charles led the way. Sixteen, tall and leather-hard, he clasped Younger Wolf's hands with a grip of iron. Louis two years younger, made an awkward bow, but little Tom, eleven, rushed over and threw an arm around Younger Wolf's waist.

"Ayyyy!" the Wolf howled. "It's good your family's come to visit."

"Yes," Freneau agreed, smiling broadly. "I hoped we would be welcome. There's much talk that the Tsis tsis tas are angry, and white men aren't welcome near their camps."

"They've brought mostly trouble," Younger Wolf replied. "But there's time for such matters later. We must collect the young ones and let them visit."

In a short time Younger Wolf summoned Little Dancer, Red Hoop and Little Hoop. The tiny ones accepted gifts and led their cousins to the fire kindled by their mother. Hoop Woman provided food, and Tom eagerly entertained his little cousins with a story.

Charles and Louis soon found their way to the young men's lodge, where Iron Wolf, Goes Ahead, and Porcupine rushed out to renew their kinship. Dreamer, who as

117

a dutiful pony boy was watching the horses, arrived later.

"It's as if we never left," Freneau said when he and Younger Wolf spotted the boys swimming together. "The color of their flesh doesn't matter. They're brothers."

"Are they?" Younger Wolf asked. "You have other sons, and a daughter."

"Mary has gone to St. Louis," Freneau explained. "To school. There's not much future here for a white girl."

"And Peter?"

"You know something of his troubles," Freneau said, frowning. "He thought to make his way scouting, but it didn't rest easy on him, bringing settlers into this country. Most of the people who come west see only what there is to take from the land, and they're blind to the world we've known."

"We saved him from the Lakotas," Younger Wolf reminded Freneau. "They would have killed him for the death he brought."

"I'm grateful, Brother."

"It's said your son rides with the bluecoat soldiers now."

"He does," Freneau confessed, gazing warily into Younger Wolf's eyes. "Not here, though. Far south, in New Orleans."

"And the other one?"

"John," Freneau said, shaking his head. "He, too, has gone to St. Louis. He studies to become a priest, a medicine man."

"It was in his heart before," Younger Wolf recounted. "Is it a hard road, the white man's medicine path?"

"For some," Freneau confessed. "I don't think John

118

will find it so. He was never at ease out here, and his letters say he's found a place to belong."

"I think sometimes that's all any man can hope for."

"Yes," Freneau agreed. "We whites aren't like the Tsis tsis tas. We're cut off, alone. It's what I value most when I'm with you."

"Being cut off accounts for the crazy ways of most *wihio*," Younger Wolf declared. "But you're no crazy man, Corn Hair. Many summers you've ridden Shell River, and seldom have you visited my camp. Why do you come now?"

"Because the world is changing," Freneau explained. "Because my sons won't be young forever."

"The grasses green in summer and turn brown under the hard face moons," Younger Wolf said, laughing. "Nothing stays the same."

"More than that will change," Freneau declared. "You must sense it. Stone Wolf does. His sons swim the river, but he has yet to welcome me. He knows."

"He's had dreams," Younger Wolf explained. "They trouble him."

"I've had no dreams, Younger Wolf, but I'm troubled also. When I ride east to exchange hides for trade goods, I see new villages growing on Shell River. I see soldiers and forts. I hear talk of Oregon, of opening this country to settlement."

Younger Wolf stared blankly. *Oregon?* What did the word mean? And how could the pale ones build forts and villages on Shell River? The Tsis tsis tas traveled that country often, and they'd seen nothing.

"So you see," Freneau said, nervously shifting his weight from one foot to the other, "I've come to warn you. To share this last good time. And to help if I can."

"I don't understand," Younger Wolf said, gazing at the pale blue sky overhead. "There are no clouds there, and yet you talk as if a storm is coming to sweep us all away."

"A storm *is* coming."

Younger Wolf was bewildered. What way was this to talk when visiting a brother's camp? Something unspoken, a terrible truth, flooded Freneau's face, and a sensation of peril crept through the Wolf's heart.

"We must go and talk to Stone Wolf," Younger Wolf declared. "I'll ready a pipe. We can consult Mahuts. The Arrows will guide us."

"Maybe so," Freneau muttered. "I pray they will."

"Come," Younger Wolf urged as he gripped his white brother's wrist and led the way from the river. "There's much to do."

Only very rarely had Stone Wolf surprised his brother. Such was the case when Younger Wolf and Corn Hair Freneau brought the pipe.

"I know what you want to know," Stone Wolf said as he declined the pipe. "This is not an appropriate time. I must begin making preparations for the New Life Lodge. Later we'll talk."

"All we ask is that you consult Mahuts," Younger Wolf said, gripping his brother's hands. "I've entered Arrow Lodge with you a hundred times, Nah nih, and often I've seen you introduce a question to the Arrows. When has it ever required so long a time?"

"Never," Stone Wolf admitted. "It will this time."

"Why?" Younger Wolf demanded.

"Because it's a complicated matter," the Arrow-keeper explained.

"You haven't heard the question yet," Freneau pointed out.

"I have," Stone Wolf told them. "I've seen this very moment in my dreams. Younger Wolf will tell you how I spoke of this visit. Can anyone believe the question a secret? It's in your eyes, Brothers! You want to know the path ahead. To invite such a vision requires greater effort than I can offer now. Later, when New Life Lodge is erected, and the hunt is well begun, I can seek an answer. Not now."

"The danger is near," Freneau insisted.

"But not the answer," Stone Wolf replied. "Later. After New Life Lodge is finished, and the earth is remade."

"It will be as you say," Younger Wolf announced when Freneau started to argue anew. "Come, we'll walk some," he added, leading Freneau aside.

They didn't walk far. Instead Younger Wolf made his way through the camp, collecting his nephews and such other young men as were unoccupied. The Freneau brothers, too, came along.

"Soon it will be time to remake the Earth," he told the young men. "Some of you have danced and sung. I ask someone to step forward now and vow to hang from the pole in New Life Lodge, vowing your blood and pain as a sacrifice so that new power might flow into Mahuts."

"I'll do it," Silver Arm replied eagerly.

"I, too," Goes Ahead added.

"It's a difficult task," Four Wounds noted. "It's for me to do."

"I'll join my brothers," Iron Wolf insisted.

"As I will," Porcupine vowed.

"Is it permitted for me to do, too?" Louis Freneau asked.

"I've heard of this," Charles said, studying his companions soberly. "It's hard. You're young, Louis. I should do it instead."

"Porcupine's only a year older," Louis argued. "And no taller."

"Would we be welcome?" Charles asked Younger Wolf. "We've swum and hunted with the People, but would we be accepted in such a sacred place?"

"It's not for *wihio*," Four Wounds argued.

"Aren't these boys my relations?" Stone Wolf asked, joining them. "Long ago I dreamed of guiding the People through a difficult time. It's a task I couldn't do alone. I was to have help. Perhaps the blood of these *wihio* can bring the spirits close."

"Yes, it's a good thing," Younger Wolf agreed. "Courage, young ones. It's a hard thing you're attempting."

The boys returned Younger Wolf's admonition with solemn eyes.

The New Life Lodge ceremony was a great event in the life of the People. All the ten bands assembled, and their lodge circles dotted the country north of Shell River. There was a wonderful feeling of strength with so many close by, and the dancing and singing renewed Younger Wolf's spirit even as the sacred ceremonies made the earth over.

Of all the sacred rituals, none was more profound than the torture endured by the young men. Each year in fulfillment of vows or to enhance their power, young men entered New Life Lodge. There they would have the skin of their chests pierced and slivers of flint introduced. Rawhide thongs were attached, and the young men would be bound to a sacred cottonwood pole. As they danced and blew on eagle bone whistles, they would try to tear themselves free of their tethers. Blood ran over their chests, and pain tormented their bodies. Often fever would ensue. Most managed to tear themselves free after much suffering, but some, collapsing, would be torn free by helpers or relations.

It was a highly respected undertaking, more so if done by a boy as young as Porcupine or Louis Freneau. Those two young ones were among the last standing, and when they eyed each other, spit out their whistles, and fell back together, screaming, New Earth Lodge exploded with howls. Both broke free, and the moment was celebrated with the giving of many presents.

"It's a great thing, this suffering by the boys," Younger Wolf said afterward, when he and Stone Wolf prepared the medicine prayers that would begin the hunt.

"It shows the pale ones also bleed," Stone Wolf noted. "We've known this."

"It proves Tsis tsis tas and *wihio* can be of similar heart and mind," Younger Wolf added. "All of us respect courage. From respect flows understanding."

"It's not Corn Hair's sons we must kindle this understanding with," Stone Wolf argued. "But I take it as a favorable sign. Soon we'll ride north, you and I, *See' was' sin mit.* We'll journey to Noahvose, where Sweet Medicine first found Mahuts, and where the bones of our grandfather rest. There, where Man Above is closest to the People, we'll make a fire. You'll watch, and I'll pray, even as we did as boys. And if there's knowledge to be found, we'll discover it."

"Nah nih, there are Crows roaming that country, and it would be good to invite some younger men along to watch out for them."

"No, it can only be you and I this time."

"We need the others," Younger Wolf argued. "I'll choose well. No one will ride with us who will spoil the medicine. Even as Mahuts are the heart of the People, you are our eyes. My obligation is to keep the Arrow-keeper safe."

"You will," Stone Wolf assured him. *"See' was' sin mit,* our lives may not prove to be long, but when have we desired such? No, we ask only to walk our path in a sacred manner, and to devote ourselves to the well-being of the People. This journey is the last one we'll make together, I fear. Our paths soon will take us in separate directions. Whatever waits on Noahvose to fill my dreams, I would share it only with my brother. We'll smoke and talk of it. Then we can bring the vision back to the People."

"You ask me to take upon my shoulders a great burden."

"Has it ever been otherwise?" Stone Wolf asked. "You were my watcher when first I accepted the obligation of Arrow-keeper. Then my dreams were clear, and my path straight. I would have it that way again. When we return, I'll leave you to your new obligations as a chief."

"Nah nih, you've seen so much," Younger Wolf noted solemnly. "Once I envied you, but now I see knowledge is a burden, too. I'll do as you ask, and we'll share this time together."

"It's good I have a man I can trust nearby."

Younger Wolf sighed. His fears of an uncertain future were not calmed by the concern etched across his brother's face.

Eleven

As the green grass moon of midsummer glimmered high in the heavens overhead, the Rope Men erected their camp on the broad prairie north of Shell River. The aroma of roasting buffalo filled the air, and even the yapping camp dogs were quiet and content as they gnawed leg bones or chewed rib meat. The hunting had been good. Young boys pranced about the camp, boasting of their exploits and swatting each other with buffalo tails. Yes, it was a fine time for the People.

Younger Wolf busied himself packing meat on the backs of the spare ponies and waiting for his brother to appear. Porcupine and Dreamer stood nearby, holding the other horses. Hoop Woman watched from beside her cook fire, and Younger Wolf read the anxiety in her eyes. He trusted Stone Wolf's decisions above all things, but he'd nevertheless asked Four Wounds and Silver Arm to watch over his family. The nephews would keep an eye on their cousins.

"See' was' sin mit, my preparations are complete," Stone Wolf finally announced.

"Then it's time we left," Younger Wolf replied.

"Ne' hyo, you should wait for morning," Iron Wolf argued. "We could ride with you a time."

"You have other concerns," Stone Wolf told his eldest son. "Continue the hunt. See to the welfare of the People. It's for me and my brother to ride to Noahvose."

"Will you be gone long?" Dreamer asked.

"Who can say?" Stone Wolf answered. "Only Man Above knows such things."

The boys stepped to their father's side and whispered their farewells. Younger Wolf accepted his nephews' warnings and clasped their hands. He'd already spoken to Hoop Woman and the little ones.

"We'll keep the camp safe," Wood Snake vowed as he stepped out from behind the horses. "Find our future in your dreams, Arrow-keeper. Keep him safe, old friend."

Younger Wolf declined the Snake's offer of a new rifle and mounted a young buckskin stallion.

"I have the Buffalo Shield," Younger Wolf explained. "My medicine flows from the old ways."

"Old ways are fine," Wood Snake admitted. "But Crow rifles strike hard and far."

"Crow," Younger Wolf muttered as he nudged his pony to one side so that Stone Wolf could mount the midnight black mare he had grown fond of. "I don't fear them."

"It's never the things you see that kill you," Stone Wolf remarked. "It's the unseen peril we must watch for."

"You should wait for daylight," Iron Wolf again urged.

"Ah, the sun's a friend to the young, but old men know the night," Stone Wolf said, sighing. "Darkness, too, is my brother."

Stone Wolf then kicked his horse into a trot. Younger

Wolf took the ropes tied to the spare horses and eased the buckskin into motion. Soon the brothers were riding north and east—toward the sacred center of the earth, Noahvose.

As journeys are measured, theirs was not a great distance. A man in a hurry could have reached the sacred butte in three days. Stone Wolf took his time, though. Nightly he smoked and prayed, and twice he danced until fatigue overcame his strength. There was a party of Crows to avoid as well. Ten times the sun crossed the sky before Younger Wolf spied Noahvose, and they were yet another threading their way up the ridge.

"We'll camp in the old place," Stone Wolf announced, pointing to a clearing on the side of the butte. Beyond stood the scaffold poles where old Cloud Dancer's body had been laid.

"It's a good place to pray," Younger Wolf observed. "Here Nam shim' began the long climb up Hanging Road."

"Man Above is near," Stone Wolf noted. "Often I've heard the spirits walk here. White Buffalo Cow first came to me here."

"It was she who gave the People the power of the Buffalo Shield. When hunger gripped the helpless ones, she led us to her children and gave them over to make us strong again."

"Maybe she will show us a way to escape the new trouble that's coming," Stone Wolf said as he halted his horse. With some effort he dismounted. A weariness seemed to possess him, and Younger Wolf climbed down and offered him assistance.

"I'll attend to the horses," Younger Wolf said as he helped his brother to a nearby boulder. "Sit here and rest. Later I'll make beds of pine needles where we can rest."

"There can be no resting now," Stone Wolf answered. "Build a fire. Bring me a pipe to prepare. I must smoke and pray."

"There's time after you rest, *Nah nih*," Younger Wolf argued.

"No, bring the pipe. Already the wind's whispering to me."

There had never been any arguing with Stone Wolf. Even when they were boys, he had been the one to decide things. Now the Arrow-keeper appeared old, bent, wearied by years of trial and obligation.

Younger Wolf located a pipe and brought it to his brother. While Stone Wolf prepared the pipe, Younger Wolf kindled a small fire. Then he busied himself unpacking the horses and seeing they had good grass to chew and water to drink.

Two days and two nights they sat by the fire together. Stone Wolf smoked and chanted the old medicine prayers. Younger Wolf heated buffalo strips and fried corn cakes, but Stone Wolf accepted nothing. The fasting hurried the vision, as did the strips of flesh the Arrow-keeper cut from his arms and chest. Fever racked his scarred frame, but he continued to dance and sing. Finally Stone Wolf's legs buckled, and he collapsed beside the fire. Only then did Younger Wolf drape a buffalo robe over his brother's trembling figure.

"Man Above," Younger Wolf prayed, "hurry this

dream. He's no longer a young man with the strength to suffer torture. Give his eyes power to see what lies ahead."

As was his duty, Younger Wolf kept the fire burning brightly. He also walked the ridge, watching the valley below for signs of danger. Once dust curled skyward from a band of horsemen, and Younger Wolf readied his bow, but they were only Lakota boys scouting game.

Of greater concern was the torment suffered by his brother as night draped the mountainside. Even a second buffalo robe failed to chase the chills from the Arrow-keeper. He continued to thrash about, muttering and screaming as if a thousand demons were plaguing his dreams. It was almost more than a brother could bear, but Younger Wolf fought the instinct to disturb the dream. Stone Wolf had suspected its terror, but he had prayed even harder for the vision.

"Help him, Man Above," Younger Wolf again prayed. "Give him peace."

The dream continued its torments. Then the wind stirred. The leaves on the cottonwoods below danced in the breeze, and the tall pines seemed to shiver. Stone Wolf's arms grew still, and his face was flooded by an expression of great calm.

"Thank you," Younger Wolf whispered to the wind. He then stoked the fire and continued his vigil.

Stone Wolf awoke the following morning with the sun. He said little, but he stepped out into the clearing and made the morning prayers.

"You had your dream, Nah nih," Younger Wolf observed afterward.

"The vision came," Stone Wolf confessed. "It requires contemplation. Understanding."

129

"You should eat and drink. Rest."

"Yes, I must recapture my strength. We'll stay here a day. Then we must return to the People."

"It's not long to rest," Younger Wolf noted. "We could—"

"I saw much," Stone Wolf argued. "I must share it. There can be no delaying our return."

Younger Wolf sighed, but he had accompanied his brother on many journeys, and he'd learned not to question Stone Wolf's wisdom. It would be as he decided.

They rode south and west with a sense of real urgency. Younger Wolf tried to slow the pace, to ease the burdens his brother placed on himself and the ponies.

"We and they must endure the pain," Stone Wolf insisted. "We have to return."

"We are returning," Younger Wolf countered. "It would be a good thing to have live ponies to carry us."

"It's not far, See' was' sin mit."

"The camp?" Younger Wolf asked.

"The danger," Stone Wolf explained.

"Tell me of it, Nah nih."

"It's better I save my words for all the chiefs," Stone Wolf said somberly. "They would only trouble you."

They trouble me already, Younger Wolf answered silently. He would say nothing, though, that might increase his brother's burden.

The camp had moved north, following the path of Bull Buffalo, but Younger Wolf had little difficulty striking the trail and leading the way homeward. All the

People rushed out to greet their Arrow-keeper. Men slapped their thighs with bows and howled in celebration while women shouted a welcome. Boys ran alongside the weary ponies, alternately offering to tend the animals and begging news of the journey.

"I've much to say," Stone Wolf told the People. "First I want to rest and take a sweat. Then I'll smoke with the chiefs and speak of what I saw."

"*Ayyyy!*" the young men howled. It was good their medicine chief had returned.

Younger Wolf dismounted and stumbled to where Marcel Freneau stood waiting with the nephews. "See to the animals," he told Iron Wolf. "Gather wood and good stones for the sweat lodge. Your father has no time to spare for delays."

"Yes, Uncle," Iron Wolf nodded, motioning Goes Ahead to the horses before waving for Porcupine to follow him toward a nearby line of cottonwoods.

Younger Wolf spoke a moment with Freneau, greeted friends, asked how the hunting had gone, and hurried to his lodge. Hoop Woman was waiting there, as were the children. Younger Wolf wasted no time drawing them close to him. Hoop Woman's touch was more comfort than a hundred warming fires.

"Come, Husband," she urged, leading him inside the lodge. "Rest. We'll bring you food. You appear tired from your long journey."

"I'll rest," Younger Wolf agreed. "But make my best clothes ready for a council. Soon we'll meet to consider serious matters."

"Ne'. hyo, you've not attended to your shield," Little Dancer observed.

"Go and tell Iron Wolf to bring it here," Younger Wolf

said, sighing. *How could he have forgotten such a matter? The medicine of that shield would be needed if the trouble Stone Wolf had foreseen was coming.*

"There's time later," Hoop Woman argued when Younger Wolf turned back toward the door.

"No, it can't be put off," he explained. "I'll speak the sacred prayers and return it to its stand."

As always she stepped aside and allowed him to walk his own road. Ceremonies couldn't be rushed, but he vowed not to postpone his return to the lodge a second time. Not for anything.

He was glad of that decision, for weeks of riding and solitude had kindled a great need in both of them. Laying with her renewed him as much as the evening passed with Stone Wolf and the nephews later in the sweat lodge.

It required more than a week to assemble the forty-four chiefs on Shell River. Even the swiftest young riders among the Rope Men were two days searching out the scattered bands of the People, and many chiefs needed time to put their camps in order before departing. Nevertheless the council did gather. Younger Wolf spoke briefly of the journey before turning to his brother.

"Stone Wolf has words for us," Younger Wolf explained. "The spirits spoke to him atop Noahvose."

"Ahhh," the chiefs murmured in expectation. They gazed attentively as the Arrow-keeper stood and stepped closer to the fire.

"Brothers, I've seen much," Stone Wolf told them. "Many days the vision has bothered me, and I've tried to make sense of it."

"Tell us," Wood Snake urged.

"I saw myself walking the valleys with White Buffalo Cow where we've camped and hunted these many summers," Stone Wolf explained. "I saw the place where my sons took their first steps, where the old ones climbed Hanging Road, and where we swam as boys."

The chiefs nodded. They, too, remembered those days. Eagerly they awaited Stone Wolf's next remarks. The Arrow-keeper had great difficulty forming words, though, and he paced before the fire, gathering his thoughts. Finally he stopped and stared at each of the chiefs in turn.

"Long ago Sweet Medicine brought Mahuts to the People," Stone Wolf reminded his companions. "He warned of the white people who were coming, and he foretold the arrival of Horse. I've seen many dangers in my life, and I've often found a road around them. This new peril is different."

"What did you see?" Thunder Coat asked.

"As White Buffalo Cow and I walked the valleys," Stone Wolf continued, "a great white flood came from the east. Like grasshoppers in late summer, the *wihio* came, choking the sky with their numbers. Like a monster with an enormous mouth, they swallowed our world. They swept the prairie with their white flames, rubbing out Bull Buffalo, carrying away the trees and the grass, emptying our rivers, striking down first the little ones and finally even the bravest warriors. They stole our hearts with their fine presents and blinded us with their whiskey and false promises. It will be as Sweet Medicine warned, and I see no way to stop it."

"We'll kill all these strange ones," Thunder Coat suggested.

"We'll move our camps," Wood Snake added.

"These are good notions," Stone Wolf admitted, "but what use will they be? We can't kill all the whites — they are too many. How far can a man move? Even the moon and the clouds are no safe refuge from what is coming."

"What can we do then?" Younger Wolf cried.

"Keep ourselves apart," Stone Wolf urged. "Turn away their presents, their strange manners. Discard the new things they've brought us. Keep to the old, sacred path."

"We've heard all this before," Wood Snake observed. "Your medicine forbids you to use the white man rifles, but they are good for hunting. Our enemies use them to kill our young men. It's fine to make stone-tipped arrows, to carry medicine shields, but these good guns kill us anyway. We need them."

"If the whites are so bad, why do you call such a man your brother?" Thunder Coat asked.

"Corn Hair's been long among us," Younger Wolf answered, "but if my brother says we must send him away, it will be that way. His son has hung by the pole and suffered in the old, honored way, but if he must go, he will. But perhaps, he can help us turn the *wihio* away from their foolish practices and save the People."

"I've considered that," Stone Wolf confessed. "He knows us as well as any white man, and he's been among the *wihio* in the east who make up the great bands that are coming."

"The whites are all crazy," South Wind grumbled.

"We should band together with the Lakotas and Arapahoes," Thunder Coat declared. "We'll be many, and we can run them out."

"No," Stone Wolf said, frowning. "We could fight a short time, but the white flood would still sweep us away.

134

Even if we painted the buffalo valleys red with their blood, others would follow and strike us down. My dreams have shown it all, Brothers. We could enjoy some good days, but if we won every battle, we would still find no victory. Other *wihio* would come like coyote in the night and gnaw at us. They would kill the helpless ones in their sleep. They'd run us like antelope and strike us down with their bullets like so many trapped rabbits."

"Would you have us go to them like old women, begging scraps from their kettles?" Thunder Coat asked angrily. "We're not camp dogs! If these are men, we should stand tall and treaty with them. Once we prove ourselves in battle, they'll see us for worthy enemies and respect us."

"A man who doesn't understand you will never truly see you," Stone Wolf argued.

"Nah nih, what do you suggest?" Younger Wolf asked.

"I've told you what I've seen," Stone Wolf explained. "I see no solution. We can die slowly, from spotted sickness and hunger, or we can follow Thunder Coat's advice and make a stand. Maybe they won't be blind to our ways forever."

"It's hard to know the right thing to do," Wood Snake muttered.

"What does Mahuts advise?" Younger Wolf asked.

"The Arrows are silent," Stone Wolf replied. "My dreams only fill with Sweet Medicine's admonition. Too often we've failed to heed his warnings. Perhaps it's too late."

"I have small children," Younger Wolf declared. "I refuse to think their days are shorter than my own. I'll talk with my brother, Corn Hair, and maybe we'll ride to the fort on Shell River. We can go east and speak with the bluecoat soldiers. Every *wihio* can't be crazy!"

"Most are," Thunder Coat lamented. "I've traded with many, and they are all chasing paper money and gold. Their bellies are hungry for food, yes, but their eyes are always on what they can take from another man. How can you talk to such men?"

"I don't know," Younger Wolf confessed. "But I know we must. How can the People live without Bull Buffalo?"

"Go to them, See' was' sin mit," Stone Wolf urged. "But be careful."

"I will take great care," Younger Wolf agreed.

Twelve

Younger Wolf again prepared to leave the camp of the Rope Men. If his heart had been heavy before, it now seemed to have grown into a great pounding stone. Even as he sat beside the cook fire, holding Hoop Woman with one arm and pulling the little ones closer with the other, he envisioned the difficulties of the task which lay ahead. He spoke only a little of the *wihio* tongue, and he understood even less about their strange manners. All his life he had avoided their odd habits. Now he felt the need to know all.

"It will be very hard to leave again so soon," Hoop Woman observed. "But it's good a man of the People rides out to talk to the *wihio*. If Fire Hawk and the other bad hearts go, there will be great trouble and much death. A man with ears willing to hear their words should listen to what they say. My husband is the best choice."

"You know I'd rather stay," he answered.

"I'll tend the little ones while you're away," she promised. "They'll be obedient, won't you, children?"

"We will," Little Dancer spoke for the three of them.

"Soon, Ne' hyo, I'll be tall and strong. Then I'll ride with you when you undertake such difficult tasks."

"That will be a good day, Naha'," Younger Wolf told the boy. "Until then I must rely on my brother, Corn Hair, and his sons."

"He, too, has an understanding heart," Hoop Woman observed. "He'll be a good guide."

Younger Wolf knew it to be the truth, and he welcomed both Marcel and young Tom that next morning when they appeared with ponies packed and eager for the journey.

"Someone has to watch the ponies," Tom said as he greeted Younger Wolf. "Dreamer would have come, too, but he's needed by his brothers."

Younger Wolf nodded. In truth, the child would only make a meeting with the whites more complicated. Tsis tsis tas children were prone to mischief-making, and the *wihio* were rarely as tolerant as their darker-skinned brothers.

More to the point, Younger Wolf had little time for looking after a nephew. There was so much to learn, and each moment as they rode eastward along Shell River, he asked Freneau about the *wihio*.

"It's hard to explain," Freneau said as they splashed across the river, avoiding the children swimming and wrestling nearby. "For you, Younger Wolf, everything is centered. You always understand your place is among the People, within your band and your tribe. Among the whites each man is essentially alone. He has his family, yes, and his home. But it's separate and apart from others. He can choose his leaders if he lives in a town, but he is bound to decisions even if he disagrees with them."

Younger Wolf stared at Freneau, unable to comprehend. If a man didn't agree with a chief, he should leave and strike out with someone of greater merit.

"Then there's the land," Freneau continued. "Here's the heart of the disagreement between the tribes and the Americans. To the great *wihio* chiefs in Washington City, ownership is determined by papers. Whoever holds the paper, saying he owns a place, is entitled to hold the land. He may be faraway, and he might never have stepped onto the ground of that place, but if the paper says it's his, all the power of the *wihio* soldiers and the great councils will support the claim."

"Who makes up these papers?" Younger Wolf demanded. "I've not seen them."

"You remember the story of the time long ago when Cloud Dancer witnessed a giveaway of fine presents. There certain chiefs touched a pen to paper. The words written there said many things. Mostly they gave the Tsis tsis tas lands to own."

"Man Above gave us this good country," Younger Wolf growled. "No *wihio* can say it's ours, or that it's not."

"That's not what the leaders of the whites believe," Freneau explained. "They believe all the land between the great eastern sea and the Shining Mountains is theirs. They grant you the right to live in certain places, but in their hearts they believe they retain the right to decide where you can live and to take back lands if they need them."

"How can they take back what they never had?" Younger Wolf cried.

"I know," Freneau said, laughing. "To you it seems their view has no merit, but to them it's everything. Let me see if I can put it another way. If the Rope Men came to a valley and found a bear living in a cave nearby, they wouldn't bother him. They would consider that the bear had been there before they arrived and will remain after they leave. Only if the bear came among the lodges, threatening the People, would the men string their bows and attack the bear.

"That's how it is with the *wihio*. They ride along Shell River, encountering Pawnee and Lakota, Arapaho and Cheyenne. Tsis tsis tas. They don't bother you so long as you aren't in their way. Only when your camps block the path or your young men take horses is there trouble. Too often, though, the *wihio* don't take into account that you are men, like themselves, and disputes can be settled without bullets."

"It's true," Younger Wolf noted. "They shoot us without concern. They take our belongings. If a bear came to our camp, we would make medicine and try to understand what was disturbing the harmony of his world. We would probably go away, judging we were at fault. These *wihio* are intruders here, but they come as if it's we who are in the wrong. In this way they're mistaken."

"You can share your feelings, show them how they are perceived," Freneau suggested. "Some will close their ears and hear nothing, but many will listen and a few will grow to understand. It's these few we must hope will speak loudly for peace. There are always plenty eager to start a war."

"Yes, among the Tsis tsis tas, too," Younger Wolf confessed.

"If Stone Wolf's right, it will only grow worse," Freneau said, frowning. "And I'm afraid he will be. Men who return east tell of shining mountains and wide rivers, of good land and plentiful game. Talk like that always brings settlers, and it's already happening farther east. The

Pawnee are forced south and west. The Lakotas north-ward."

"It's a bad thing," Younger Wolf grumbled. "Bull Buffalo once fed everyone, but even he needs grass to chew."

"Already he's gone from the woodlands back east. The day he's gone from the Platte, from Shell River, I will have lived too long."

"And the Tsis tsis tas will be no more," Younger Wolf said, sighing.

Such discouraging talk chilled Younger Wolf's spirit, and he would often put an end to it by riding ahead. Freneau would then speak of other matters, or they would make camp and shoot rabbits for their dinner. Other times Tom would fish the river, or the three of them would revive themselves by sharing a late afternoon swim. Younger Wolf was never entirely able to escape the memory of Stone Wolf's prophecy — of the white flood sweeping westward — but for a short while he would shake off his gloom and taste the sweetness of life.

They were a day short of the *wihio* fort when Younger Wolf spied a line of canvas-topped wagons cutting ruts alongside the river.

"It's a wagon train," Tom announced when he saw Younger Wolf pointing.

"West of the fort?" Freneau cried. "Already?"

"As before," Younger Wolf noted, recalling the party Peter Freneau had led west not long before.

"I didn't know," Freneau muttered. "Maybe we should turn back and warn the camp. These wagon people will run right into the camp in a few days."

"We came to speak with the soldiers, or to people at the fort," Younger Wolf argued. "To go back now, when we have come so close . . ."

"I could go," Tom volunteered. "To warn of the wagon people."

"Would anyone listen?" Freneau asked.

"He can tell what we've seen," Younger Wolf suggested. "Scouts can come and look for themselves. It would be good to move the camp north."

"I'll tell them, Uncle," Tom said, turning the pack horses over to his father. "I might not have been born to the People, but I can ride far just the same."

The boy gave a shout, then kicked his pony into a gallop and rode off. Younger Wolf nodded gravely at Freneau.

"They don't stay small forever," Freneau noted. "Do you want to turn north and avoid these people or meet with them before going to the fort?"

"We should know their intentions," Younger Wolf said. "We'll talk to them."

"Then follow me, Brother. They're sure to respond better to a white man."

"Approach slowly, Corn Hair," Younger Wolf warned. "I remember the other wagon people. They shot a Lakota boy who approached them."

"Have you known many yellow-haired Lakotas?" Freneau asked, pulling off his hat.

"Show them," Younger Wolf said, motioning toward the wagons. Already several men were approaching, rifles in hand.

"Friends!" Freneau shouted, holding up his right hand to show it was empty.

One of the wagon men raised his rifle and fired a shot. The ball whined harmlessly overhead, and Freneau laughed.

"Either they can't shoot," he said, "or they're saying good morning."

"A poor greeting, Brother," Younger Wolf observed. "I should answer it. With a great scream, he kicked his horse into motion and charged the first wagon. Howling and waving his bow, he drew up short, gestured wildly, and raced back to where a startled Freneau stood, frozen.

The whites raced about like ants on a disturbed hill, crying and shouting.

"Friends!" Freneau bellowed again. This time a solitary man rode out from the others. Dressed in wool britches and a buffalo hide coat, the *wihio*'s appearance wasn't so different from others Younger Wolf had seen. He, too, waved an empty right hand, but there was no trace of friendship on his bearded face.

"Get clear of this train!" the man demanded. "You got no business blocking our trail."

"We only came to talk," Freneau answered. "I'm Marcel Freneau. If you've been to the fort, you'll have heard of me."

"I'm Ben Waxman," the wagon man answered. "Been to the fort. Some there think you're dead. Scalped by Sioux."

"Those who'd know wouldn't say so," Freneau argued. "I'm with my brothers, the Cheyenne. This is one of their chiefs, Younger Wolf. You're near his camp. And in his country."

"On Platte River according to the map," Waxman replied. "Got a party of missionaries bound for Oregon Territory."

"If they expect to get there in one piece, they'd do better greeting riders with an open hand than firing bullets," Freneau warned. "We're headed to the fort, but we'd speak with the folks first. My brother here has questions."

"I'm not in the habit of talking with Cheyenne," Waxman growled. "Let him chew on his questions. We've got miles to cover."

"There's hundreds of Cheyenne two days ride from here," Freneau said, gazing intently into Waxman's eyes. "Not all are overly friendly. You could do worse than have Younger Wolf's friendship."

"Him?" Waxman asked. "Old fool's carrying flint-tipped arrows. I don't hold much fear for such."

"No?" Younger Wolf asked, grinning. "You would strike us down with your lead balls. Too many ride into our land without understanding. You may die there."

"He speaks English?" Waxman asked, growing pale.

"Been learning. Speaks better than some white men," Freneau explained. "Now, we going to have a parlay or not?"

"I'll tell the folks. We'll make camp and put coffee on to boil. I expect you'll find us pure congenial."

"It would be wise," Freneau said, gazing past Waxman toward the wagons. "People always view each other more kindly once they've broken bread together."

"Broken bread?" Younger Wolf asked.

"Eaten," Freneau explained. "Christian phrase. *Wihio* medicine."

"Ah," Younger Wolf said, nodding. He had heard of the black robes and their silver crosses. John Freneau was one of them now.

Waxman returned to the wagons, and the men gathered to talk. Soon the wagons formed a circle, and men freed the horses from their harness. Only now did Younger Wolf and Freneau approach, and what they found troubled the Wolf. Women, even children, were among

144

the band. Such people came not to trade or hunt but to stay.

When they gathered later to eat and talk, Younger Wolf was surprised to find that women joined their men in the council. One in particular spoke boastfully of how the *wihio* would tame the wilderness.

"Soon we'll have you calmed down, Friend Wolf," she assured Younger Wolf. "You'll have no need to pray to spirits or make your wild naked dances around the fire. We'll teach you to plant corn and raise pigs. You won't have to steal horses or scalp white women."

"I've only seen a few white women," Younger Wolf told Freneau. He added, in the language of the People, that he'd never thought to scalp any before meeting this long talker.

"What did he say?" the woman demanded.

"That he's never scalped a woman," Freneau translated. "In truth, Younger Wolf isn't much on scalping."

"I thought all Indians—" the woman declared.

"You look at me," Younger Wolf interrupted, "but you don't see me. You think I'm someone you hear about from somebody far away. We are the original people, the Tsis tsis tas. Not Pawnee. Not Crow. You come into our country, but you ask no permission. You meet us on Shell River, and we call out as friends. You shoot guns and tell us to go. What way is this? I've heard talk here of what good work you will one day do among us, but you speak only of changing, not understanding. We were here before you! This is our country!"

"Now there you're wrong," Waxman argued. "I've seen the treaty papers myself. All of Platte River's open to us. Free passage to Oregon."

"Who told you that?" Freneau asked.

"It's well known," the woman insisted. "When we approached the government about coming west, they explained it all. We asked about what tribes we might encounter, and they told us Cheyenne were here. It didn't worry us. Cheyenne chiefs signed the treaty."

"What is this treaty?" Younger Wolf demanded.

"The paper I explained," Freneau said. "But this is news. Who signed?"

"As I recall, it was some fellow called Yellow Coat or something."

"I know nobody with such a name," Younger Wolf said angrily. "No one man may speak for the People. No bluecoat soldier brought any paper to the council of forty-four! This paper is a lie."

"Certainly," Freneau said, trying to calm the Wolf. Around the fire the wagon people were growing alarmed. Men drew their wives closer, and some fingered their rifles.

"We must ride to the fort," Younger Wolf announced. "You and I, Corn Hair. Tomorrow. We must tell them of this lie and take back Shell River. This road they would travel cuts our country as a knife carves out a man's heart."

"We'll go," Freneau agreed. "But let me do the talking. You grow angry, and these people become afraid. Fear makes a man foolish."

"Yes," Younger Wolf agreed. "You know the traders at the fort. Speak. But tell them their paper's no good."

The next morning they left the wagon train to continue its journey. Freneau led the way to the fort. There were only a handful of traders there, together with some trap-

146

pers and a party of Lakotas. The old fort had grown, and the new place was called Fort John. The traders welcomed Freneau and offered Younger Wolf presents.

"We haven't seen many Cheyenne yet this year," a trader named McIntyre observed. "Gone north, it's said."

"Many camps are close by," Younger Wolf told them. "The Tsis tsis tas prefer to keep the old ways, though. We hunt with stone arrows."

"You're the brother of the Arrow-keeper," McIntyre said. "I've heard of your medicine. It's said you can turn bullets just by looking at them. I'd be honored to know Younger Wolf was my friend."

"It's fine to talk that way," the Wolf answered. "But I hear much talk of treaty papers, of sending people along Shell River to kill our game. Their horses will chew the grass, and when they choose, they'll camp on the rivers and steal our land."

"There's room for everyone," McIntyre argued. "Besides, a new treaty's been made."

"Have you seen this paper?" Younger Wolf asked. "It's a lie. No Tsis tsis tas chief gave up our hunting grounds."

"Could be," a trader named Parth muttered. "Don't matter. Things change faster'n you can spit. Pretty soon they'll drag their kids along, build towns up everywhere! Why, beaver's practically gone. Be elk and buffalo next."

"No," McIntyre objected. "I've talked to Waxman's batch. They're bound for Oregon, only passing through. They'll muddy the river a little, but it'll come back just fine."

"Maybe they won't stay," Parth admitted, "but others will. They always do."

"I was wrong to come here," Younger Wolf muttered. "I've found nobody to treat with, and all I hear turns my

147

heart away from peace. Fire Hawk is right when he urges the young men to fight. We will kill some of these *wihio*. Then they will respect our power."

"That's not what will happen," Freneau argued. "You can kill a few, but Tsis tsis tas, too, will die. The whites will send an army and run you across the land. They are too many."

"They?" Younger Wolf asked, staring hard at his white-skinned companion.

"We," Freneau agreed. "Remember Stone Wolf's dream. The flood! You can't quiet the wind, Brother. You can't stop the wagon people, either."

Thirteen

Younger Wolf rode west with a heavy heart. Change was coming, and even the power of the Buffalo Shield, even the Arrow medicine of his brother, could not turn it from the People. The traders and even the wagon people would not be the end. Already he grieved for the boys who would never know Bull Buffalo, for the girls who would never throw the hoop or wait at their father's lodge for a boy carrying a flute to arrive.

"It's a hard thing we're facing," Freneau remarked. "I'd rather wrestle a bear."

"Yes," the Wolf muttered. "It's the unseen enemy who's most deadly. The sun's high, though, and summer days remain. We should hunt and swim and share the good time that's left to us."

"We will, Brother," Freneau promised. But even as he spoke, the distance was growing between them. When they arrived at the Rope Men's camp, Fire Hawk and a band of young Foxes were mounting their horses.

"We're going to punish the wagon people!" Fire Hawk shouted.

"What's happened?" Younger Wolf asked.

"Silver Arm is dead," Goes Ahead explained as he climbed atop his pony.

"He went among the wagon people," Dancing Lance added. "He wished to trade an elk hide for tobacco."

"They took the silver bracelet from him," Goes Ahead said, dropping his chin onto his chest. "When he tried to take it back, they shot him."

"We rode to rescue him," Four Wounds said, "but it was too late. Silver Arm no longer breathed."

"We must punish these murderers," Fire Hawk declared. *"Ayyyy!* They'll bleed!"

"We should meet with them and discuss this terrible thing," Younger Wolf argued.

"The time for words has passed, old man!" Fire Hawk grumbled. "Come, Brothers, it's time we left!"

"Ayyyy!" the young men howled. "We'll punish the murderers!"

As the riders departed, Younger Wolf dismounted and walked to the Arrow Lodge. There he shared his failure with Stone Wolf. Later, they spoke with the chiefs, telling them of the *wihio* paper and the news other wagon people would come.

"Already many bands go south, to ride among the Arapaho and fight with Pawnees," South Wind noted. "Maybe we'd be wise to join them."

"Bull Buffalo guides us to this country," Stone Wolf argued. "The *wihio* are everywhere."

"Even in your lodge," Wood Snake pointed out.

"Corn Hair is my relation," Younger Wolf objected. "He's no *wihio*."

"And his sons?" Thunder Coat asked.

"His sons are my sons," Stone Wolf answered.

"Even he who wears the blue coat?" Thunder Coat asked.

"It's better he should go away," South Wind said, folding his arms. "Many of the People hold anger for the *wihio*, and his presence disturbs the harmony of our camp."

"It's so," Thunder Coat agreed. "The boys often fight with the white skins. They're too strange to understand."

"Corn Hair's never brought us harm," Younger Wolf insisted.

"Nor brought much good!" South Wind barked. "The Crazy Dogs won't stay in the camp if a *wihio* remains!"

"Many of the Foxes, too, will leave," Wood Snake added.

"It's for you to go to Corn Hair and speak with him," Thunder Coat told Younger Wolf. "You will know the right words to say. We hold no anger for him in our hearts, but we are pledged to insure the welfare of the People. They must come first."

You dare to tell me this? Younger Wolf thought. *Me?*

They were right to speak of harmony, though. He swallowed his anger and agreed with their decision. That afternoon he shared the news with Marcel Freneau.

"It's for the best," Freneau said, sighing. "I feel the anger on my back. I came as a brother to help, and I won't remain if it brings trouble to your lodge. My sons have hunted with the Tsis tsis tas and come to understand the sacred path. Maybe a day will come when anger can again be put aside and we'll be brothers once more."

"I pray for that day," Younger Wolf replied. "But it's a distant dream."

"Yes," Freneau agreed.

It saddened Younger Wolf to see the Freneaus leave, but Stone Wolf had deemed it wise.

"You weren't here to listen to the hard words spoken to the boys," Hoop Woman told Younger Wolf afterward. "Even Little Dancer was rebuked for walking with Tom to the river. *Wihio* Heart', they called him. It was dangerous for them to remain. Blood would have been spilled."

Younger Wolf considered it likely, especially after Fire Hawk's return. Two young Tsis tsis tas had died fighting the wagon people, and there was much mourning.

"We struck their camp at daybreak," Four Wounds explained as Younger Wolf helped treat the young man's injuries. "Mostly there were small ones about, and we had to hunt down the men. Fire Hawk kept busy killing children. He's good at that. We others felt the sting of the *wihio* rifles."

The sight of Fire Hawk presenting his sister with three yellow-haired scalps didn't improve matters, either. Clearly these were young ones killed, and Younger Wolf understood well the heartache their fathers would feel.

"We must move our camp again," Younger Wolf declared in the council. "The *wihio* will hunger for vengeance. They'll urge the soldiers to come and punish us."

"Let them come!" Thunder Coat growled. "We'll strike them down."

"They will be too many," Stone Wolf said, frowning. "Brothers, I've seen many things, but none as terrible as the white flood that's coming. The People have never known such a bitter time. Let's go north and hunt this summer. The wagons will pass, and we'll return when they've gone."

"Run away?" Thunder Coat cried.

"No one chases us," Stone Wolf pointed out. "We go because the welfare of the People demands it. Let this present trouble pass us by. Later, when we must, we'll fight."

"Yes," the chiefs agreed. "We'll go north."

Seasons came and went, and the Rope Men roamed the plains as never before. Stone Wolf spoke to the Arrows often, and Mahuts directed the People away from Shell River and into the wild country to the north one year and the broad southern plains the next. Younger Wolf watched his nephews grow tall and strong. He gazed on Little Dancer with approving eyes as the boy passed his eighth summer wrestling and swimming and riding. Red Hoop and Little Hoop were a great help to their mother and a delight to their father.

Nevertheless, Younger Wolf worried. Wagon trains continued to plod their way westward, scarring the land with their ruts. The *wihio* travelers cut down the timber, and their animals chewed the grass so that Bull Buffalo sought pasture elsewhere. All manner of tins and discarded belongings marked the trail. The strange ones even cut their words into the rocks.

"There's no harmony among them," Younger Wolf declared.

"No, and each summer more come," Wood Snake observed. "Soon we must take up our lances and stop them."

Not all the tribes objected to the wagon people. Many, mostly Crow and Pawnee, greeted the intruders warmly, swapping ponies or hides for tobacco and beads. Soon they acquired new, much-improved rifles with which to fight their old enemies, the Tsis tsis tas. The old days of brave heart fights when a man stepped out to strike his enemy were vanishing faster than Bull Buffalo. Now Crow and Pawnee concealed themselves in rocky ravines and killed from afar.

"Once we were a brave People," Wood Snake spoke to the council of forty-four. The Fox leader had been named one of the old man chiefs, a leader of the ten bands.

"Yes," Stone Wolf agreed. "All our enemies trembled at our approach. What's become of our brave hearts?"

"The power Mahuts brought us is no good against the *wihio* magic," South Wind declared. "Even the Buffalo Shields fail to turn back the enemy."

"What must we do?" Thunder Coat asked.

"Be brave," Younger Wolf answered. "Face the enemy as we once did, boldly, so he may see we have no fear of him. Treat with the *wihio* and help them understand the harmony they disturb."

"They have no ears to hear!" Thunder Coat complained. "We should run them. Kill them. Punish them for the death they've brought amidst us."

"A man learns only hatred when he is whipped," Stone Wolf argued. "No, we must find a road we can walk among these strange ones. One they can walk, too. Guide them, show them the true road."

"It's a warming thought," Younger Wolf agreed. "But will they welcome it?"

"We can only try," Stone Wolf replied. "See' was' sin mit, you ride with the young men. Turn them to this harmonious path. Bring it into their hearts."

"I'll try," Younger Wolf promised. "My time as a chief grows short, though. Soon others will speak louder in the council, and I'll be another old man with memories to share by the winter fire."

"No, Brother," Stone Wolf argued. "They follow you. They respect you."

"No, most follow Fire Hawk and Thunder Coat. They listen to Talking Stick and seek his medicine. You taught him as a boy, and many say his power is growing. It's for the young to follow the young, even as we did, Nah nih."

"Their visions are clouded with anger."

"Perhaps," Younger Wolf admitted. "But our world is passing. It's for them to direct the People tomorrow."

Tomorrow was still tomorrow, though. Younger Wolf remained a chief. When a party of *wihio* riders approached the Rope Men's camp north of Fort John, it was to him they offered presents.

"Uncle, there's trouble on Shell River," Charles Freneau announced.

"What trouble?" Younger Wolf asked, noticing how like his father Charles had grown to be. Eighteen now— taller and much stronger.

"A party of boys from one of the wagon trains has become lost," Charles explained. "Three days ago they walked into the hills beyond Laramie River, and no one has seen them since."

"Why come to me with these people's trouble?" Younger Wolf asked. "Our young men hunt Bull Buffalo. Ask the Lakotas who camp near the fort."

"They showed us a trail," Charles said nervously. "They won't go there, though. It's a Tsis tsis tas place."

"White Face Hills," Stone Wolf said, shuddering. "Where the Windpipes place their dead."

"Yes," Charles admitted. "The wagon chief admits the boys went there."

"Is there no finish to their outrages?" Wood Snake

155

cried. "The bones of my relations rest there. Would they disturb the spirits and bring ghosts down onto the plain?"

"They wouldn't understand," Charles explained. "They're new to this country. Mostly sons of corn growers."

"It's a bad thing they've done," Younger Wolf growled. "They should be punished."

"But not killed," Charles said, nervously eyeing his companions. "We tracked them from the burial ground, Uncle, to a small creek where they made a camp. Many horses visited the place, and the boys have disappeared."

"Yes?" Younger Wolf asked. "Why come to me with this story? Go and follow the horses."

"That country's well known to many people," Wood Snake added. "Lakotas and Crows hunt there. Even Rees."

"We tracked the horses," Charles explained. "They came from this camp."

"Uncle, many hunters have gone north," Iron Wolf said, frowning. "Only Fire Hawk went east."

"Fire Hawk?" Charles asked anxiously. "He has no love of white people."

Charles informed the other *wihio* of the news, and they spoke angrily.

"Come along, talk to Fire Hawk," Charles pleaded. "There may be time to prevent these boys' deaths."

"I will come," Younger Wolf agreed. "But first it must be understood what these boys did was wrong. To violate a sacred place is a terrible thing. It must not be done a second time. If the place has been disturbed, a giveaway should be made. The Windpipes should be satisfied."

Charles translated, and afterward Younger Wolf told the wagon men directly of his offer.

"We'll do as you say, chief," a tall *wihio* named Fraser agreed. "I can promise you the boys will be punished, too. Just help us return them to their mothers. They're all of them young and can learn from mistakes if they live long enough."

Younger Wolf agreed. He quickly sent Dreamer to bring a horse, and several others collected ponies as well. Dancing Lance and Four Wounds, in particular, agreed to go, for their group of hunters had already returned from its foray. Ten men in all followed Younger Wolf and the wagon men eastward.

Locating Fire Hawk proved rather easy. Smoke from his campfires painted the sky, and the hunters had selected a low hill overlooking Laramie River for their camp. As for the *wihio* boys, they, too, were in clear sight. Younger Wolf counted six.

"That's all of them," Fraser noted. "What are they doing to them?"

"Nothing," Younger Wolf explained, pointing to the stick-thin figures sitting naked beside a blazing fire. The Hawk would have some devilment in store for them, but as yet they appeared more fearful than injured.

"Wait here," Freneau urged when Younger Wolf and Four Wounds rode on. "Let them settle the matter."

"But the presents," Fraser objected.

"Later," Younger Wolf said, pausing but a moment. "First we must convince Fire Hawk to give the boys up."

"You're his chief!" Fraser exploded. "Order him."

"Explain to him our ways," Younger Wolf told Charles. "While I try to win the boys' freedom."

Younger Wolf tried to ignore the heated words of the

157

wihio as he rode ahead. Four Wounds kicked his horse into a trot and led the way, singing a Fox chant and waving a bright red cloth. Fire Hawk immediately set out to greet his visitors. Only when he spied the others farther back did his smile fade.

"You bring *wihio* to my camp?" the Hawk cried. "Brothers, why?"

"They're seeking some lost boys," Younger Wolf explained.

"We have these boys," Fire Hawk readily admitted. "Lost? No, they walk among the scaffolds of the dead, stealing their possessions, tossing their bones on the hillside like hide balls. We found medicine charms in their clothes, bone breastplates, even finger bones. The ghosts of the disturbed ones will walk the country now, for no one can put right this terrible thing."

"What are you planning?" Younger Wolf asked.

"To scatter their bones," Fire Hawk explained. "Cut them into pieces as the Crow do, fingers and toes, arms and legs. Those who see it will remember and think long before disturbing our sacred places."

"Yes," Younger Wolf agreed. "Fire Hawk, their fathers are there, behind us. Seeing this, what will they do?"

"Weep like old women," Fire Hawk boasted. "Wet themselves."

"Kill you," Younger Wolf declared. "And punish the helpless ones. No, you can't do it. Returning cruelty in kind brings no satisfaction, restores no harmony. Come, let's speak to the boys. Tell them of your plans. Let fear chill their bones. Then we'll go and talk to the fathers. We'll come to an agreement."

"We should kill one at least," Fire Hawk suggested.

"I remember the three scalps you brought to camp,"

Younger Wolf said, frowning. "The hair of boys brings a man little honor. The presents you càn take the Wind-pipes and the things we'll return to White Face Hills will make you a great man among the People. Generosity is a good thing. And the *wihio* will fear you for the words you share with them."

"Then it will be as you say," Fire Hawk agreed. "Your words appeal to me, and you stand high in the eyes of the council. You won't be a chief forever, though. Soon it will be my turn to decide things. That day the *wihio* will truly shake."

Younger Wolf sighed. The Hawk would never under-stand how gladly a chief would set aside his obligations. For now it was enough to see the boys returned to their fathers, and the *wihio* riding south, away from the Rope Men's camp. No one could doubt others would come, and more trouble would follow. But every day of peace was welcome. Every moment.

Fourteen

Other wagon people rode Shell River road that summer, and often they encountered groups of young men. Occasionally one of the ten bands camped near the fort to trade. Such was the case when Younger Wolf moved the Rope Men to Fort John. A circle of wagons was there already, and the Wolf was inclined to leave.

"Uncle, we've not visited our *wihio* cousins in many moons," Iron Wolf complained. "Already this visit has been long delayed. We'll make no trouble with the wagon people."

"It's not easy to know what a *wihio* will do," Younger Wolf warned. "But you're children no longer. Tell Corn Hair his brother camps on Shell River. We'll smoke and eat and talk."

"I'll tell him," Iron Wolf promised. Together with Porcupine and Goes Ahead, he rode on toward the fort.

Even before the People began to raise their lodge poles, Marcel Freneau and his three younger sons appeared outside the fort.

"Welcome, Brothers," Freneau called. "It's a good day

that's brought you here. We'll feast on buffalo steaks and swap the old, remembered stories."

Children howled at the notion, and the young men greeted Charles, Louis, and young Tom warmly. Only Fire Hawk and a few others scowled. They had but one use for white men. They collected bundles of elk hides and carried them to the trader's store to exchange for powder and lead for rifles.

Toward midday the boys of the camp splashed into the river to swim. Cool water was a welcome remedy for the blazing heat of the midsummer sun, and soon many of the wagon boys stripped off their clothes and joined their Tsis tsis tas age-mates. Racing each other through the shallows, catching fish with their hands, or wrestling in the mud, boys were boys. One needed no language other than laughter to share in that good time.

"I sometimes think we should leave the making of treaties to them," Freneau said, pointing to the boys. "They understand better than anyone what's important. Accept a man for what he is. Don't labor to change him."

"It's the fathers who make agreements," Younger Wolf said, pointing out the nervous men watching warily from the wagon camp. Many held rifles in their arms, and none was smiling.

"It's easy to suspect men who are different," Freneau declared. "Too easy. Those of us who understand must bring our peoples together."

"Once I thought we could do it," Younger Wolf lamented. "But I'm a young man no longer. Winter reminds me of the wounds I suffered in the hard fights against the Crow and Pawnee. Perhaps our sons will mold agreements that will last."

"That would please us both."

Later that evening a band of young Foxes arrived with fresh meat, and a great council fire was lit. As the Rope Men danced and sang, many of the wagon people approached. Some of the boys recognized among the dancers companions from the river and joined in the celebration. Women offered food to the uninvited guests, and quickly the two camps became one.

Younger Wolf watched, amused, as small *wihio* children stumbled and fell in their awkward efforts to match the movements of their Tsis tsis tas friends: The wagon people had their own songs, and they shared one when the drummers paused to rest.

"We're not so different, Chief," a large woman told Younger Wolf. "I never did believe some of the tales spread about blood-thirsty savages. People are people. A man who loves his children is a man to be trusted."

"Yes," Younger Wolf agreed, surprising the woman with his comprehension of English. "The young should be an example to us in their behavior toward strangers. And it should be the task of grandfathers and grandmothers to decide when to take up the war pipe. They know the price paid for fighting."

"You are so very different in many ways," she observed. "But not in the ones that are important. Soon my husband and I resume our journey westward, to Oregon. I hope the tribes there will be as understanding."

"It's easy to welcome people who come with open hearts," Younger Wolf declared. "You'll find what you look for in them."

"I suspect you're right," she answered, bowing. "Now I must fetch the little ones to their beds and start my preparations for the journey."

"Dawn always comes too early," Younger Wolf noted.

"Peace to you, friend."

"And to you," she replied.

Three days after the wagon people left, the first spots appeared on Red Hoop's face. Other children were similarly afflicted, and those among their elders who had not suffered the spotted sickness before now became ill.

"It was the wagon people," Stone Wolf said after a fever took Horned Moon. His brother, Two Moon, was bent over in sorrow, as was the young men's aunt, Hoop Woman.

"We should never have come to the fort," Younger Wolf told her. "The *wihio* strike us first with rifles. When their lead can't find us, they send us sickness instead. *Ayyyy!* Who can fight such an enemy?"

"Yes, it's hard," she agreed. "But you've always done the hard things, Husband. You and I both."

Neither had known as difficult a day as when the spotted sickness struck down Red Hoop and Little Hoop. The spots appeared on Little Dancer, too, but they troubled the boy less.

"Once before we fought this *wihio* fever," Stone Wolf said as he chanted over the children. "When the Crow woman I took as a wife brought it from the traders' camp. It's said it troubles a man only once."

"Then you and I are safe from its torments," Younger Wolf said, wiping Little Hoop's feverish forehead.

"As are my sons," Stone Wolf added. "We can separate the sick and tend them safely."

"Before, when death came close, we set up a sweat lodge and burned the sickness out."

"Yes," Stone Wolf agreed. "Even so, many climbed

163

Hanging Road. Maybe it's not so bad as before."

"Look into their eyes, Nah nih, and tell me that," Younger Wolf said, gazing at his daughters. "There lies my heart. We must bring them back."

"I'll send my sons to gather wood and good stones. We'll erect the sweat lodge, and the little ones will go there."

"Will it bring them back to me?" Younger Wolf asked.

"Only Man Above can do that, See' was' sin mit."

"You will devote your powers to them, though."

"They're my blood, too," Stone Wolf said, steadying his brother's trembling hands. "Once I had a daughter, and her ghost is never far from my thoughts. Enough have died already. We'll make these well again."

The sweat did drive the fever from the girls, and to others besides, but the mourning cries of the Rope Men swept across the plain like a winter wind, chilling everything it touched. Two children of every three climbed Hanging Road, and many mothers and fathers walked alongside. Freneau rode out to offer the help of a wagon man familiar with the *wihio* sicknesses, but all the man could suggest was keeping the sick from the rest and burning what they had touched.

"Look at the smoke that climbs from our camp," Fire Hawk observed. "This is what the *wihio* brings us. They're no good, and we must punish them."

"No good?" Younger Wolf asked. "You carry their rifles, shoot their lead balls, and cut meat with their iron knives. If these things are bad, why do you bring them among us? You say their hearts are bad, but you wear the scalps of their young ones. It's a road both our peoples walk, this hating. We can keep ourselves safe only if we avoid these strange ones."

"How?" Thunder Coat cried. "They're everywhere!"

"We must seek medicine to protect ourselves," Talking Stick, Thunder Coat's brother, declared. "Mahuts can show us a way. Or we can climb the high places and make prayers."

"We've sought visions before," Wood Snake said, gazing at Stone Wolf. "They offer us little hope and no future."

"Maybe the Arrow-keeper's power is broken," Talking Stick suggested. "My dreams hold power. I'll find a path we can walk."

"It's for Mahuts to decide," Younger Wolf argued.

"You won't lead us forever, old man!" Fire Hawk barked. "The day's coming when your voice will be a half-remembered whisper."

"When you are older and have proven yourself, you may speak to a man of the People with words worth hearing," Wood Snake declared. "Now it's your voice that is not of value here. Go and prove your merit before calling yourself chief."

"Yes," other older men murmured in agreement, and Fire Hawk dropped his head and marched off toward the pony herd.

"I fear the day Fire Hawk will lead our People," Younger Wolf told his brother.

"That one won't ever sit in the council of forty-four," Stone Wolf replied. "His heart is bad, and his eyes never see danger. He'll die young."

"Then many will die with him," Younger Wolf said, frowning.

"Yes," Stone Wolf agreed. "My dreams have told me that."

"What else?"

"That it's a bad day for the Tsis tsis tas. And worse times are ahead."

* * *

Once health returned to the camp, and the burned hides and lodges were replaced, Younger Wolf called a gathering of all the men.

"My brother has seen many dangers in our path," he told the others. "Already we're weakened by the *wihio* sickness. We must avoid these people. Don't ride among their camps or visit their lodges. Remain apart, and we'll grow strong again."

"Where will we do it?" Fire Hawk asked. "Our old winter camps on Shell River are heavily travelled. Game is scarce there. The Lakotas have moved into the good eastern country. North? The Crow remain strong there, and bands of Rees ride there now, too."

"We could join our Arapaho friends in the south," Wood Snake suggested.

"Many are there already," Thunder Coat said. "We don't know that country well."

"We must follow Mahuts," Younger Wolf declared. "Nah nih, we'll bring a pipe and ask the Arrows."

"Yes," the other chiefs agreed. "Stone Wolf will seek a dream. The Arrow-keeper can direct us."

But even before Younger Wolf located a pipe, word came of a *wihio* band that had strayed onto the buffalo range.

"See how they come among us even here?" Fire Hawk cried. "Let's go and punish them!"

"We'll go," Younger Wolf agreed. "But we must be cautious. They may carry another sickness. Maybe we can turn them back to Shell River."

Fire Hawk grumbled, but the head men were all of like mind. Ten of them gathered around Younger Wolf, and the chief took down his Buffalo Shield. He was determined to be prepared for whatever trouble waited for them.

They had no difficulty locating the *wihio* camp. The whites burned green wood in their fire, and the thick gray smoke was visible across a great distance. Already a band of hunters stood watching from a nearby ridge. Dreamer was among them, and he galloped down to meet his uncle's party.

"They have a bad wheel, I think," Dreamer explained. "Also, their animals are thin from overwork. The wagons are heavy, and the pulling difficult."

"Yes," Younger Wolf agreed. "I'll go and speak with them. They must go back from this country. They don't belong here."

"Ayyyy!" the others shouted in agreement.

Younger Wolf left his shield tied behind him, and he discarded his lance and bow. Instead he approached the wagons unarmed, calling out his intentions in English.

"We could use your help, friend," a ragged man with a great long beard answered. "We've gotten ourselves lost."

Younger Wolf studied the faces of the others. The men's faces were red and swollen, and their eyes watery. The solitary woman had difficulty walking, and the children huddled behind wagon wheels or heavy barrels, terrified.

"It's easy to stray from a river when your head is full of whiskey," Younger Wolf observed.

"Yeah, we've emptied a jug or two," the *wihio* said, laughing. "Got our wagon broken down. Clem here come along to help, but his horses can't pull him back to the train."

"I don't know how to repair your wheel," Younger Wolf said, "but we can guide you to your people. They will help you."

"Sure, and that'd be a great service, Chief."

Younger Wolf then returned to his companions, explained the wagon people's trouble, and instructed the younger men to remain on the ridge, watching over the wagons. He would take the *wihio* on his spare horse to the other wagon people.

It should have been easy, but the whiskey prevented the wagon men from staying atop a horse. None of the boys were familiar with horses, and walking would take too long.

"We'll follow their trail to where the others are camped," Younger Wolf finally declared.

"Just head for the river," the *wihio* urged. The other men nervously glanced back at their rutted path, and the children hid themselves.

"They're telling only part of the truth," Thunder Coat observed. "Let's discover the rest."

Younger Wolf, too, felt uneasy. He had intended to seek out the other wagons alone, but now he instructed his companions to follow. The ten of them rode eastward in a single file. They had but a short distance to travel before coming upon the unspoken horror. Near Shell River, amid a great wallow, lay the skinned carcasses of a hundred buffalo. Bulls, cows, even small calves were slaughtered. Meat enough to feed a dozen camps lay rotting under the summer sun.

"Now we know why the wagons were so heavy," Thunder Coat muttered.

"I always knew the *wihio* were a crazy people," Younger Wolf said, sighing. "Here's the proof of it!"

"Look there!" Four Wounds cried, pointing to the river. A handful of young whites raced about in the shallows, swatting each other with buffalo tails. Their elders were farther ahead, even now trading hides for whiskey.

"I know that one," Thunder Coat said, motioning toward the trader.

"Fire Tongue Goss," Four Wounds said, spitting.

"He walks the earth no longer!" Fire Hawk screamed, kicking his horse into a gallop. Riding like fury, the young man raced toward the *wihio* camp, waving a lance as his comrades cheered him on. With a single blow the Hawk rammed the lance into Goss's chest, then climbed down and took the trader's scalp.

"Indians!" the whites shouted as they scattered.

"Wait!" Younger Wolf urged as the startled boys splashed out of the river. Fire Hawk remounted his horse and blocked their retreat. With a rawhide strip he whipped them past the slaughtered buffalo and on to the waiting Tsis tsis tas warriors.

"Stop," Younger Wolf insisted when Fire Hawk jumped down and drew a knife. "Look at them. They're only boys."

The warriors' blood was up, for the smell of death nearby choked them. Even so, gazing down at the pale, naked boys, they found their hatred dying. Suddenly two shots shattered the calm. Fire Hawk turned and gazed with surprise at the *wihio* wagon people. The men hurried to reload their rifles as the women drove their children to shelter.

"Nothing lives long," the Hawk muttered as he staggered a step closer to the boys.

"Only earth and mountain," Thunder Coat added as red blood streamed out of Fire Hawk's back.

"No!" Younger Wolf cried as the others drew out war axes and knives. The moment Fire Hawk fell, the other Tsis tsis tas fell upon the white boys.

"Stop this madness!" Thunder Coat screamed as the younger men dismembered the bodies. "It's not them we should fight."

"It's their fathers!" Younger Wolf added. "Don't darken your hearts with this work."

But there was no stopping it. Fire Hawk lay dead, and the boys were at hand. No Crow was ever mutilated in such a fashion, and it sickened Younger Wolf to know a Rope Man could perform such a dark and terrible deed.

"Now we'll kill the rest!" Talking Stick vowed as he waved a scalp at the line of wagon men nervously approaching.

"Hasn't there been enough?" Younger Wolf asked. "Will you strike down the women, the babies?"

"Every one," Talking Stick vowed. "Our brother is dead. His killer must be punished."

"And what have you done there?" Younger Wolf said, pointing to the slashed *wihio* bodies.

"Which of them killed Fire Hawk?" Thunder Coat asked, gazing at the wagon men.

"The two in the center fired," Four Wounds explained as he wiped blood from his knife. "Who can say which ball killed him?"

Thunder Coat took aim with his own rifle and struck down one. He then took his brother's rifle and dropped the second.

"Now it's done," Thunder Coat said as the wagon men broke and fled. "We'll take our brother home and mourn him. There can be no more killing here."

The others dropped their chins and stared at the butchery. Slowly, with heavy hearts, they tied Fire Hawk's body to his horse. Then, mounting their own animals, they rode westward.

Fifteen

Fire Hawk had always been a man to value himself above his fellows. He had never taken a wife, and his sister's family had died of the spotted sickness. Nevertheless he was mourned by most of the Rope Men, for the story of his charge and killing of the *wihio* whiskey trader was deemed honorable. Younger men, who had so often followed his bad heart raids, considered his death a great loss.

"He warned of the *wihio*," Talking Stick recounted. "He was not a man to have visions, and he was too often foolish, but his was a brave death. *Ayyyy!* He was a man to know!"

When the three days mourning was finished, the Foxes placed Fire Hawk on a scaffold in the hills north of Shell River. Many good arrows were placed in a quiver beside him, and a brightly-painted lance was close at hand.

"If his enemies find him on the other side, he will be prepared," Goes Ahead noted.

Strange how he is better respected in death than in life, Younger Wolf thought. In truth, he thought it a good thing such a careless man was gone. Now was a time for caution, for thought and contemplation. But once the Hawk's mourning rituals were finished, the young men marked his death with new, violent attacks on the Shell River road. Each day small bands returned, waving scalps and recounting coups struck against the *wihio* wagon people.

"See these good guns I took off a hairy-faced *wihio!*" Dancing Lance shouted. *"Ayyyy!* We've counted many coups and taken many horses!"

Not all the raiders enjoyed such success. Yellow Dog led one party south and didn't return. Younger Wolf and his nephews rode out to find the boys. After searching the nearby hills, Goes Ahead picked up their trail. Near the wallow marked by the sea of buffalo bones, the young men lay, shot down by *wihio* rifles.

"They undertook no preparation," Younger Wolf said, scowling at the corpses. Already the animals and birds had been at work, but the remains bore no charms.

"They carried only hunting bows," Iron Wolf observed. "Yellow Dog enjoyed tricks, and he probably intended to frighten the wagon people."

"He'll frighten no one now," Younger Wolf noted. "We'll make a pony drag and carry their bones to the ridge. It's too late to prepare the bodies, and our camp is far."

"Dragging bodies there would be hard," Iron Wolf agreed.

"No. It will be hard telling their relatives," Younger Wolf argued. "These were good young men. I remember crafting arrow points for Yellow Dog."

"We hunted elk under the dirt-in-the-face Moon," Goes Ahead said. "They'll be missed."

"Will any of us survive this crazy time, Uncle?" Porcupine asked. "So many of my age-mates have made the long walk already. Like me, they had not yet won a brave heart name, taken women to their lodge, or fathered children."

"That's true," Younger Wolf said, resting a hand on the sixteen-year-old's shoulder. "The Tsis tsis tas have known hard times before, though. Your father will find an answer to this new trouble. He sees with the far-seeing eyes, and he has Mahuts to guide him."

"Yes, but I've seen a change in his eyes," Iron Wolf said somberly. "He's seen too much. Death. Sickness. Change. Once I blamed it on the woman who was my mother. Now I'm older, and I see it's no different with many others. Pain wearies a man."

"Life is pain," Younger Wolf said, pointing to the sun. "We don't question why Man Above painted the sun yellow. We don't wonder why grasses brown in winter and become green again to fatten the ponies. It's enough for us to keep the old ways, to walk modestly this road we find before us."

"I hoped to discover a better trail," Goes Ahead confessed.

"Perhaps you will," Younger Wolf said, nudging the young man along toward a nearby cottonwood. "We'll cut poles from this tree and make the drag."

The others hurried to help, and all welcomed the labor. Work, as it often did, helped the sadness to pass.

The cherry-ripening moon marked the passing of summer, but it didn't see the last of the wagon people, who continued to creep westward. These later bands often had poor wagons and pitiful livestock. But while it was a simple enough matter to pursue such people, striking them down was another matter. Too often the warrior societies who formed raiding parties neglected to prepare the young men. Leaders led wild charges, but when the *wihio* companies collected their senses and formed boxes or circles of their wagons, brave heart charges were often bloodily repulsed.

"*Wihio* don't fight in the old manner," Thunder Coat grumbled. "They don't stand in the open and face a man. No, they hide in rocks and shoot when our backs are turned to them. What honor is there in killing this way?"

"They don't fight for honor," Younger Wolf explained. "They count no coups. They shoot to survive, and most would pass by peacefully if given a choice."

"They're all our enemy now," Talking Stick insisted. "Since the spotted sickness. From the day Fire Hawk fell."

"Ah, where were you, Talking Stick, when Sweet Medicine's warnings were ignored?" Younger Wolf asked. "Then was the time to strike boldly. Now we must use every advantage. Darkness is our friend. Cover our best shield. Steal their horses first. Set them afoot. Then attack."

"Yes, it's a good plan," the Stick agreed.

"Make your preparations, though. Carry a pipe to Mahuts. Make the Arrow medicine. Make medicine against bullets and wear the correct charms. Enhance your medicine and use the power to run the enemy."

"All these things are good," Thunder Coat said, "but many of us are young. Others have never led the fight. You, Younger Wolf, would find many eager to follow you against the *wihio*. My brother and I would willingly ride at your side. All know the concern Younger Wolf has for his friends. Haven't we heard your many rescues recounted in our councils?"

"I hold no great anger for the *wihio*," Younger Wolf told them. "It's true their coming brings trouble, but I never make war on the helpless ones. I'll kill no children or women. These can be made captive or driven back to the trader fort. If I lead, all who ride along must purify themselves in the sweat lodge and make medicine to turn the *wihio* bullets."

"It will be as you say," Thunder Coat agreed. "Show us, Uncle, and let us learn."

"It's right for me to do so," Younger Wolf told the young chief. "Soon the leading will be for you to do. My days as a chief grow short."

"They'll ask you to remain in the council," Thunder Coat declared. "Who else stands as tall in the eyes of the Hev a tan iu?"

Younger Wolf frowned. Ten years was enough. A chief's burdens too often took a man from his lodge. He longed to show Little Dancer so many things, and the girls were growing older. Soon there would be marriages to arrange. Afterward grandchildren would come.

In truth, he was tempted to pass those final days as a chief in his lodge, singing with the children or blowing notes on the courting flute. Hoop Woman would have welcomed it. But as always, a man of the People put the desires and needs of others before his own.

Younger Wolf never considered the raid his own. Thunder Coat had spotted the wagon camp, and Talking Stick had carried the pipe to his mentor, Stone Wolf.

"When you were a boy, I thought you would walk at my side, traveling the medicine trail," Stone Wolf told the young man. "Now you've set your feet upon war's road. Come. Ask Mahuts your question. Find the answer."

Younger Wolf entered the Arrow Lodge with Thunder Coat and Talking Stick, but it was the Stick who made the Arrow offering, and it was to him that Stone Wolf spoke. After tying eagle feathers and a silver charm to the medicine bundle, Stone Wolf invited the question.

"We plan to strike the wagon camp," Talking Stick said. "We ask Mahuts to shield us from harm and warn us of any danger there."

Stone Wolf swallowed the question and studied the Arrows as they turned in the light breeze. "There are good guns among the *wihio*," he finally said. "If you charge them, many good men will fall. Let the land plague them. Take their ponies and blister their feet. Make them hungry for the lands they've left behind. Send them back to tell of hardship and death. In this way others may become discouraged and remain where they are."

"It's a good notion," Thunder Coat agreed. "But how can we do it?"

"Take their horses," Younger Wolf explained. "Once, long ago, the bluecoat soldiers came to Shell River. They weren't killed. No, the People crept close and took their animals. And their clothes. The sight of so many naked *wihio* was truly humorous. Many Rope Men got good guns from that raid, and we saw few bluecoats afterward. Yes, it was a good way to treat the soldiers."

"There were only a few of them, though," Thunder Coat said, shaking his head. "There are many wagons. We can't steal their clothes. The horses we may drive off, but it will take some good men. As to—"

"Yes," Younger Wolf confessed. "We must plan carefully. But it's possible. We'll organize the ceremonies and take a sweat. Then we'll paint the young men and make charms. Finally we'll fight."

"Ah, it will be a remembered day," Thunder Coat predicted. *"Ayyyy!* We'll run the *wihio!*"

* * *

They rode out that autumn, the Foxes, singing the old songs and vowing a remembered fight. To Younger Wolf, the fights most remembered were ones where old friends had fallen, where promising young men had been struck down by the enemy. There were twenty warriors following him south, but he saw other faces — ghosts long absent from the camps of the Tsis tsis tas. Silver Arm, who had walked a troubled path even as a boy. Red Woodpecker and Spring Hawk trailed behind, their torn bodies testifying to the death that stalked warrior's road.

"You're troubled, Uncle," Iron Wolf observed as he pulled his pony even with Younger Wolf's buckskin.

"I've seen too many fights," Younger Wolf explained.

"This won't be the last," the young men said, urging his horse onward.

"No," the Wolf agreed. "We'll face other struggles."

"*Ayyyy!*" Thunder Coat howled. "We're Fox warriors. Courage. Difficult tasks lay ahead for us!"

"*Ayyyy!*" the others cried.

"Don't worry, Uncle," Porcupine said as he galloped alongside. "The Buffalo Shield will turn their bullets."

Younger Wolf nodded. How could he explain he didn't fear the *wihio?* No, it was the death the People would leave behind that chilled his heart and soured his stomach.

For a time, it seemed the anxiety was wasted, though. Shell River flowed as always, clear and untroubled. No wagon people camped there. Scouts rode out in both directions, but they found no enemy to fight.

"Summer's gone," Thunder Coat grumbled. "The *wihio* will wait for the grass to green again."

"No, they're near," Talking Stick insisted. "I'll find them."

The Stick built a small fire and smoked with the chiefs.

Then he rode out with his brother toward Fort John.

"What are we to do?" Goes Ahead asked. "Wait? Return to our camp?"

"Wait," Younger Wolf answered. "Talking Stick will find what he seeks. I read that much in his eyes. We can stay here, fishing the river, and preparing ourselves for the fight that's coming."

"*Ayyyy!*" the others howled. "We're not too late."

The Foxes repeated their medicine prayers and painted themselves for battle. When Talking Stick and Thunder Coat returned the next day, the young men hurried toward them.

"You found the *wihio?*" Porcupine asked excitedly.

"Many wagons," Talking Stick answered. "Just as I saw in my dreams. They send out no scouts, and many stray far from the main band."

"They don't guard their animals," Thunder Coat added. "It will be an easy thing to steal them."

Younger Wolf nodded, but he expected the raid would prove more difficult than the brothers foresaw. He quickly split the party into four groups. With nightfall, each would approach from a different direction, hoping to catch the *wihio* unaware and run their ponies.

"We'll wait for the sun before striking their camp," Younger Wolf added. "We may convince them to abandon their wagons and return to their camps beyond Fat River."

"Is that our intention?" Thunder Coat asked. "We mean to punish them, make the *wihio* consider their mistakes."

"We should kill them all," Talking Stick argued.

"Is that the war you would make?" Younger Wolf asked. "We've fought many times, but always warriors killing warriors. Women and children were always made captive. Would you anger Man Above by striking down the helpless ones? This invites our enemies to do the same."

"They have already," Thunder Coat complained. "Their spotted sickness has emptied many lodges. How many Tsis tsis tas children have climbed Hanging Road because the *wihio* brought death to this country?"

"Yes," others agreed. "Let's kill them all."

"We'll fight the men," Younger Wolf insisted. "Only them. It's my medicine that offers you protection, and it's useless if you slay the helpless."

"Ah," the young men groaned. The arguing ended, for no one wished to ride against rifles without the power of the Buffalo Shield.

That night Younger Wolf's party slipped silently past the camp guards and drove off the *wihio* horses. Great lumbering oxen, too, were run through the shallows and on past the wagon camp. Behind them, the *wihio* shouted and ran about in confusion. Morning found them staring anxiously from the cover of their wagons, rifles in hand.

Younger Wolf rode out to treat with them. His empty right hand raised high, he explained the choice. If the *wihio* left their wagons and walked east, they would not be harmed. If they stayed, the raiders would strike them hard.

"We have many good things to trade," the *wihio* leader cried. "Give us our oxen and leave us in peace. We'll give you presents. Beads. Looking glasses. Good cloth."

"We have all we need," Younger Wolf answered. "You come and scar this good country. You paint it brown with dead grass and red with the blood of our brother creatures, our young men. Make your choice."

179

The *wihio* men gathered in a circle and discussed the proposal. In the end they merely repeated the offer of presents.

"Then it's decided," Younger Wolf declared. "Make your farewells. We'll strike you hard."

The Foxes were eager to hear the *wihio* answer, and many greeted it with enthusiasm.

"Courage!" Thunder Coat yelled. "We go to kill them."

"It won't be easy," Younger Wolf insisted. "They hold good ground. The river behind them's too deep to cross, and they have good guns to protect their front. We must strike one end hard. Many of us will be hurt."

"Nothing lasts long," Thunder Coat shouted. "Who will follow me and strike the enemy?"

Many raised their bows and lances, and half the party assembled behind Thunder Coat. He was also a chief and a shield-carrier, and they trusted his power almost as much as that of Younger Wolf. As for the Wolf, he and his nephews rode toward the center of the wagon camp, waving bows and lances as they shouted taunts at the wagon people.

Younger Wolf held the Buffalo Shield so that it caught the sunlight and blinded the *wihio* riflemen. Their bullets fell short, as was intended. Then Thunder Coat and the others struck the far side of the camp.

Soon the fighting was wild and furious. The *wihio* wagons exploded in splinters as the Tsis tsis tas fought their way into the heart of the camp. There the rifles struck hard, killing many horses and driving the raiders back.

Thunder Coat's horse was shot down, and together with Talking Stick and Dancing Lance, they huddled behind the animal's corpse and covered their companions' withdrawal.

"Now's our time to ride, Foxes!" Younger Wolf shouted. He kicked his horse into a gallop and charged a band of *wihio* who were closing in on the three Foxes. Howling wildly, Iron Wolf and Porcupine followed. The wagon people weren't prepared for this new menace, and they managed only a few wild shots. Two balls bounced off the hard hide of the Buffalo Shield, and others were turned away. Younger Wolf urged the buckskin on, and the *wihio* scattered like frightened boys.

"Ayyyy!" Thunder Coat cried as he climbed up behind Younger Wolf atop the buckskin. Iron Wolf rescued Talking Stick, and Porcupine carried Dancing Lance away. They rode furiously away from the wagon camp, shouting defiantly.

"Now we'll strike the other end," Thunder Coat suggested when the raiders reassembled.

"No," Younger Wolf said, frowning as he examined the many wounds the young Foxes had suffered. Three had been left behind in the wagon camp, dead. It was enough of a price to pay.

"What then, Uncle?" Iron Wolf asked. "They, too, have been hurt."

"I must recover my shield," Thunder Coat insisted.

"Yes," Younger Wolf agreed. He dismounted and approached a fresh horse. Thunder Coat, too, mounted a spare pony.

"It's for us to do, old friend," the Coat suggested.

"I will lead," Younger Wolf said, slapping the pony into a gallop. The two chiefs raced toward the wagon camp, screaming and waving. Younger Wolf held his shield to turn the enemy bullets, and Thunder Coat raced past to where his shield lay, retrieved it, and escaped while Younger Wolf drew the enemy fire.

When they returned, a stillness settled over the land. The wind shifted, blowing hard toward Shell River and carrying the odor of death away to the south.

"They wish to treat," Goes Ahead observed, pointing to the wagon chief, walking out unarmed and alone.

"Speak with him," Thunder Coat said, turning to Younger Wolf. "But offer him nothing new."

The Wolf rode out to the wagon chief and listened to another offer of presents.

"There can be no peace now," Younger Wolf explained. "Blood has been spilled. Take your people away."

"We have no horses to pull our wagons."

"You have your lives, some of you!" the Wolf shouted. "It's all I offer."

The wagon chief stumbled back to his companions, and Younger Wolf returned to the raiders.

"When do we strike again?" Talking Stick asked.

"It's not for us to do," Younger Wolf said, taking out a flint and some kindling. "Porcupine, go to the hill and fire the grass."

"Ayyyy!" the Foxes howled. The wind would carry the fire into the wagons, and the river would prevent its spread.

"It's right fire should punish them," Thunder Coat said. "As their fevers tormented us."

Younger Wolf found no satisfaction in the blaze. The flames raced south furiously, and although the *wihio* fought to save their possessions, they had no luck. Coughing and crying, the wagon people fled to the safety of the river and swam over to the far bank. Behind them flames devoured the camp.

"When they speak of this day, they'll shudder," Talking Stick declared.

"No longer will they come and spoil our country," Thunder Coat added.

Younger Wolf heard another voice, though, that of his *wihio* brother. "You can't quiet the wind," Corn Hair Freneau had said. "You can't stop the wagon people."

Sixteen

Younger Wolf rode homeward with a heavy heart. While his companions exchanged boasts and recounted their coups, the Wolf fought to erase the haunting echoes of dying cries, the sight of the flames devouring the wagon camp. Three young men who had ridden out with such high spirits had climbed Hanging Road. Was that an event to celebrate?

"The *wihio* will sing of this fight," Talking Stick declared. "They'll remember their burning lodges and speak of it to others. No more will they ride Shell River!"

"Do you believe that?" Younger Wolf asked. "You're a man of vision, Talking Stick. You have strong dreams. Do you see the *wihio* road once more covered by tall grass, by grazing buffalo?"

"Brother? Is that what you've seen?" Thunder Coat asked.

"I will," the Stick assured his companions. "These pale people are easily frightened. Did you see how they shuddered when we charged? *Ayyyy!* They're not to be feared."

"I didn't see many run before the flames came," Younger Wolf argued. "My brother also dreams. Stone Wolf's flood is yet to come."

"He's an old man now," Talking Stick said, frowning. "Once he was a great man, but his dreams are dim. He's like the fat ones who sit at the fort and trade for the *wihio*. They've forgotten the power we hold."

"Perhaps," Younger Wolf responded. "I'm old myself. Age allows a man wisdom, and old men know that it's the sweetness of life a man can lose when he dies. I mourn those who ride no more with the Foxes. I mourn the *wihio* who won't see his sons grow tall. And I respect tomorrow for the mystery it holds for us all. You say the *wihio* are afraid, but they fought well enough. They don't walk the earth in the sacred manner, but they have their own medicine. And there are many of them. Such an enemy merits your respect. Don't ride like Fire Hawk, blind to the danger, and let them kill you."

"I won't," Talking Stick vowed. "Nor will I hide in Woman's Lodge, fearing their bullets."

"Ayyyy!" the younger men howled when Talking Stick raised his lance and screamed.

Younger Wolf slowed his pony and let the others surge ahead. He followed, accompanied by his nephews and Four Wounds.

"The Stick's words are like squirrel chatter," Iron Wolf declared. "Nothing to note."

"He stands tall in the eyes of many," Porcupine argued. "I don't like to hear Ne' hyo insulted."

"Once the Stick walked the Medicine Trail in Stone Wolf's shadow," Younger Wolf muttered. "Now he envies my brother the esteem of the People."

"Talking Stick wishes to keep Mahuts," Goes Ahead observed. "Ne' hyo hopes our brother, Dreamer, will next keep the Arrows."

"It's more appropriate for a son to take his father's place," Iron Wolf agreed. "One of us might have chosen to follow the medicine road, but we were directed elsewhere."

"Yes," Younger Wolf noted. "It's not yet time to erect a scaffold for Stone Wolf, though. We'll choose no Arrow-keeper today. Come along. Ride harder. The others are far ahead!"

The young men gave a whoop and followed their chief as he galloped toward Talking Stick, Thunder Coat, and the others. Soon the whole party was racing across the prairie, eager to return to their families and share their triumphs.

The returning Foxes were greeted warmly, and many gathered to hear the story of the wagon fight. Afterward, though, the celebrating was rather brief. The three who were killed were mourned, and coups were recounted in the Fox warriors' council. Later, when the embers had burned low, Wood Snake drew Younger Wolf aside.

"Brother, soon you will have sat in the council of forty-four ten years," the Snake observed.

"Yes," Younger Wolf replied. "I've carried my burden a long time."

"Others have spoken to me of it," Wood Snake continued. "They say, 'Younger Wolf is a great man. He's struck down our enemies. He's led wisely, always putting the welfare of the People above his own desires.' "

"That's a chief's obligation."

"As you've led the Rope Men, the Tsis tsis tas now say you should lead all the bands. When it's time you pass on your obligations, join me in the center, where the old men chiefs sit. Help guard the welfare of our tribe."

"Who asks this?" Younger Wolf asked. A chill seized his heart. How many times had he longed to pass on his obligation, the great burden a man of the People bore? To be one of the four principal Tsis tsis tas chiefs would be to add yet more weight to responsibilities which already threatened to crush him.

"All the People speak your name," Wood Snake explained. "The young men know of your many rescues and the modest way you ride to war. Older ones recall your generosity, the way you share your meat with the helpless ones. Boys speak of the arrows you've made for them or the remembered tales shared beside your fire. *Ayyyy!* No man stands higher in our eyes."

"You honor me," Younger Wolf said, gripping his friend's hands. "But I have young daughters, a son who needs my help to walk man's road. I'm sick from the many hardships I've endured. I must restore harmony to my heart."

"We can wait for you to do that."

"I will never be a chief again," Younger Wolf told the Snake. "It's for someone else to do. These days that are coming require a man with the heart to strike hard at the *wihio,* and I have no such anger inside me. Even as I burned the prairie and drove the wagon people away, I cried for the children with fathers left behind, knowing the starving times that wait ahead for them. I know starving days will find us, too, for Stone Wolf has spoken of it to me. I've seen too much. I only long to taste Hoop Woman's cooking and draw my children close to my side."

"No one as able remains to us," Wood Snake argued. "It's in the hard times that good men are most needed."

"I won't do it," Younger Wolf vowed. "I've led long enough. In the days remaining to me, I'll do what I can to provide for the helpless ones, but I won't sit in the council, nor will I lead the way in battle. I'm tired. My path has made me old."

"And can you follow another?" Wood Snake asked, studying the Wolf's eyes. "When the Rope Men turn into danger, will you share it?"

"I will do as any man is free to do," Younger Wolf replied. "I'll follow when a good choice is made. For a time, though, I think I'll seek my own path. There are high places close by where a man can enjoy peace. Stone Wolf and I can find one, as we did when we were boys. We'll pray and smoke and remember."

"It won't change anything," the Snake complained.

"It will give myself back to me," Younger Wolf explained. "Cast off the demons haunting my soul. Let me be a father and an uncle, teaching and sharing the secrets of life with the little ones. *Ayyyy!* It's enough."

"It's a dream," Wood Snake muttered.

Later others came to suggest Younger Wolf reconsider, but although he listened politely to each one, he continued to refuse.

"I've been a chief ten years," he told them all. "It's enough. Give me back to my family for a time. Let me show them the way now."

Stone Wolf observed the reluctance in his brother with concern.

"We've always known our lives were not our own," the Arrow-keeper reminded his brother. "From the first day we followed Cloud Dancer's footsteps, there could be no turning back. When did we ever know a day when the People's hardships were not our own?"

"That's true, Nah nih," Younger Wolf admitted. "But what good has it brought us? Sometimes I envy our father his brief life. He tasted the sweet fruits of glory and avoided the pain which later tormented the People."

"I believe he would have endured the pain to see us grow tall, See' was' sin mit."

"I wish to see my own son set his feet on man's road. This won't happen if I continue to place myself before the *wihio* rifles."

"My brother isn't afraid," Stone Wolf argued. "He carries the Buffalo Shield!"

"Will its power be enough to turn all the bullets the *wihio* have? Can it avert the sicknesses the strange ones bring into this country? I'm tired, Brother, and I'm finished with the council. I'm a simple man, and I wish only to be left alone."

"Yes," Stone Wolf agreed. "It's a temptation. You'll never be a simple man, though. You carry Cloud Dancer's blood, and it will always demand sacrifices."

"I won't sit in the council again."

"You've decided then," Stone Wolf said, turning and gazing at the distant hills. "Your way's become confused. We should ride into the hills and seek a dream."

"As we have so many times before," Younger Wolf agreed. "This time we'll take the young ones with us. They should learn of your medicine."

"A new Arrow-keeper will one day be needed," Stone Wolf noted. "If not my son, perhaps yours."

"It's important Mahuts be protected," Younger Wolf agreed. "They are both small, though."

"It's best a man begin walking the medicine trail when he's young. There's much to learn."

"Yes," Younger Wolf agreed. "It will be hard for them. Darker days are ahead."

"The People will need them," Stone Wolf observed. "As they need you, See' was' sin mit."

Before departing the camp, Younger Wolf devoted half a week to hunting so that Hoop Woman and the girls would have all they needed. Afterward he, Stone Wolf, and the young men undertook a sweat. It was hoped the steam would cleanse the chief of his doubts and restore the lost harmony. In part, it did. But even the medicine prayers of an Arrow-keeper and the tender touch of Hoop Woman couldn't cast from him the fear of the *wihio* and the changes they were bringing.

"You should ride to Fort John and speak with Corn Hair, your brother," Hoop Woman advised. "He may be able to make sense of it."

"He's my brother," Younger Wolf noted. "He's ridden beside me, eaten at my cook fire, and shared the buffalo hunt. Our sons have grown tall together. But he's a *wihio*. He can never understand the fear I feel for the changes his people bring to the world."

"Stay here with me, husband," she pleaded. "There's nothing in those hills to soothe your pain. I alone can do it. Give your troubles over to me. Let me drive them away!"

"No, I must go," Younger Wolf insisted. "It is true I never know such belonging as when we're together. I may even forget the peril that awaits us tomorrow. Even so, it remains. I will go to the high places and seek an understanding of what I must do to drive away this danger. From you. From our son and daughters. From our people."

"You're a chief no longer," she grumbled.

"No, that burden is gone," Younger Wolf admitted. "But Cloud Dancer, my grandfather, put me onto man's road with the understanding I must be watchful and devoted to the welfare of the other Tsis tsis tas."

"Another might complain it's a chief's duty," she said, swallowing other, unspoken words.

"My wife has an understanding heart," Younger Wolf boasted.

"You won't stay long? I smell winter on the wind."

"No, and we'll remain nearby," he assured her. "I'll bring your son back to you."

"I knew that much," she said, smiling. "I think he'll be taller, though."

"It's the way of things," Younger Wolf told her. "The little ones don't remain small forever."

* * *

191

They passed another day preparing for the journey. Iron Wolf selected good ponies for the ride into the hills, and Stone Wolf collected medicine herbs and a pipe. Younger Wolf busied himself with Dreamer and Little Dancer, making certain the boys had hunting arrows for their bows. Hoop Woman rolled hides and blankets while Dove Woman filled water skins and a food sack.

"Ah, it's different than when we rode out as boys," Stone Wolf observed when the boys began packing the spare ponies. "Then we set off with only our bows and our ponies."

"The hunting was better," Younger Wolf noted.

"It had to be," Stone Wolf replied.

"New dangers haunt the country," Younger Wolf argued. "It's wise to be prepared."

"Crows rode these hills even then, See' was' sin mit, and there were just two of us."

"Yes, we have good men with us now," Younger Wolf agreed as he eyed Iron Wolf, Goes Ahead, and Porcupine. Dreamer stood taller now in his eleventh summer, and even Little Dancer appeared less a boy.

"Everything's been done, Ne' hyo," Iron Wolf told Stone Wolf. "We should leave."

"Yes," the Arrow-keeper agreed. "The hills last forever, but we're growing older."

"Mount your pony then, Nah nih," Younger Wolf urged as he climbed atop his buckskin. "Let's seek a high place."

They left the camp amid encouraging howls from young men and the concerned glances of others.

"It's not right these good men should leave our camp

unprotected," one woman complained.

"Wood Snake remains," Stone Wolf chided her. "Your ponies are safe."

"There are plenty of fighters in the Rope Men's camp," Iron Wolf said when they passed from the view. "No one remains with the wisdom to keep the People from harm. That's your duty, Ne' hyo, and yours, Uncle. That's what troubles the women."

"Maybe one of us should have stayed," Porcupine suggested.

"My wife is there," Stone Wolf countered. "Do they imagine I would leave her in a dangerous place? No, they are safe. We won't ride far, either."

"Not far," Younger Wolf agreed. "Just high."

Indeed, they wove their way through the low hills and climbed a rocky bluff. It was a good place, once favored by the *wihio* trappers who kept a trading post there. The store had moved to Shell River now to sell supplies to the wagon people, and the bluff was rarely visited.

"In my father's father's time, this was a place where spirits walked," Stone Wolf explained, waving at the ledges above where the skeletons of burial scaffolds remained even now.

"You can see great distances from the top," Younger Wolf added. "And touch the heavens."

"Ayyyy!" Goes Ahead cried. "It's a good place then."

Good, yes, Younger Wolf thought. *Strange as well.*

It appeared so, for as they climbed the narrow trail leading to the summit, Younger Wolf felt an eerie touch to the breeze. It turned his flesh cold, and he had to urge his horse on ahead. The ponies were uneasy, and their riders no less so.

"Ne' hyo, is it far?" Dreamer called.

"Not far, little brother," Goes Ahead answered. He drew out a flute and whistled a tune, and the brave heart song emboldened them all.

Once atop the bluff, the fine view took Younger Wolf's breath from him.

"Yes, it's been a long time," Stone Wolf said, dismounting. "It is good we are here."

"It is as it has always been," Younger Wolf agreed. "Let's build up a fire, quickly. I feel a chill in the air.

The boys agreed. After tending to the ponies, they eagerly collected wood and kindled the fire. Then, formed in a circle around the blazing logs, they chanted an old song.

"It's right we share this remembered time here, at the top of the world," Stone Wolf said as he drew the pipe from its skin cover. "Here, where my brother and I once sat as boys with our grandfather, we'll smoke and pray and seek to renew ourselves."

Little Dancer appeared concerned, but Goes Ahead placed a reassuring arm around his small cousin, and the boy relaxed. Then Stone Wolf performed the pipe ritual. He and Younger Wolf smoked, and Iron Wolf, too, inhaled the smoke. The others reverently touched their lips to the pipe and passed it along.

After the pipe had circled the fire three times, Stone Wolf emptied its ashes and returned it to its cover. Then, chanting a brief prayer, he gazed solemnly at his sons and young nephew.

"Once, when the world was young, the Tsis tsis tas roamed this good country afoot," Stone Wolf began.

"Horse was still a distant dream, and he had only dog to drag his possessions to the winter camps."

"That was a hard time," Younger Wolf observed. "Many enemies struck our camps, and helpless ones were often carried away. Young men fell to their woodland enemies, and many children never lived to walk man or woman's road."

"Even so, the People never despaired," Stone Wolf resumed. "For they had Mahuts, the sacred Arrows, to guide the way. And men of the People, who set aside their own desires and made the world safe for the defenseless ones. Our blood, and the blood of our fathers, has always been devoted to our People. Often we've fallen in battle as young men. Sometimes we've walked Hanging Road as boys because our fathers gave away food to others. Never have we taken from those more in need, nor made ourselves safe by sacrificing another."

"This is the heritage we bring to you," Younger Wolf added. "It's a hard road to walk, and it makes a man weary. When his heart grows heavy, he should climb the high places and look out across the land. See how great the world is? And yet you can't see even a single man! Our troubles are nothing. We are nothing. Man Above strives to paint harmony, and our goal is to accept what's decided."

"We may think to change our fate," Stone Wolf declared, "but we can as easily blow mountains to dust or change the wind."

The last phrase tore at Younger Wolf's being, for weren't those Corn Hair Freneau's words as well?

"This day we'll share remembered stories, and eat

the good things the women have prepared," Stone Wolf continued. "As night comes to this place, we'll dance and pray and seek a new direction. Dreams may come to tell us what we should do. We'll suffer, and afterward we'll return to the People and help them to walk the sacred path."

"Ayyyy!" the boys howled.

"It's good we've come to this holy place with our fathers!" Iron Wolf shouted.

"We'll learn much!" Goes Ahead added.

The voices carried across the ridge, echoing again and again. It warmed Younger Wolf, hearing the confidence in his nephews' voices. And later, as the boys danced beside the fire, cutting their flesh so that their blood ran down their bare chests, he couldn't hide his pride.

"Help me, Ne' hyo," Little Dancer asked as he took the old stone-tipped knife from Goes Ahead. "I don't know what's to be done."

"I'll show you, Naha'," Younger Wolf told the boy. "Cut lightly," he explained, making the first mark himself. "As the blood runs, say 'Heammawihio, I make this sacrifice to invite a dream. Give me power! Show me what I must do.'"

"Heammawihio, I make this sacrifice to invite a dream," Little Dancer shouted, wincing as he touched the knife to his skin. "Give me power! Show me what I must do."

The others, too, shouted and prayed, and the dancing continued until the flames died into memory. They spread their blankets beside the embers and lay quietly as the stars danced overhead. Younger Wolf deemed it a good thing, the sharing of that time with the young ones. And he hoped they would have sons and grandsons as worthy of sharing such a remembered moment.

Seventeen

They passed three days and three nights atop the bluff, and Younger Wolf's dreams filled with many images. He saw old Cloud Dancer and relived his first buffalo hunt. Again he turned back the Crow with his Buffalo Shield. All those things were in the past, though. To him came no vision of future events.

Stone Wolf did glimpse the days ahead, but he spoke little of what he saw. Instead he sat beside the fire, smoking and whispering medicine prayers. As for the young ones, they dreamed of fighting the wagon people or turning back Crow raiders.

"And you, Little Dancer?" Younger Wolf asked his son.

"I saw clouds carried on a great wind, Ne' hyo," the boy explained.

"Nothing more?" Iron Wolf asked, lifting his cousin's chin.

"I saw my father much honored by the People," Little Dancer explained. "But I didn't understand many of the words that were spoken."

"In my dream, I saw a tremendous buffalo trapped in a snowdrift," Dreamer explained. "I tried to help him free himself, but the snow was too deep. I became trapped myself."

"I saw it, too," Stone Wolf said, frowning. "The snow. It was the *wihio* flood now frozen by winter's cold. Naha', you have the power to see ahead. It's good."

"Yes," Iron Wolf agreed. "Ne' hyo will soon have company on the medicine trail."

"It's good," Porcupine agreed.

"First I'll ride with my brothers, though," Dreamer insisted. "I must walk man's road soon, and they'll show me how."

"Our uncle's a better teacher," Goes Ahead said, glancing at Younger Wolf. "And he has better horses to give away."

The boys began exchanging taunts, but Stone Wolf put an end to that.

"It's time we returned," he announced. "Ready the horses. Pack up our belongings. Soon the People will need us."

When they arrived at the Rope Men's camp, Stone Wolf sent for the chiefs.

"I've had a dream," he told them. "After consulting with Mahuts, I've decided the People must go south. We'll winter in the flat country."

"The Pawnee camp there," Thunder Coat grumbled. "Have you forgotten how they stole Mahuts from us and turned back our power?"

"It's not such good country for hunting," Wood Snake declared.

"No, we'll know no easy days there," Stone Wolf confessed. "But here we face graver perils. We must go."

Some argued against the move, and small bands broke away from the main camp. Most trusted the vision of their Arrow-keeper, though, and heeded Stone Wolf's advice. Men broke down their lodges and assembled pony drags while the women bundled their belongings. Soon the whole camp was fording Shell River and heading southward.

For many, the migration south took them into an unknown land. Many winters had been passed along Shell River or in the shadow of Noahvose farther north. The older people recalled the south country as the place where old Cloud Dancer had brought Horse to the Tsis tsis tas. Many bands passed the summer and winter there, as did friendly Arapaho parties.

Once, before peace was made with the Comanches and Kiowas, the Tsis tsis tas had found great peril on the prairies. Now only two enemies lurked there—the hated Pawnee and the crazy *wihio*. Except when the snows were deepest, *wihio* traders made their way to the Mexican lands to the south. Some of these whites traded captive children to the Mexicans, and little ones dreaded the telling of stories of the terrible lives waiting for them there.

"Don't stray, little brother," Goes Ahead warned Dreamer one morning. "You wouldn't like life among the Mexicans."

"Are they crazier than the Shell River *wihio?*" the boy asked.

"No, but some say they're meaner," Goes Ahead

answered.

"Who?" Dreamer asked. "Nah nih, you've never even seen a Mexican. I don't believe any of it."

"That doesn't make it less true," Iron Wolf said as he waved both brothers along. "We've all seen Pawnees. They wouldn't cut you up into more than fifty pieces."

Dreamer read no jest in Iron Wolf's eyes and hurried along. Even boys of eleven knew how the Pawnee had tricked the Tsis tsis tas and captured Mahuts. A warrior named Bull had carried the Arrow bundle on his lance, and when he stopped to kill a fallen Pawnee, the Pawnee tore the Arrows away and fled with them. Younger Wolf had led three charges in an effort to break the enemy, but the Pawnee had held. The disheartened Tsis tsis tas had lost their great medicine.

It was Stone Wolf who remade the Arrows. Now two of the original four had been reacquired by diplomacy and trade. Even now it was said the Pawnee carried two of the captured Arrows and worked their own medicine to thwart the old enemy.

"The Pawnee have good weapons," Wood Snake had warned a party of young hunters. "They have many *wihio* friends who bring them powder and new guns. These rifles have made them reckless, and they strike us often. They're great horse stealers, too. Guard your ponies."

In spite of warnings, the Rope Men soon fell afoul of Pawnee tricks. First twenty horses were stolen by a party of young Pawnees. When the Crazy Dogs set off in pursuit, they were caught in a trap and driven home. A band of Tsis tsis tas buffalo hunters was attacked and driven north soon afterward.

"We must collect our best fighters and run the Paw-nee!" Thunder Coat declared. "If we don't punish them, we will have to fight other tribes as well. We are Tsis tsis tas! It's wrong any people should laugh at us. And for Pawnees . . ."

"Yes," Younger Wolf agreed. "It's well to talk hard, but what will you do? The enemy knows the country better, and he sets traps for our men. Be careful. Don't give yourselves over to an ambush!"

The young men's blood was up, though, and many were ready to paint their faces and ride against the Pawnee.

"Are we old men to sit and talk?" a young man named Magpie cried. "Those dogs are waiting."

"They'll be waiting tomorrow," Younger Wolf argued. "Listen to me, Brothers. Remember the last time we fought the Pawnee. Don't make the same mistake. Make the proper preparations. Carry a pipe to Ma-huts. Seek the guidance of my brother, the Arrow-keeper. We'll make good medicine."

"It's a wise idea," Talking Stick said, nodding. "Stone Wolf sees many things. We can invite Mahuts to offer us protection."

"The Pawnee will be safe in their camp," Magpie grumbled.

"You are a man, Magpie," the Stick said, turning to the young warrior. "Take a pipe and carry it around the camp. See if you are a chief who men will follow."

"Yes," Thunder Coat added. "You've counted coup on rabbits and mice. Take up your rifle and run the

Pawnee."

The others laughed at the notion. Magpie, for all his strong words, was but a boy of eighteen summers. He had counted no coups, nor had he ridden in the war parties against the *wihio* wagons.

"It would be a good thing to enjoy Mahuts' protection," Magpie admitted. "Carry your pipe to the Arrows, Talking Stick."

"There will be time to run the Pawnee afterward," the Stick promised. "If the signs are favorable."

They weren't. Although Talking Stick and Stone Wolf climbed the hills and sought a vision to guide the young men, neither found a dream that spoke of success.

"I saw many brave hearts eaten by coyotes," Stone Wolf explained.

"It's a bad time to strike," Talking Stick agreed. "Our medicine will hold no power to turn the enemy bullets."

It appeared the matter was settled. However, the next day a body of angry Arapahoes arrived at the Rope Men's camp. Their chief, Little Beaver, was hot to fight the Pawnee.

"They struck my camp," the Beaver explained. "Brave brothers have fallen to their bullets, and many small ones were carried off. My sister is among them. Who will sing his war song and follow me to bring the helpless ones home?"

"I will," Magpie quickly volunteered.

"I, too," others shouted.

Soon twenty young men had vowed to join Little Beaver. When Stone Wolf reminded them of the bad medicine dreams, they only laughed.

"You didn't see the Arapaho, old man," Magpie declared. "We're strong now. *Ayyyy!* We'll run our enemies!"

"We are strong, Uncle," Iron Wolf told Younger Wolf while preparing a horse for war. "Now these Arapaho fighters join us. They know the country. We'll rely on their eyes to avoid the Pawnee tricks."

"And who would lead you?" Younger Wolf asked. "Thunder Coat? His brother, the Stick?"

"Talking Stick will not go," Iron Wolf explained. "He's dreamed bad things. Thunder Coat will not question his brother's dream. Our chiefs have grown afraid, it seems, but Little Beaver is eager to have us with him. He'll lead."

"What do you know of him?" Younger Wolf asked.

"He fights," Iron Wolf answered. "It's enough."

"In my life," Younger Wolf said sourly, "I've seen many men eager to lead others into danger. I've followed some and seen the death they bring to their companions. I know Little Beaver. His mother was Pawnee, and it's said his father was *wihio*. This is no strong blood for a man to have. He's eager to punish his mother's people, I think. He'll know no caution, as a chief should. The leader of a war party must practice patience and make every preparation. This won't happen. Stay here, Nephew. Don't hurry your death."

"We can't hide our faces from the enemy, Uncle," Goes Ahead said, joining his brother. "You bear the marks of many wounds, and there's nothing you need to prove. We're no longer boys suckling their mother's

204

breasts. It's time we counted coup."

"We'll ride together, we three," Porcupine vowed. "No one of us will be alone. Our strength comes from this bond, and it will carry us from every danger."

"Or hurry you into peril," Younger Wolf observed. "For if one is in harm's path, the others will step there, too."

"You could lead us," Goes Ahead suggested.

"I'm a chief no longer," Younger Wolf insisted. "I'll lead no young men to their deaths."

The chiefs spoke loudly their concerns for the young men, but Little Beaver had no ears for their words. And when he rode out of the camp, many Tsis tsis tas followed.

"It's a bad thing," Wood Snake observed as he stood with Younger Wolf, watching. "I've lost too many relatives in such foolish raids. Now my nephews ride with yours."

"They're young," the Wolf replied. "They can't hear us. They must make their own mistakes."

"Even Talking Stick sees the folly in this raid," Wood Snake grumbled. "I've read death in his eyes."

"I, too," Younger Wolf said, staring at his feet. "What's to be done, old friend?"

"What we've always done," the Snake explained. "We must follow and rescue the young fools."

"They can't know," Younger Wolf insisted. "We may be wrong."

"We aren't wrong. We'll stay well behind, though, so that no one can see us."

"Two men can't do much."

"Two?" Wood Snake asked, laughing. "Others have sons and nephews. We won't be alone."

And they weren't. Half a day after Little Beaver led the way south, ten others left the Tsis tsis tas camp. Younger Wolf was a chief no longer, but his eyes were good at spotting sign, and he was respected by all. He led the way.

"It's a hard thing, holding back," Wood Snake observed whenever they spied the dust thrown high by Little Beaver's party. "I'm a stranger to this country, but I would have trapped them three times already. They post no night guards, and they spread themselves out as if scouting Bull Buffalo. This is no way to ride to war!"

"We could slip in and steal their ponies," Dancing Lance suggested. "Then they would have to return."

"I don't want to break their spirits," Wood Snake argued. "And when they saw their horses among the herd, they would harden their hearts toward us. The Arapaho, too, would be bad hearts."

"We must wait for the Pawnee to strike," Younger Wolf agreed. "Be patient, Dancing Lance. When you're as old as we are, you won't hurry a thing to its end."

"I only want my brothers to grow as old," the Lance explained.

"Nothing lives long," Wood Snake muttered. "But we'll save most of them."

Two days after leaving camp, Younger Wolf spotted two Pawnee. They were boys, surely sent to scout the prairie for signs of the enemy. They watched from a low hill, and when Little Beaver approached, they mounted their horses and galloped straight toward the Arapaho, shouting and waving their rifles.

"Decoys," Wood Snake observed. "Where are the others?"

"There," Younger Wolf said, pointing to dust trickling skyward from a nearby ravine.

"Fools!" Dancing Lance said as he watched Little Beaver charge after the Pawnee boys. It was an old, often-repeated trick, and a war chief should have held back. Nevertheless the Arapaho fired their rifles at the decoys and urged their Tsis tsis tas companions to follow.

Younger Wolf grimly watched the ambush develop. He found scant satisfaction in the fact that his nephews remained to one side with Four Wounds, Wood Snake's nephew. Those four showed some trace of caution. Magpie, who had spoken so loudly for war, raced toward the second Pawnee boy, caught up with him, and struck him a hard blow on the shoulder with a war ax.

"*Ayyyy!*" Magpie shouted as he jumped down, smashed the decoy's skull, and lifted his scalp. "I'm first!"

The second decoy fell, too, but their sacrifice brought the enemy into the trap. Vengeful Pawnees screamed wildly as they hurried from the ravine and surrounded their surprised prey. Little Beaver was set upon by five of them and lifted from his horse. The Pawnee fell on the Arapaho chief and cut him to pieces.

Stunned, Arapahoes fled in every direction. Six were shot down quickly, and others were trapped in twos and threes by the Pawnee. Fighting was hard, and Pawnee blood stained the prairie. But the enemy held all the advantages.

Magpie was the first Tsis tsis tas to fall. Afoot, he was easily ridden down. The Pawnee began their cutting when he was still alive, and his shrill screams were terrible to hear.

"It's time," Younger Wolf said, pointing to a low mound where Four Wounds was gathering the survivors. They dismounted and let their weary animals escape. Iron Wolf stood between his brothers and shouted defiantly at the Pawnee line preparing to charge.

"Now!" Wood Snake shouted, and the ten followers split the air with their cries. Riding like thunderbolts, they struck the Pawnee line from behind and broke it apart. Younger Wolf struck down two men and unhorsed a third while his companions likewise scattered the enemy. The surprised Pawnee tried to rally themselves around a tall chief wearing two eagle feathers on his hairless scalp.

"It's for me to do the difficult things!" Younger Wolf sang as he turned his horse and charged the Pawnee leader. Holding the Buffalo Shield on his left arm, he balanced his lance in his right and hurled it into the chest of the bald Pawnee. The Pawnee tried to deflect the lance with his rifle, but the lance pierced his arm and passed on, striking him in the belly and driving on through to the spine. The Pawnee chief rolled off his horse as if struck down by Thunderbird.

"Ayyyy!" the surviving Tsis tsis tas young men shouted as they bolstered their courage. Emboldened, they stepped forward and drove off the last of the charging

Pawnees. Shaken and leaderless, they scattered past the ravine and sought the shelter of the low hills beyond.

"Collect your horses!" an Arapaho named Sparrow Hawk urged. "We can still run them."

"No, we return to our camp," Wood Snake demanded. "We've done enough."

"You've saved us, Uncle," Four Wounds said, dropping his eyes toward the ground.

"Younger Wolf has again rescued the helpless," Iron Wolf observed. "We were foolish to ignore our uncle's advice."

"Learn from this mistake," Younger Wolf replied as he helped find horses for the young men. Others set off to collect the dead and tie them on ponies for the hard ride north. Some paused to scalp the dead Pawnees or take discarded rifles.

"We've killed twenty," Sparrow Hawk boasted. "This will be a day to sing about!"

"In the Pawnee camps, perhaps," another Arapaho suggested. "Little Beaver's dead. Many others, too."

"All of us might have fallen," Four Wounds said solemnly. "No, we'll sing no brave heart songs of this day."

"It's enough that we have breath to sing at all," Goes Ahead said, nodding sorrowfully.

"Let's go," Wood Snake urged. "This is Pawnee country, and there are surely others about."

"Lead us, Uncle," Four Wounds replied.

"No, that's for another to do," the Snake said, motioning toward Younger Wolf.

"Lead them, Brother," Younger Wolf said in turn. "You're the chief. I'll follow and watch."

"As you've always done," Wood Snake said, nodding. He then turned his horse and headed for the distant camp of the Rope Men. Some who trailed sang brave heart songs and others began the mourning howls. The mixture haunted the prairie, and the riders hurried their horses.

"Are the Pawnee chasing us?" Porcupine asked.

"Perhaps," Younger Wolf said, glancing back at the empty horizon. "Something is."

"What?" Goes Ahead asked.

"Ghosts," Younger Wolf explained. "Doubts." The first he only suspected. He was certain of the other.

Eighteen

As they rode homeward, a great anger grew in Younger Wolf's heart. As he helped tend the wounds of old friends and young men, it seemed to him as if the world was ablaze in a firestorm of blood. He searched his memory for such a time and found nothing to compare. Worse, they rode the great prairie without spotting a single buffalo. It appeared that Stone Wolf's dreams were coming to pass.

When they returned, the council assembled to discuss the failed raid on the Pawnee. Many voices argued that now, while the Pawnee mourned their fallen chief, was a time to raid again.

"Why should we succeed now?" Wood Snake asked. "The Arapaho are gone, and winter is browning the grasses. It's a bad time to leave our women and children."

"To remain here is to invite the Pawnee to steal our ponies and raid our camp," Talking Stick argued. "They'll judge us weak and strike hard."

"Will they?" the Snake asked. "What medicine tells you so?"

"It's always been this way," Thunder Coat said, rising

and pacing before the fire. "In my father's day, we always rode out to strike the Crow before erecting our winter camp. They would hold fear in their hearts and leave us alone. These Pawnee laugh at our efforts to punish them. They'll come."

"A Pawnee can grow as cold in winter as a Tsis tsis tas," Stone Wolf said, frowning. "You say how it was in your father's time, but you only remember stories. I walked the earth and remember how it was. Only when the Crow came into our country did we strike at them, or when we moved north into the Crazy Woman's River country in search of Bull Buffalo.

"We've fought the Pawnee, yes, and stolen their horses. Sometimes parties have taken women and little ones, but mostly they've been bought back or gone of their own choice. When you brought a pipe, I consulted Mahuts. The Arrows warn against such raids. The enemy is elsewhere."

"How can we be sure?" Talking Stick asked. "When I was young and slept at your side in the Arrow Lodge, you shared the knowledge of your medicine, Stone Wolf. You told me which herbs cure sickness and which powders turn the enemy bullets away. I watched you suffer and pray, but I saw no signs that would tell you what to do. Your power is in your dreams. I, too, dream, and my vision tells me the People must be strong. We must fight."

"My power flows from Mahuts," Stone Wolf insisted.

"Some grow old, and their eyes no longer see as a young man does," Talking Stick noted. "Many winters you've sacrificed for the welfare of the People, and the burdens you have carried show in the lines of your fore-head. I honor the good you've done, and I respect your power. But maybe the years blind you to the truth. You see what you wish and disregard all else."

"It's true," Thunder Coat agreed. "When has he of-fered us counsel that could give us a victory? Always he speaks for turning away from war, for running from our enemies!"

Younger Wolf listened to the chiefs' complaints with a heavy heart. He saw the pain flowing across his brother's face, and it kindled a rage inside. When had Stone Wolf ever misled them? When had he ever turned his medicine to his own use? The welfare of the People had always come first. Always!

"I'm a chief no longer," Younger Wolf finally said, rising. "But my voice is a familiar one, and the chiefs may find use for it now."

"Speak," Wood Snake urged.

"Forty summers I've walked this earth at my brother's side," Younger Wolf began. "When the time came for our grandfather to give over to another the care of the Arrows, I hoped I would be the chosen one. Instead Mahuts came into Stone Wolf's possession. *Ayyyy!* It was a better choice. I am quicker to anger, and I would never have made the sacrifices necessary to maintain the harmony required in the Arrow Lodge. Now I hear young men say Stone Wolf is old, that his vision is weak. I'm glad the Arrows rest in the hands of an expe-rienced man. He's felt the sting of enemy arrows and tended the dying. Only a man who's mourned a dead child can truly value life.

"Since Stone Wolf has tended Mahuts, great peril has come to the People. Each time a warning has been ignored. Stone Wolf spoke against trading with the *wihio*, but it was done. The spotted fevers which emptied our lodges came. Stone Wolf spoke against ignoring the ceremonies and rushing Mahuts into danger, but it was done, and the medicine was lost. It was my brother who brought Mahuts back to the People, who restored our power.

"Many times young men have proposed raids. Some have consulted the Arrows. Whenever Stone Wolf has warned of calamity, he has been ignored. Many have died because the chiefs didn't listen. It's the same now. The blood of our brothers even now stains the grasses, and yet you speak for another raid, for taking others to their deaths."

"Yes, the bloodstains are there!" Talking Stick shouted. "They cry for revenge!"

"My days are coming to their end," Younger Wolf said, studying the concerned faces of the men around him. "Soon others will stand in my place and say what should be done. Take these words of mine for the iron that's in them. Heed Mahuts. Don't ignore the wisdom that's shared with you. Only death can come of such foolish behavior."

"You've spoken, old man," Talking Stick grumbled. "Now be quiet and let the chiefs decide."

"Is Talking Stick now a chief?" Wood Snake asked.

"He's a man of power," Thunder Coat declared. "He speaks with my heart, and his words are mine."

"The Crazy Dogs are willing to strike the Pawnee,"

South Wind declared. "I remember the days Younger Wolf speaks of, for I'm no young man. Many times I've fought our enemies, counting coup and taking his hair. I respect Mahuts, and I listen to Stone Wolf's advice, but the Stick is right. The Arrow-keeper is old."

"He lacks the all-seeing eyes," Thunder Coat added. "We'll form a war party and ride against our enemy."

"Have you no ears to hear the truth!" Younger Wolf exclaimed.

"We've heard you," Thunder Coat said, frowning. "But now it's for us who to decide."

"Choose as you will then," Younger Wolf said, turning away. He left the council and marched angrily to his lodge.

"What's happened?" Little Dancer asked, touching his father's arm.

"The People have turned away from the sacred path," Younger Wolf said. "We're led by fools. The young men hunger for honor, and they would sacrifice the helpless ones."

"Ne' hyo, you should have remained a chief," Little Dancer declared. "All the young men say so."

"Perhaps they say it, but their eyes turn to others. Even now they are eager for war."

"What will you do, Husband?" Hoop Woman asked as she stepped outside and greeted Younger Wolf.

"No choice remains," the Wolf said, sighing. "If I stay, I will disturb the harmony of our camp. I must leave this place and seek my own way."

"Alone?" Hoop Woman cried. "With winter coming?"

215

"Stone Wolf will be with us," Little Dancer declared. "My cousins and I will protect you, Nah' koa."

"Stone Wolf must remain," Younger Wolf insisted. "The People need Mahuts more than ever. No, we'll go alone. There are high places that will conceal us from enemy eyes. I'm not so old that I can't guard my family."

"It will be hard," Hoop Woman argued. "You've been angry at the others before. Go and talk with them some more. Make peace with them."

"I'm finished with them," Younger Wolf said, pulling the Hoop close. "We'll break down our lodge and set out tomorrow. I won't leave my family in danger, and this camp won't be safe. It will be good, sharing the winter silence with you, Hoop. I'll have stories to share with the little ones, and there will be no war parties to take me away."

"I will enjoy your company," Hoop Woman confessed. "But I worry that it's wrong you should go."

"I must be true to my heart," he told her. "To remain will be to agree with the men who lead the Rope Men. To go tells the others they have decided poorly. Maybe they'll call us back."

"Maybe," Hoop Woman whispered, though neither one of them expected it to happen.

Younger Wolf shared his thoughts with no one, but only a dead man could have ignored the breaking down of a lodge occupying an honored place in the camp circle.

"See' was' sin mit, you are leaving?" Stone Wolf cried in surprise as he approached his brother's cook fire.

"It's necessary," Younger Wolf explained. "I can't follow those who now lead the Hev a tan iu. I would only create disharmony by staying."

"The People need you," Stone Wolf argued. "It's known you would have sat in the chief's council. The young men look to your advice."

"They must find their own way now," Younger Wolf declared. "I'm seeking my own direction. I wish no chief's burden, Nah nih. I long to winter in quiet and solitude, with my wife and children close."

"I've grown to rely on having you at my side. You know I can't leave. My obligation is to keep Mahuts among the People."

"I understand," Younger Wolf said, sighing. "Nah nih, I've ridden at your side these many years, but I can't stay here now. The nephews no longer require someone to craft their arrows, and the older ones can instruct Dreamer in what he needs to know. It will be hard to leave you and them, but I will find no peace here."

"There's peril in this country."

"I know, but I have eyes to see my enemies. It's the danger from within our band I have always been blind to."

"As I have," Stone Wolf said, frowning. "You spoke for me, I know, but I would rather you have kept silent and remained here."

"The words needed to be said," Younger Wolf asserted. "Don't concern yourself for my welfare. I'm like

217

a colt running wild—free to find my own pace and to seek my own direction."

"Run then, See' was' sin mit, but return to us. The People need their best men to face the trouble ahead."

Younger Wolf had no easier time bidding farewell to his nephews. Young men like Four Wounds and Dancing Lance, who had shared so many hard fights, collected their belongings and packed their horses.

"I've always found Younger Wolf a man to follow," Four Wounds said. "I'll travel with him again."

"You have relatives in this camp," Younger Wolf objected, thinking of Wood Snake in particular.

"I'm a boy no longer," Four Wounds boasted. "I seek my own path,"

"It will be good to have you with us," Younger Wolf then said, grinning.

Soon others heard of the Wolf's departure. Men stopped to question his departure. Others arrived to offer thanks for kindnesses or encouragement. Later, four families broke down their lodges and prepared to follow.

"It's a bad thing you're doing," Thunder Coat complained. "Now, in this hard time, we need all our band together."

"I can't follow the direction you've chosen," Younger Wolf answered. "Others agree."

"You'll be easy prey for the Pawnee," the Coat warned.

"I've never been an easy man to kill," Younger Wolf replied. "Good men are going with me. It's you who will bring the People into danger by ignoring Mahuts.

218

You've been a good fighter and will make a good chief if you remember what you've seen. Seek my brother's advice. Be cautious. Then you will have many things to mark when it's time for you to make your winter count."

"I wish you well, Uncle," Thunder Coat concluded. "You're wrong, but you have never turned away from the difficult tasks. I respect your decision."

"It's good to know," Younger Wolf noted, turning back to his labors.

Not long afterward the lodge was broken down, and the belongings were placed on pony drags. The nephews helped gather Younger Wolf's horses, and Iron Wolf assisted Red Hoop and Little Hoop atop a pair of gentle mares. Little Dancer climbed on his favorite paint, and Younger Wolf mounted the reliable buckskin. Hoop Woman, who usually preferred walking, rode a white mare. She knew theirs was certain to be a long journey, and she took her place between the girls.

"It's a sad day my brother leaves us," Stone Wolf called from the edge of the broken camp circle.

"Yes, it's hard going," Younger Wolf replied. "My road takes me north."

"We'll meet when it's time to remake the earth," Stone Wolf vowed. "Man Above will guide you there."

"I hope he watches over you, Nah nih," Younger Wolf said, frowning. "Be watchful."

"As is my obligation," Stone Wolf declared.

They traveled north a week before crossing Shell River and climbing into the hills beyond.

"No Pawnee will find us here," Four Wounds observed. "This is the heart of our old country. We know it well."

"Crow travel here," Younger Wolf pointed out.

"Lakotas mostly," Dancing Lance declared. "We have relatives among them. I don't fear Crow."

"Nor anything that's known," Younger Wolf boasted. "Only the future offers peril, for there is much about it we can't know."

They formed their small camp circle a day's ride east of Noahvose, in the sacred country where Stone Wolf had so often sought medicine dreams. Younger Wolf felt at ease there, for game abounded, and the men returned daily after killing deer and elk. Good winter coats were made, and meat was smoked against winter's need. Already the autumn buffalo hunt had provided much. Now even the hungriest boy could eat without concern.

Once the snows began to fall, the men ventured out less and less. Younger Wolf passed the short days beside the fire, making medicine charms, crafting bows, or sharing stories with the children. Sometimes, when the sun warmed the snow-coated land, he walked the ridges with Little Dancer, sharing such knowledge as a boy of eight summers could digest. There were medicine cures to teach and prayers to pass on. And the legacy of a proud family.

"Ne' hyo, does it trouble you we're cut off from our People?" the boy asked one morning.

"Look around you, Naha'," Younger Wolf answered. "Our world is closer here than ever. Are we cut off?"

"There are few Tsis tsis tas here, though," the boy lamented. "Only a few other children."

"Yes, we're few," Younger Wolf admitted. "But we can walk the sacred path here. Harmony fills the air. It's as good a place to be as we might find under the heavens, Naha'. I'm at peace with myself and the world beyond. Do you feel that peace?"

"Yes," the boy admitted. "But I miss my cousins."

"We'll be together again when it's time to collect the ten bands," Younger Wolf promised. "I hope the peace here will have prepared me for the trials we'll face next summer."

"The *wihio* wagons will come again."

"Yes, Stone Wolf says they will."

"We'll fight them then. And the Crow, too, maybe."

"We have many enemies."

"That's not what troubles you, though."

"You see much," Younger Wolf said, pulling the boy closer. "Soon you will be old enough to learn from others, Naha'. Already Dreamer is learning the medicine prayers, the rituals an Arrow-keeper must perform."

"You think I should learn them, too?"

"It is good for more than one person to prepare to lift my brother's burdens. You, Naha', watch the small things. I've seen you study the smallest creatures. You follow Butterfly's flight, and you trace Deer's path through the thickets. No ordinary man watches so closely. Even if it's not your destiny to keep Mahuts,

221

you may come to be a man of power. The People will need you."

"If you think it's wise, I'll go to my uncle."

"His sons have come to me," Younger Wolf noted. "It's appropriate."

"Is it a hard path, the medicine trail?"

"All paths a Tsis tsis tas must walk are hard, Naha'. The world changes before our eyes, and the old, accustomed ways are no more. Once it was enough to throw the lance and shoot arrows. Now the *wihio* has brought rifles to change all that. A man proved himself when I was a boy by striking the enemy with his hand, counting coup. Now the young men long to strike the heart, and prove they've killed by tying scalps to their lances.

"It's all crazy. Maybe we can restore the old harmony in this high place. I pray so, for a world without harmony can't be understood even by a man of great power."

"A man such as yourself, Ne' hyo?"

"Perhaps," Younger Wolf said, smiling. "And as my son may come to be."

Nineteen

It was remembered as the year of the deep snows in the winter counts of the old people. Younger Wolf couldn't remember a time so bitter cold. Snows choked the mountains and ate the sun. Children coughed and shivered. Even cloaked with heavy buffalo and elk robes, Younger Wolf felt the bitter bite of winter. It penetrated deep into a man's soul, chilling him through every inch of his being.

He knew it was worse for the little ones. Nightly he and Hoop Woman let the girls crawl between them. Red Hoop and Little Hoop were so small! By comparison, Little Dancer appeared grown. As he nestled under his father's arm, Younger Wolf felt the boy's heart pounding as it sought to pump warming blood through the trembling child.

"Perhaps it was on such a night," Younger Wolf said one night as shrill winds bombarded the lodge, and snow fell in great clumps, "that the Star Boys climbed into the sky."

"Who were they, Ne' hyo?" Little Dancer asked.

"Ah, once they were boys much like you," Younger

223

Wolf explained. "They loved to swim the rivers and chase antelope across the prairie. But when winter came, painting the country white with snow, they grew fearful. They had no warm lodges to sleep in and no roasting meat to eat. Hunger and cold tormented them, and they searched in vain for shelter. Finally they found a place. Dark, damp, deep inside the heart of the mountain, it was. A cave."

"Like the ones on this mountain?" Little Hoop asked.

"Yes, little one," Younger Wolf told the six-year-old. "They thought at last they had found refuge, but it wasn't so."

"There was a bear living there!" Little Dancer cried.

"Yes," Younger Wolf agreed. "A great silver-coated bear large as the mountain itself. With a bellowing growl, it cried, 'Who dares to come into my den?' "

"What did the boys do, Ne' hyo?" Red Hoop cried.

"They stared through the darkness at the fiery eyes of the beast. 'We're poor boys, who have come into your home to avoid the snow,' one of them explained. 'We mean you no harm, Uncle. We're only cold.'

" 'Yes,' Bear answered, 'and you would steal my coat to warm you! I've known humans before, and they're no one I care to pass the winter with. Out!' "

"Did they run, Ne' hyo?" Little Hoop asked.

"Ah, not in the beginning," Younger Wolf explained. "They thought to hide from Bear, but the beast had their scent, and when they didn't leave, he set out after them, snapping the air with his big, sharp teeth and shaking the earth with his heavy feet. The boys ran from the cave, but outside the cold struck them like a heavy club. They were blinded by the falling snow, and freezing finger by finger, toe by toe. 'Man Above,' they cried, 'Save us from the beast. Save us from the cold.' Man Above shook the snow from a tall pine and bid them climb it. There, high above the ground, they would be safe from Bear."

"So they climbed the tree?" Little Dancer asked.

"Yes, but their eyes were still blind, and when they reached the top, they went on climbing. First one cloud and then another they stepped upon. Finally, when they were high above the snow clouds and near the warming sun, they saw what they had done.

" 'Man Above, you've brought us high into the sky,' they said. 'Here it is safe, and we have Sun to keep us warm. Let us stay, and we'll be good company.' So it was that they stayed. Even now, when the sky is clear, you can see them dancing in their half circle overhead."

"Is it true, Ne' hyo?" Red Hoop said, gazing deeply into her father's eyes.

"There were seven boys. Now they're up above. Look yourself. Count them. The seven are there even now."

"I wonder if they would take another?" Little Dancer asked. "I'm cold."

"Yes, Naha' we're all cold," Younger Wolf admitted. He rubbed the boy's chest and flanks, then did the same for the girls. A shine came for a time to their eyes, but the cold returned too soon.

"Are we being punished, Ne' hyo?" Little Dancer asked. "Is it cold in the south country, too?"

"Cold everywhere," Younger Wolf said, frowning. "Imagine how the *wihio* fort people are freezing inside

225

their thick stone walls with no hides on the floor! No fire burning in the center of the lodge! *Ayyyy!* They'll freeze!"

"It wouldn't be such a bad thing," Little Dancer suggested. "They've brought us much trouble."

"Our cousins are there, though," Red Hoop argued. "Tom said he would come and see us when the grass grew green once more."

"He isn't welcome," Little Dancer grumbled. "Soon he'll be a hairy face like his brothers. He, too, will join the bluecoats and kill us."

"Who told you that?" Younger Wolf asked.

"The boys speak of it often," Little Dancer explained. "Once, before the sun darkened my skin, they called me Corn Hair Heart. They say it's turned Mahuts against the People, bringing a *wihio* into our family."

"Do you believe it?" Younger Wolf asked.

"No," the Dancer said, huddling beside his father. "It's only talk. They wish to hurt me. They envy my father's shield, his power, the honor paid him by the young men. It's why they turn away from your counsel, I think. Iron Wolf says so."

"Does he?" Younger Wolf asked.

"They don't understand why you turn away from the chiefs' council, why you don't wear a bonnet of many feathers like other men who have counted coups."

"Do you understand it, Naha'?" the Wolf asked.

"My father is a modest man," the boy replied. "His power comes from the old ways, from stone-tipped arrows and the sacred Buffalo Shield. He won't carry a rifle or wear a war bonnet. I think sometimes Younger

226

Wolf walks a difficult road. But I'm glad he's my father."

Younger Wolf warmed at the touch of the boy's arms, and glowed as the girls gazed up lovingly. Later, when Hoop Woman enveloped him under the hides, and they became one, he wondered if any man deserved such good fortune as a devoted wife and loving children.

The worst of winter passed into memory. Nightly the lodge filled with the sounds of stories and the playing of flutes. Songs and comforting arms drove away the torment and left a warming glow behind.

The first thaw brought the camp to life once more. Younger Wolf and the other men shot fresh game, and the cook fires burned brightly as roasting venison awakened new hunger in the people.

"Summer will come early this year," Dancing Lance declared. "Will we join our brothers for the counting? Will we share in the remaking of the earth?"

"You must do as you think best," Younger Wolf replied. "I will stay here."

"You told Stone Wolf you would come, Ne' hyo," Little Dancer reminded his father. "It's expected."

"Nothing has changed there," Younger Wolf grumbled. "We've found peace here. I now know my children."

"Husband?" Hoop Woman asked. "Can we walk?"

"Yes," he said, excusing himself from the others. Once out of hearing, Hoop Woman stopped.

"It's not right to cut yourself off from the Tsis tsis tas," she told him. "You're needed."

"I'm needed here, too," he insisted.

"Yes, and I would hold you here, away from the

others, if I thought it was the right thing to do. But it is not," she told him. "When I first took you to my heart, you warned you would always belong first to the People. I knew it even before. It's the source of your generosity, of your warming heart. You've been ours alone for a time, and we are grateful. But as each moon passes, your concern for the others will grow. It will devour you in the end. Go now, when all the People assemble together. If the chiefs remain deaf to your words, we can break down our lodge and come back here."

"You don't expect that to happen, though," he muttered.

"No, nor does my husband," she replied.

"Once, long ago, an old man told me I would have a choice to make in my life," Younger Wolf explained. "I might choose a quiet life, a rich and long one with many children and a loving wife. I would know many winters, but I would mark my passing with no great deeds."

"And the other choice, Husband?"

"A short but remembered life," he answered. "Filled with difficulties. Hard fights. At my heart would always be the welfare of the weak and helpless. I would sacrifice, as would my family. And one day I would give up my life for my People."

"I know your choice," she said, sighing. "You never doubted it before."

"I was young then, Hoop. Now I feel the aches of many wounds, and I sense the day's coming when I'll be asked to give up my life. These times are too precious, too sweet. I don't wish to climb Hanging Road when my children remain so small."

"How often have you told me no man truly decides anything? Man Above has laid a road before your feet. Walk it, as you always have, with courage, as a man should. If you die, we will survive. You've given us your strength, whether you're with us or not. Many are devoted to you, and they won't let your family suffer."

"It's true enough," Younger Wolf agreed. He glanced back at the camp where Dancing Lance and Four Wounds were playfully teasing the girls. Stone Wolf lived, as did his sons. Hoop Woman and the little ones would be provided for.

"It's necessary we begin our preparations," she said, turning him back toward the camp. "We must fatten the horses if they're to carry us to Noahvose for the New Life ceremony."

"Why there?" Younger Wolf asked.

"Because I know your brother. If winter has wearied the others as it has ourselves, Stone Wolf will seek the greatest medicine he knows. That flows from Noahvose, where Sweet Medicine brought Mahuts to the People."

"You're right," Younger Wolf agreed. "I'll go and tell the others."

It was a remembered time, the summer morning when Younger Wolf led the way to where the Rope Men were making camp in the shadow of Noahvose. The young Foxes rushed out, whooping and shouting, for they were eager to have their old war leader back among them. Older men shouted greetings, and even Thunder Coat and Talking Stick welcomed him.

"It's a good day!" Stone Wolf shouted. "My brother's returned."

"You look well, Nah nih," Younger Wolf observed. "The cold has left you well."

"Better than many," Stone Wolf confessed.

"The nephews?"

"All taller and stronger. Even Dreamer is becoming a man. He plucks his chin hairs."

"We've become old, Nah nih," Younger Wolf said, sighing.

"Not so old that we can't join in the feasting," Stone Wolf insisted. "I have much to do, but first the others must arrive. We'll eat well while we wait."

"Hunting is good here then?"

"Always, when our family is together," Stone Wolf boasted. "Bring your lodge inside the circle beside my own. It belongs there, in its honored place. When the poles are raised, we'll cook a buffalo hump roast and share news of the winter apart. First the lodge, and then the food."

Younger Wolf agreed, and the brothers set off to tend to their separate tasks. Later, when the lodges stood side by side, and the brothers, their wives, and the children sat in a circle, eating roasted hump, Younger Wolf told of his band and the deep snows.

"We, too, suffered," Stone Wolf said, staring anxiously at the smaller circle of lodges that composed the Rope Men's camp. "It was as I foretold, and as you expected. The raiders found no Pawnee, but the enemy struck our camp in their absence. Seven men were killed, and three women taken. Some children, too, but they returned, having escaped with the aid of an Arapaho.

"Many of us have bad hearts toward the chiefs who made such a thing possible. Your name has been spoken often, and Mahuts enjoys greater respect. Even so, only Wood Snake insists the old ceremonies be performed and appropriate prayers made before hunting."

"The Snake's a man to note," Younger Wolf declared.

"As is my brother," Stone Wolf added. "I believe Thunder Coat will give his place in the council over to his brother soon. Talking Stick now leads the young men. South Wind is sick and speaks only rarely. Snowbird, who also led us, fell to the Pawnee. They will ask you to sit in his place."

"I'm finished with being a chief," Younger Wolf grumbled. "I won't do it."

"Then it's certain the young men will insist Thunder Coat remain and the Stick sit in the vacant place."

"Snowbird has sons," Younger Wolf objected.

"Wed to Lakotas," Stone Wolf explained. "Gone to ride with their wives' people."

"Then Thunder Coat and Talking Stick will sit in the chiefs' council," Younger Wolf said, frowning. "Brothers have sat there before."

"Yes," Stone Wolf said. "Men of strong hearts. Once, when Talking Stick was still a boy, I had such hopes he would be a good man. White Horn, he was called then, and a braver boy I never saw. *Ayyyy!* His heart held the welfare of the People foremost, and he learned the medicine cures quickly. He hung from the pole to bring the sick good health."

"He turned aside from the medicine trail," Younger Wolf noted. "He tasted glory as a warrior. Now he hungers for it."

"More each day he brings me to think of Fire Hawk."

"Then it's a sad day for the Rope Men," Younger Wolf lamented. "Soon maybe they'll consider Dancing Lance as a leader. Later your sons will stand tall in the eyes of the young men."

"Now only you, See' was' sin mit, can counter the Stick."

"It's more than a man should be asked to do, Nah nih."

"When have you ever turned from the difficult tasks?" Stone Wolf asked. "There's no one else. Ride with the young men. Keep them safe."

Younger Wolf only sighed. More than ever he felt the end of his days creeping closer. He wished no burden of responsibility. He hungered for peace, for solitude, and he knew it wouldn't be his.

That night the council met around a small fire, and many things were discussed. Talking Stick was, indeed, selected to take a place of his own, but even as the Stick spoke of turning south to punish the Pawnee for their raid, a band of young men marched toward the fire, howling and slapping their bare thighs with stringless bows.

"We're Foxes," Four Wounds boasted as he led the way. "We have always done the difficult things."

232

"We're Foxes," Iron Wolf added. "We've struck our enemies hard and taken many horses."

"Always we've stayed behind to protect the defenseless ones," Dancing Lance said, raising his bow. "When the council has sent us word a raid must be organized, we've been the ones to do it."

"Now we come before you, our chiefs, to undo a great wrong," Four Wounds said. "Before the first snows of winter fell, you also met. Many matters were discussed, and good advice was offered. One who spoke wisely, from experience, was ignored. His honored name was insulted, and he broke away from his brothers."

"It's time he was brought back to the heart of the Rope Men," Iron Wolf argued. "Here he is, Younger Wolf, bravest of our leaders. Will you welcome him to your council, Wood Snake, and recognize him for the great man he has always been?"

"Gladly," Wood Snake said, stepping over and clasping the arms of his old friend.

"Ayyyy!" the young men howled. "Our brave heart is back among us!"

"You, South Wind, who have led the Crazy Dogs into many a remembered fight," Dancing Lance said, turning to the second chief. "Would you also welcome this good man to the council?"

"As a chief?" the Wind asked.

"As a wise man whose counsel is respected," Iron Wolf explained.

"He has always been welcome to speak here," Spring Hawk said, wearily sliding over to make a place available beside the fire.

"Thunder Coat?" Dancing Lance asked. "You've ridden with us often. What do you say?"

"I say we've known great hardships since he left us," Thunder Coat said, frowning. "We've missed his strength. His strong arm is welcome."

"I, too, welcome him," Talking Stick added. "But it must be remembered, a two-headed horse never finds the true path. We must be of one mind here."

"Agreed!" Iron Wolf shouted. "Let's hope it will be the voice of wisdom that's spoken now. Enough mistakes have already been made."

Twenty

Once the earth was renewed, the ten bands dispersed across the plain. Younger Wolf devoted himself to the buffalo hunt, for many had known hunger during the long freezing winter, and he was eager to fatten the children. Some appeared far too frail to be sons of the Hev a tan iu.

"Our chiefs brought us to this, Uncle," Iron Wolf grumbled. "They ignore Ne' hyo's warnings, and they have no nose to tell them of approaching snows. There were boys among us with no fathers, and some who might have provided for their needs neglected the obligation."

"We had food enough to share," Younger Wolf confessed. "We left the helpless ones to others."

"It was for a chief to do," Dancing Lance complained.

"Wood Snake took in many," Iron Wolf explained. "But Thunder Coat, who has no sons to feed, busied himself with other matters."

"No child should go where he's not wanted," Younger Wolf declared. "But food should have been offered."

Younger Wolf was even less pleased with the organization of the hunt. More than once the prayers were neglected, and often men rode among Bull Buffalo, wildly shooting their rifles so that bulls stumbled along, bleeding, for a long time before death overtook them.

"Better to use arrows and killing lances," Younger Wolf told the young men who followed him. "White Buffalo Cow, seeing such needless suffering, will grow angry and take her children away from us. Always the Tsis tsis tas hunt in the old way, showing respect, and praying forgiveness for striking down our fellow creatures. Has the world turned crazy?"

"No, Uncle," Iron Wolf answered. "Only people."

Even before the hunting was completed, word came that the wagon people were again making their way along the Shell River road. A party of Lakotas first shared the news. Later Corn Hair Freneau came to add his warning.

"There's much talk of bringing soldiers out to fight the tribes," Freneau explained. "Terrible stories have been told of murderous Indians. Be wary. These new travelers may shoot anyone who approaches their camp."

"It's no different now," Younger Wolf grumbled. "The others did the same. They don't understand this is our country. If a man violates your mother, you would strike at him. So it is when these *wihio* scar Earth Mother."

"They should stay away!" Iron Wolf shouted.

"They won't," Freneau declared. "It's their way to come. Be careful, Brother. I would miss you."

Corn Hair returned to the trader fort, but Louis and Tom remained. With their hair grown long, and their

236

flesh browned by the sun, they seemed odd Rope Men indeed. Tom, whose hair grew lighter under the summer sun, was particularly strange. His legs were far too long for the rest of him as well.

"We have a name for him at last," Porcupine declared. "White-haired Frog."

"*Ayyyy!*" the young men howled. "It's a good name.

Louis also obtained a name. Being seventeen and a boy no longer, he was taken to the Fox council and received with considerable ceremony.

"My cousin has ridden to the hunt with us," Iron Wolf declared. "He's shared the river with us and raced his pony. *Ayyyy!* His heart and ours are the same. He has no good name, so it's necessary we give him one."

"Yes, he should walk the earth as a Hev a tan iu," Younger Wolf agreed. "He's come among us, to be born over."

"I will give him a name," Stone Wolf announced, stepping toward the tall young man. "As his heart is one with ours, he should be called Yellow Rope. May he always be bound to his brothers."

"*Ayyyy!*" the others howled. "It's good."

Porcupine and Goes Ahead then presented horses to boys in need of mounts, and other presents were also given away. It was a fine time, for there was dancing, singing, and feasting.

Younger Wolf was glad the young men could celebrate the naming, but he wondered how long a *wihio* would be welcome in his camp. Some already stared hard at the young Freneaus, and others spoke hard words against them.

"Is it wise they stay with us, See' was' sin mit?"

Stone Wolf asked.

"They're teaching Little Dancer and the girls the *wihio* tongue," Younger Wolf explained. "I still don't understand many of their strange customs, but some I've learned. If we're going to fight these *wihio,* it's necessary to know them better."

But few Rope Men agreed.

"They come to steal our medicine," young Two Bows accused. "They're no better than the Pawnee who killed my father."

Younger Wolf saw the sting of the words and drew his *wihio* nephews aside.

"It's their pain that's speaking," the Wolf explained. "Their hearts have grown bad."

"There's reason," Louis noted. "Maybe we should return to the fort."

"You must do as you consider best," Younger Wolf told them. "But you're welcome to stay. Some direct insults at me as well, but I let the words pass like rain that falls on my lodge. It's nothing."

"It's because of our skin," Tom said. "We can braid our hair and paint our faces, but there's no changing our skins."

"It's more," Louis argued. "We've hunted, and we've joined the games down by the river, but we've never fought alongside our cousins. They don't trust us."

"When the hunt's finished," Tom said, "many of the young men speak of raiding Crow ponies. We should go along."

"Yes," Louis agreed. "As we share the danger, we'll be accepted."

"You're already one of us," Younger Wolf declared.

"Those who don't know this won't change their minds."

"You won't refuse to allow us to go?" Tom asked.

"You're boys no longer," Younger Wolf observed. "What you are considering is dangerous, but the choice is yours. Today the Crow are no enemy of yours. Afterward they will be."

"We can always clip our hair and wipe off the paint," Louis said.

"It's not so easy to change what's inside," Younger Wolf warned. "If you ride against a people, you will know them as an enemy afterward. Making peace is more difficult than you can imagine."

"I trust your words, Uncle," Louis said. "But here I'm at home. It's different at the fort. I'm always alone there, cut off from the land. I've spoken with my cousins, and they don't understand such feelings. I wish I didn't."

"Tell me this," Younger Wolf said, pausing to breathe deeply. "The time's coming when we may fight the *wihio*. Can you be certain you can stand with us if that happens?"

"It would be a sad day for us all," Louis suggested. "I have a brother who is a soldier. I can't be certain what I would do."

"Honesty is a good quality in a man," Younger Wolf said, smiling. "But consider that moment before riding to war with your cousins."

"It's only to take horses," Louis argued.

"Yes," Younger Wolf said, laughing. "But what if the Crow choose to keep their ponies? Maybe you will be clever, and maybe their scouts will see you. Perhaps a man can ride on a cloud. Who knows?"

Once the hunting camps broke up, and the summer camp was made in the hills near Crazy Woman's River, the young men gathered to discuss raiding the Crow pony herd.

"Ayyyy!" Four Wounds cried. "They have many good horses. We'll take them and be wealthy men."

"Yes!" Dancing Lance agreed. "We've been too long away from this rich country. Let's run the Crow and steal their ponies."

The two young friends carried a pipe to Stone Wolf and sought the advice of the Arrows.

"Mahuts urges caution," Stone Wolf told them. "The Crow know many tricks, and they have eyes everywhere in these hills."

"Will we find success?" Four Wounds asked.

"If you make strong medicine," Stone Wolf told them. "Many times the Rope Men have set out after ponies and struck Crow camps instead. Be mindful of the principal task. Don't darken the world with killing. Devote yourselves to the young ones who ride with you. Then all will return safely, and this will be a remembered raid."

"Ayyyy!" Four Wounds screamed. "It will be done."

Before they left camp, the young men faced a more difficult problem. Half the camp wished to join them. Such a large body would never escape the notice of the sharp-eyed Crow, but it wasn't for a young man to turn away his brothers.

Four Wounds took up a second pipe and brought it to Younger Wolf.

"Uncle," the young man said, respectfully offering

the pipe, "We go to run the Crow ponies. Many are eager to go, but we need a good man to lead us."

"It's time you led," Younger Wolf responded. His hands remained at his side, and he made no effort to accept the pipe.

"I've ridden at your side many times," Four Wounds said. "Our blood has stained the same ground. I trust your judgment, as do others. My heart tells me to lead, but I feel my feet are not ready for the trail. Show me the way, Uncle."

"There are others," Younger Wolf argued.

"Stone Wolf warns we must look to the safety of the young ones. No one is better at the task than Younger Wolf. All sing of your many rescues. Too many of us are strangers to warrior's road. We need an experienced leader."

"Then I will go," Younger Wolf said, reluctantly accepting the pipe. "We'll smoke and make medicine. And I will show you what must be done. Learn well, for I'm no longer young. You soon will do the teaching."

After smoking the pipe, Younger Wolf, Four Wounds, Dancing Lance, and Iron Wolf chose twenty from the eager young men who wished to go. Louis Freneau was among them. Of the ten pony boys added to the party, young Tom stood out from the rest. At his side rode Dreamer.

Goes Ahead and Porcupine rode out ahead to locate the pony herd, and Younger Wolf felt a mixture of concern and pride. He had taught the boys all he knew, and now they were coming to be men. Good men. It was all a man could ask.

The raiders themselves rode north a way, then

camped on a ridge overlooking Crazy Woman's River. Crows were everywhere, and no fires were lit. The men chewed dried buffalo meat and spoke in whispers. Boys nervously guarded their own ponies and waited for the chance to ride against the old enemy.

Porcupine brought word of the pony herd, and the leaders met to plan the raid. The Crow had driven their horses into a narrow valley between the river and a ridge. With guards on each side, it made stealing the ponies a difficult task.

"We will strike in four groups," Younger Wolf said, drawing the camp in the sandy ground. "The first will draw off the guards here," the Wolf explained, showing how the riders would dart down the ridge and strike the pony boys' camp. "That's for you to do, Nephew," he added, turning to Iron Wolf. "The next two will have crossed the river. When the guards chase Iron Wolf, these men and the boys who go with them will run the ponies south. There can be no pausing to chase strays. Keep the ones you can control and ignore the others. There are too many to get all of them away anyway, and if a rider wanders off, the Crow will have an easy time killing him."

"Who leads these parties?" Four Wounds asked.

"It's for you to do," Younger Wolf explained. "And Dancing Lance. I will take the last party and hold off the pursuers."

"That's where the danger lies," Four Wounds argued. "I should be there."

"You'll be with the pony boys," Younger Wolf insisted. "Don't forget Stone Wolf's words. You must see to their safety."

242

"But if there's trouble, who will rescue you?" Iron Wolf asked.

"Ah, I have my shield," Younger Wolf declared. "Its power will turn back the enemy. And I will have company. Choose the four who will stand with me."

"They'll be good men," Dancing Lance promised.

Indeed they were. Speckled Wing, lately adopted by Wood Snake, was foremost. He was short of stature for a young man of seventeen summers, but his broad shoulders made him a famous wrestler, and he rode as if he were part of his pony. Alongside galloped Thunderbird, South Wind's nephew, who though older than the Wing, attached himself to the younger man as a brother.

Bent Leg and Mountain Heart, two younger men, completed the party. They had won their names in the hard fighting against Pawnee raiders, and their scarred arms and chests attested to a resolve to stand fast.

"Are we acceptable, Uncle?" Mountain Heart asked when Younger Wolf looked them over.

"You're Hev a tan iu," Younger Wolf told them. "Can it be otherwise?"

They then allowed the others to head out toward the waiting pony herd. Younger Wolf watched the pony boys with particular interest, for this was Dreamer's first raid. The boy would devote his life to the medicine trail, but it was good he passed some moments on warrior's road.

"It's time," Iron Wolf said, waving toward his uncle. Louis Freneau followed his Tsis tsis tas cousin eagerly, and Younger Wolf sighed. If anyone besides his own party came into danger, it would be the decoys.

Iron Wolf made his charge as the sun began its descent into the western sky. Whooping and howling like crazed coyotes, the five young Rope Men galloped through the Crow guard camp, scattering dazed pony boys, tearing down lodges, upsetting drying racks, and drawing rifle fire.

"We're unwelcome here!" Iron Wolf shouted as he motioned for his companions to follow. The decoys then charged past the pony herd and tore off toward the river.

A handful of Crows managed to mount their horses and pursue. Scarcely did they depart when the second and third raiding parties emerged from the river, waving blankets and screaming. The ponies flew into motion. A great cloud rose skyward, blinding the remaining Crow guards and allowing the raiders to make off with the herd. The pursuing Crows turned away from the decoys and fought to halt the stampede. Three were knocked from their horses and trampled beneath the flying hooves. Others managed to split off twenty or so animals, but they were unable to do more.

Once the stolen ponies passed to the south, Younger Wolf turned his companions toward the confused Crow camp. A man or two rode out to chase the enemy, but the sight of Younger Wolf, standing tall with the Buffalo Shield raised to the dying sun, halted each one. Only when ten were assembled was a charge attempted.

"Courage!" Younger Wolf urged as the Crow fired their rifles. "We're Foxes. Ours are the difficult tasks."

"We're Foxes!" the others shouted.

The Crow galloped on in a ragged line, and none of

them was prepared for a determined enemy. Mountain Heart shot the lead man's horse from under him, and the second turned back, blinded by a sudden glare from Younger Wolf's shield. The others managed to close with the Tsis tsis tas, but there was no getting past them. Blows were exchanged, and coups were counted, but no one was badly hurt. Finally the Crow turned and fled, the fight gone from their weary arms.

"What now?" Thunderbird asked.

"We go home," Younger Wolf explained. "Our task is completed. We've shielded our brothers from the Crow."

They were two days making their way back to the Rope Men's camp. In all that time they spotted only two Crows, and they were boys with no desire for an early death. Even they turned back in time, leaving Younger Wolf and his companions to ride the country unmolested.

Back at the Rope Men's camp, all the People celebrated the successful raid. The raiders were generous, and every family received at least two ponies. As for the horse stealers, they had twenty or more each. Even the pony boys led ten to their fathers' lodges.

"Surely Mahuts was with us," Dancing Lance said as he brought Stone Wolf two fine mares. "Your medicine was strong."

"As your hearts were," the Arrow-keeper replied.

"*Ayyyy!*" the men cried. "We're Tsis tsis tas again. No longer can our enemies insult us."

The horse raid emboldened many to speak of raiding the *wihio* wagon parties, and when the chiefs gathered to discuss such a move, Younger Wolf was invited to speak.

245

"The young men honor your power, old friend," Wood Snake said. "Tell us what you think."

"I don't keep the Arrows," Younger Wolf replied. "If you wish to see what will happen, consult Mahuts."

"The Arrows warn of danger," Stone Wolf said.

"We're not afraid," Talking Stick boasted. "Some may chase ponies, but I'm hot to fight the true enemy."

"Yes," Younger Wolf said, frowning. "I see. But what profit would it bring? Honor? Stealing *wihio* horses is too easy, and most are no good for hunting. You'll grow fat and lazy from so small a challenge."

"I would strike the *wihio* hard," Talking Stick argued. "Kill them all."

"Even the smallest of them?" Younger Wolf asked. "To kill the helpless ones is to disturb the harmony of the world. Have we learned nothing? We must keep to the old ways. If we attack these people, we must be prepared to take the helpless survivors into our lodges."

"No," Talking Stick shouted. "There are white men enough among us."

"Once you said it was a good thing to invite the traders," Wood Snake reminded the young chief. "You said we should trade for their good guns, use their powder and lead. Now your heart is hard toward them. Younger Wolf is right. A child is like a new hide, with no mark upon it. Killing it angers the spirits, and we would be punished."

"We'll leave them for the *wihio* at the fort," Talking Stick suggested.

"The obligation would be ours," Younger Wolf argued. "If you are unprepared to accept it, then you must not fight them. War embarked upon with the intent of killing is a poor undertaking. We have always fought to achieve honor and to protect the defenseless."

"Then we'll wait," Talking Stick grumbled. He read the disapproval of the others, and he stepped from the fire and allowed Wood Snake to prevail. Younger Wolf deemed it a good thing, but he suspected it wouldn't last.

"Uncle, the *wihio* are our greatest enemy," Dreamer told Younger Wolf later. "We must fight them."

"They are a danger, yes," Younger Wolf told the boy. "They bring many hard things. But fighting them is like shooting arrows into a mountain. What harm do you cause? The *wihio* are ignorant, but there are so many of them! You can't hope to kill them all."

"Only the bad hearts," Dreamer insisted.

"It's a good notion, Nephew," Younger Wolf confessed. "Maybe you will find medicine to show us how it can be done. My difficulty has always been reading a man's heart. Would you smoke with the *wihio* wagon people and then decide who to kill? No, it's impossible."

Twenty-one

The winds of change continued to sweep across the land, but for once the Tsis tsis tas withstood their torments. Hunting was good that summer, and even better under the plum moon of early autumn. With their Crow ponies, many young men were able to take wives.

"Spring will see many new Rope Men born," Stone Wolf told his brother.

"Yes, the People are recovering their strength," Younger Wolf noted. "As always, while heeding Mahuts, we prosper."

That next spring Stone Wolf's dreams were much troubled, though. He saw many things, and when he climbed Noahvose with Younger Wolf prior to remaking the earth, the Arrow-keeper's eyes were clouded with doubts.

It seemed to Younger Wolf they must have climbed that sacred slope a hundred times. This time, with Dreamer and Little Dancer along, it seemed different. The boys asked so many questions, and their fathers found themselves neglecting the task at hand as they pointed out the cave where Sweet Medicine first received the Arrows and the haunted clearing where old Cloud Dancer had climbed Hanging Road.

"One day you will place me there as well," Younger Wolf told the boys. "Even as I helped my grandfather find his peace, you will help me find mine."

Stone Wolf put an end to such talk.

"You have many summers left to you, See' was' sin mit," the Arrow-keeper scolded. "This is a time of new life, and there can be no talking of death!"

That night Younger Wolf built up the fire, and Stone Wolf stood before the flames, cutting pieces from his scarred chest and arms. His flesh was marked by hundreds of sacrificial wounds, and the boys gazed at him with wonder in their eyes.

"He's often bled for the People," Younger Wolf explained as his brother chanted and danced, inviting the dream. "His walk upon this earth has been a weary one, but the People have benefited from his attention."

"The man who lifts his burden faces a difficult task," Dreamer observed. "Is there a man alive worthy enough?"

"One may grow to be," Younger Wolf assured the boy.

They then turned to watch over Stone Wolf, who continued to sing the brave heart songs of long ago even as his legs weakened, and his weariness grew. The Arrow-keeper ceased his prayers only when his legs buckled beneath him, and he collapsed into the soft elk hides spread below him.

No one had to tell Younger Wolf when the dream came. The sky became dark and still. Clouds ate the stars, and a great howling wind whipped across the mountainside. Younger Wolf shielded the embers of the fire with his body while the boys hurried to secure the ponies. Suddenly the earth seemed to split apart as the air exploded into yellow flame.

"Ne' hyo!" Little Dancer cried as he dashed away from an incinerated pine. Dreamer fought hopelessly to hold the horses. They raced off to find their own cover. The skies then emptied a world of icy water onto the mountain, and Younger Wolf hurried to cover his brother.

Stone Wolf never stirred. The storm lashed his exposed flesh and shook the land with a violence hitherto unknown, but the dreamer slept on.

"We should carry him to shelter," Dreamer said, trembling.

"The cave," Little Dancer suggested.

"He must remain," Younger Wolf argued. "You two may go. I will remain and tend his needs."

"No, Uncle, that's for me to do," Dreamer objected.

"Share the labor with me then," Younger Wolf said, gripping the boy's wrist. "We must cover the fire. It must continue to burn."

They held a buffalo hide over the sputtering flame and tried to ignore the sting of the smoke that attacked their eyes. Hailstones bombarded their bare arms and backs, but they didn't flinch.

"We must wake him," Little Dancer said, huddling close to his father. "He's suffered enough."

"He's with the spirits," Younger Wolf explained. "Only Man Above can release him to us."

They passed a long day and most of the morning atop Noahvose, protecting Stone Wolf from the rain and hail. Younger Wolf frowned when the sun broke through the clouds and revealed the bruised and battered flesh of the boys. But when Stone Wolf awoke, they all knew the worth of their torment.

"I've seen much," the Arrow-keeper explained. "We must stay and smoke. Then we will return, and I'll speak to the council of forty-four."

"It's good your ordeal's over, Ne' hyo," Dreamer said as he helped his father sit up and warm himself by the fire.

"Your task wasn't easy, either," Stone Wolf observed as he picked up a half-melted hailstone in his fingers. "None of us will find an end to our ordeal soon, I fear. Terrible trouble is coming."

Stone Wolf spoke no more of the dream before returning to the Rope Men's camp. There he and Younger Wolf spoke to Wood Snake.

"I'll send riders, hurrying the other bands," the Snake promised. "The chiefs will ride ahead. Soon the council will meet, and we can discuss what you have seen."

"It's good they hurry," Stone Wolf told Younger Wolf afterward. "The danger is near."

"Is there something we can do to hold it off?" Younger Wolf asked. "The Foxes are strong. We can fight."

"Not this enemy," Stone Wolf warned.

"Yes, I see the gravity of it in your eyes, Nah nih. It's a heavy burden to carry such a vision alone for so long a time. Can you share it with me?"

"No, it must wait for the council. Not knowing is hard, too, See' was' sin mit, but I know it's best. All must hear at the same moment."

Not knowing *was* hard, but Younger Wolf swallowed his anxiety and kept himself occupied making preparations for the New Life Lodge. He walked among the young men, urging many to offer a sacrifice for the welfare of the People.

"Nah nih, Wood Snake, South Wind, and myself will make the New Life Lodge this summer," Younger Wolf later told his brother. "Many young men have vowed to hang by the pole and suffer so that the People may remain safe."

"It's a good thing," Stone Wolf judged. "It will bring our leaders new power and help avert danger."

"Perhaps knowing this, you should invite another dream," Younger Wolf suggested. "Our destiny may change."

"What's coming won't be turned aside, not even by such devotion," Stone Wolf said, sighing. "But you may protect our band by your sacrifice. I pray it will be so."

Younger Wolf felt a new fear grip his heart as he read the terror in his brother's eyes. What danger could prevail over such strong medicine as the New Life Lodge?

He found out two days later when Stone Wolf revealed the dream to the council of forty-four. As the many chiefs sat and smoked, the Arrow-keeper collected his courage and prepared to speak. When the pipe was finished, and the ashes were disposed of, Stone Wolf spoke.

"Forty-four summers I've walked the earth, brothers," the Arrow-keeper began. "There is one of you here at this fire for each of those years. In all that time I've seen many things in my dreams, and often I've been afraid for the People. Never as I am now, though."

"What did you see, old friend?" Wood Snake asked.

"Death," the Arrow-keeper explained.

"Ah, we've known death before," Talking Stick declared. "I'm not afraid of it."

"Not your death, Brother?" South Wind said, motioning for Talking Stick to be silent.

"Not mine," Stone Wolf agreed. "The death of our People."

"All of us?" Wood Snake asked.

"All," Stone Wolf answered. "Death that silences the voices of the children. Death that robs the old ones of their memory. Death that leaves our lodges empty, and our ponies without riders."

"It's not possible," Thunder Coat objected.

"Once, in my grandfather's time, the Mandans walked the world," Stone Wolf said, sighing. "These people camped on Fat River and hunted Bull Buffalo there. Then the *wihio* came, bringing his sickness to the friendly Mandans, and they were no more."

"Stories for old women," Talking Stick muttered.

"No, as a small boy, I visited one of their camps," South Wind explained. "Their beehive lodges still stood, but only ghosts live there. My pony turned away, and I rode no farther."

"This is what you've seen?" Wood Snake asked.

"All that, and worse," Stone Wolf replied. "This dream came to me on a night the earth was torn by Thunderbird, and the Crooked Lance touched its fire to the trees. Hailstones poured from the heavens. Yes, it was a remembered night!"

"What will bring us to this end?" South Wind asked.

"It can only be our own folly," Stone Wolf declared. "Sweet Medicine warned us to avoid the pale people, but we traded with him, invited him to walk among us, drank his whiskey and gave our women over to him. We've exchanged our lives for rifles."

"I've spoken of fighting the *wihio,* but you always spoke against it," Talking Stick complained. "Now see what you've brought us to?"

"You would paint the earth red with their blood," Stone Wolf complained. "Even that wouldn't stop them. And such killing would turn you away from the harmony of the sacred path. I don't come among you chiefs to assign blame. Only to warn of what's coming."

"Death," Wood Snake muttered. "Is there any way to turn it from us?"

"How will it come?" South Wind demanded. "Bluecoat soldiers?"

"Sickness," Stone Wolf explained. "As with the Mandans. Already its fevers are among us, so there can be no turning it away. If we pray and dance and remake the earth, we may hope to save ourselves from the worst."

"We'll do it," Wood Snake vowed. "Already I've promised to make the New Life Lodge. My sons and nephews will hang from the pole. *Ayyyy!* Our blood will turn away the *wihio* fevers."

"We must all pray," old Otter Skin declared. "And no one can have dealings with the *wihio.*"

"Your brother has *wihio* nephews in his lodge," Talking Stick said.

"No," Stone Wolf said, rising. "I sent them away. They have returned to their father and will come here no longer."

"We may still be saved from the fevers then," South Wind said hopefully.

Stone Wolf offered no encouragement, and the chiefs grew quiet.

"We'll remake the earth and prepare ourselves," Wood Snake said. "If the sickness is certain to come, we can do only that."

Stone Wolf stood. "Yes." "Only that."

Even as Younger Wolf and the others performed the earth renewal ceremonies, the fever struck the camp of the Windpipes. Soon it spread like a prairie fire among the bands, striking down young and old, woman and man. It spared only those who had suffered before.

Already a host of young men waited to hang by the pole. Once the fever broke out, others hurried to offer themselves.

"My sister suffers," Bent Leg told Younger Wolf. "I must exchange my pain for her healing."

Dreamer, too, stepped forth.

"You should help your father," Younger Wolf scolded. "He has much to do in remaking the earth and tending the sick."

"Others even younger are hanging by the pole," the boy objected. "If I'm one day to stand among them as a man of power, I must be remembered as one who set the needs of his people above his own."

"He must hang," Wood Snake agreed. "Look in his eyes. I see your brother there."

Dreamer was approaching his thirteenth summer,

but he remained short and thin. The boy appeared too frail for the task at hand, but Younger Wolf found himself recalling the day when he approached the pole. Had he been any bigger? No.

"Find a good man to help," Younger Wolf urged.

"My brother will show me the way," Dreamer said, nodding to where Iron Wolf stood waiting.

After they left, Younger Wolf expressed his concern that many of the dancers were too small to undergo such a trial.

"If the fever strikes them, they'll be weak," he noted. "How will they recover?"

"They must find power to cure themselves," Wood Snake insisted. "This they'll find while undergoing the torture."

Younger Wolf prayed it would be so, but when the ceremony was concluded, many of the dancers quickly covered over with spots. Some climbed Hanging Road quickly. Others lingered for a time. Too many passed from the ranks of the warriors.

The suffering was terrible to behold. Anguished cries of mothers and fathers haunted every night as children burned with fever. In the hills beyond Noahvose a forest of scaffolds marked the horizon. Good men were set there, together with sons too young to pluck their chin hairs. Daughters who had never visited woman's lodge were wrapped in buffalo robes and carried to the ridge.

"I have no power to fight this affliction," Stone Wolf lamented as the small daughter of Speckled Wing was carried from the camp. "We have taken the unaffected ones off to distant hills, but still the sickness finds them. There's no turning it away."

"Once we burned the spotted fevers from our sons in the sweat lodge," Younger Wolf recounted.

"It was winter then," Stone Wolf argued. "I don't know if the little ones could tolerate more heat."

"We can try it," Younger Wolf suggested. "Nothing else is of help."

So they erected a sweat lodge and took the strongest inside. Amid the steam, Stone Wolf performed the medicine prayers and sought aid from earth and sky. The three young men seemed to recover for a time, but each passed to the other side as night fell.

"It was no use," Stone Wolf said, collapsing to his knees. "It's as I saw. The People will die."

So it seemed to Younger Wolf. He and his nephews labored to tend the sick. Each night they burned the belongings of the sick and hoped it would satisfy the anger of the spirits.

"It's good many of us had the sickness before," Little Dancer said, gripping his father's hand tightly. "Many of my friends were spared before. Now they are dying. Soon only ghosts will know this place."

"Perhaps, Naha'," Younger Wolf said, sighing. "It's a bad day for the Tsis tsis tas. Death walks among us, and we have no medicine to turn him away."

By midsummer the sickness had completed its deadly walk among the ten bands. Whole families were taken. Of many others, only small boys and girls remained. Sadder still were the fathers and mothers who could only sit and weep over their dead children.

"You should take into your lodge a child without parents," Stone Wolf advised many of them.

"The wound is too fresh," one mother answered. "I can't bear to gaze upon another girl."

"I can't bear to see a smiling boy," another remarked.

"You needn't worry," Iron Wolf replied. "They won't be smiling."

Indeed, it seemed the entire world was grieving. Of all the Tsis tsis tas, one of four was dead. Many others were too weak to hunt. Most lodges, hides, even weapons had been burned. Those hunters able to ride mounted ponies and set off to hunt Bull Buffalo.

Never before had anyone taken such care with the ceremonies as did Stone Wolf that hard summer. Only a successful hunt would prevent a second calamity. To survive the spotted sickness and freeze in the snow that winter would be more than even a strong heart could bear.

Fortune smiled again upon the People. Goes Ahead returned from scouting with news he had spotted White Buffalo Cow herself on a nearby ridge.

"Alone?" Younger Wolf cried.

"No, with many of her children," the young man explained. "I thought my eyes might be feverish, and it all a dream, but I found this," he added, handing over a few delicate white hairs caught on a prickly pear spine.

"Man Above has given us new life," Stone Wolf said.

Younger Wolf met with the chiefs, and parties of hunters were organized. Shortly the medicine prayers were performed, and the next day men rode out to strike down Bull Buffalo and bring back the meat and hides which would ensure the People's survival.

It was a remembered hunt, especially for the young

men who spied White Buffalo Cow thundering among them. No arrow or lance was directed her way, for she was sacred and protected from harm. Each dawn and each dusk she stood on the next ridge, watching over the People. Her presence renewed their faith and gave them the courage to rebuild their lives.

As summer passed into bitter memory, the Rope Men turned south once more. Stone Wolf wished to make a winter camp near Noahvose, and so they traveled Shell River for a time. It was there that Bent Leg spied a *wihio* wagon camp.

"Here are the ones who have brought this suffering to us!" the young man cried.

"Ayyyy!" many screamed. "Let's punish these killers of children!"

Before the chiefs could advise caution, or Stone Wolf could consult the Arrows, parties of young men mounted their ponies and headed for the wagon camp.

Younger Wolf insisted on performing the appropriate prayers and thus didn't reach the river until later. Already many of the wagons were blazing, and the prairie was marked with the corpses of several brave hearts cut down by the *wihio* rifles.

"Stop!" Younger Wolf shouted as Hawk Feather, a boy of twelve summers, charged the wagon camp. Bullets met him halfway, but even when his horse stumbled, dying, he continued onward. His naked chest was pierced four times, and one arm hung limp at his side. Only when a *wihio* stepped out and clubbed the boy across the face did he fall.

"There's no stopping them, Uncle," Iron Wolf lamented as he joined Younger Wolf. "Hawk Feather lost his father, his mother, three sisters, and a brother to the spotted sickness. All his relations among his father's people, the Windpipes, are dead. He had no heart to continue."

"No," Younger Wolf said, trying to steady himself as another boy charged the camp. "A brave death can at least erase the pain."

Talking Stick and Thunder Coat soon arrived with a party of Crazy Dogs, and they put an end to the wagon people. Not a *wihio* survived. The fighting was fierce, and men who had buried sons found no compassion for the wagon children. Even the smallest of them perished.

Twenty-two

The sickness and the killing darkened Younger Wolf's brow. As summer passed into memory, more and more he set off alone into the hills to hunt. Often he would sit by himself on a hillside, staring at the sky and contemplating the strange turn his path had taken.

"Husband, don't go alone," Hoop Woman pleaded more than once. "The young men have seen Rees and Crows nearby. They would enjoy killing you."

"I won't fall to a stray Ree," Younger Wolf assured her. "No, my death will be a remembered thing."

It was much that way the morning Hoop Woman and the girls set out to gather plums from the hills west of Noahvose.

"Don't talk of death, Ne' hyo," Red Hoop cried when her father vowed he was a man not easily slain. "Too many have climbed Hanging Road this summer."

"I'll prepare two ponies," Little Dancer offered. "We can hunt deer in the thickets."

"No," Younger Wolf said, gazing at his feet. "I have no heart for killing things."

"Then we'll ride," the Dancer suggested. "It's enough."

"Ask your cousins," Younger Wolf told the boy. "They would be better company."

"Do you remember, Ne' hyo, how you tended me when I was sick with the fever long ago?" Little Dancer asked. "Now it's you who are sick, and I'm the one who must help you regain the harmony you've lost."

"Perhaps you're right," Younger Wolf confessed. "Your eyes are young and keen. Maybe you can spot where I lost my way."

Little Dancer hurried to get the ponies and ready them for the ride. When he returned with them, Younger Wolf climbed atop his old buckskin, and the Dancer led the way north on a spotted stallion.

"This horse isn't much to look at," the boy said as he matched the buckskin's gait, "but he's fast. Already I've won three races with him."

"Good," Younger Wolf said, warming. A smile flooded his son's face, and the boy darted in front of the buckskin, howling and waving his arms at his sides.

"Iron Wolf taught me that trick," Little Dancer explained. "He rides as well as anyone."

"Except maybe Goes Ahead," Younger Wolf argued. "That one rides as if his pony has wings."

"I beat him often, Ne' hyo!"

"Do you?"

"Often!" the Dancer boasted. "Even when he has the better horse."

"I'm sorry not to have noticed," Younger Wolf said, frowning. "A father should see such things."

"You have been a father to many," Little Dancer said.

"It's no excuse for neglecting my own son."

"Ah, but the concern you've had for the others has brought me many brothers to guide my steps! Ne' hyo, I have no complaining to do. My age-mates envy the son of Younger Wolf."

"I've too often been away," Younger Wolf muttered.

"In summer, yes." the boy admitted. "My sisters and I missed you then. But we've had the winters together, and those have been good times."

"Have they?"

"Should I tell you the story of the Star Boys?" the boy asked, laughing. "Or of the time Trickster fooled Owl into trading his feathers?"

"It's a fine thing for a man to ride this country with his son," Younger Wolf observed. "You won't be small forever. A few summers more will pass, and then you will go to the young men's lodge with your cousins."

"Before then we'll hunt many deer, Ne' hyo, and share other stories."

"Yes," Younger Wolf agreed. "Now, maybe we'll climb that hill and sit for a time."

"Ne' hyo, not that hill," Little Dancer said, pulling his horse up short.

"Why not . . ."

"There, in the shadows of the pines," the Dancer said, pointing his small hand to where a pair of figures lurked. "Crows, I think."

"No, see how they wear their hair?" Younger Wolf asked, frowning.

"Lakotas shave their hair in that fashion."

"Pawnees, too. But these are neither."

"Who then, Ne' hyo?" Little Dancer asked.

"Rees. The scouts were right. I've rarely seen them so far south of Fat River. It's a bad sign."

"Will we fight them?"

"With bird arrows?" Younger Wolf asked, gazing at the boy's short bow and quiver of arrows. "I have only a lance, and the tall one there holds a rifle."

"Then they'll run us," the boy grumbled.

"No, they won't," Younger Wolf said, fixing the concealed enemy in his iron gaze. He untied the lance from the back of the buckskin and raised it skyward. *"Ayyyy!"* he screamed. "Come, feel the sting of my lance, Ree dogs!"

The Rees stepped out from their cover, and the one with the rifle fired it. The range was too great, though, and the bullet fell harmlessly short. Neither Ree was much more than a boy, and they had no notion of charging a scarred veteran of many hard fights. They walked to their horses, mounted, and rode away, shouting their disdain as they went.

"If you had your good bow and the Buffalo Shield, you would have run them," Little Dancer declared. "Even without them you turned them away."

"Just boys scouting game," Younger Wolf said, laughing. "No battle to tell your friends of."

"You did not wish to kill them, Ne' hyo. And I've seen enough dying this summer."

"It's been a hard time for all of us."

"So many are gone. My cousin, White-haired Frog, didn't come to us this year."

"It's for the best," Younger Wolf declared. "They must learn to walk the *wihio* road, I think. And we must find a new way, too."

264

"What way, Ne' hyo?"

"I don't know, Naha'. Too often I'm lost now, and I can't lead even myself back to the sacred path."

"It's time we took a sweat then. You once told me it would drive away ghosts and help a man restore the harmony he'd lost."

"It's true, Naha'," Younger Wolf said, nodding. "We'll do it. Stone Wolf can prepare us, and the steam can cleanse us of the darkness that's fallen over our world."

"Shall I race you back to the camp then?"

"Do your best, Naha', but remember, I know many tricks."

"Ayyyy!" Little Dancer screamed, kicking his pony into a gallop. "Then I'll need to start early!"

Younger Wolf laughed as he urged the buckskin into motion. The sight of his son galloping across the grassland eased him from the worst of his sorrow. As the wind brushed his face and swept through his hair, he was Younger Wolf once more.

"Ayyyy!" the young men howled when Little Dancer dashed into the camp ahead of his father.

"I've beaten Ne' hyo," the Dancer boasted as he rolled off his lathered pony.

"It's no great thing," Younger Wolf said as he wearily dismounted. "Your father's an old man."

"Not so old as some have thought," Stone Wolf observed.

Younger Wolf pulled his son close, and the boy embraced him.

"Ne' hyo has decided you should build a sweat lodge, Uncle," Little Dancer said.

"We must hurry to cut poles," Iron Wolf declared.

265

"Younger Wolf feels an urgency to the thing. Why else would he have ridden so swiftly across the prairie?"

The others laughed, and Younger Wolf himself managed a grin. He had managed to escape death's shadow for a time. He hoped the sweat would help restore his sense of direction. Winter was coming, and it was a terrible thing for a man to lose himself under the snowblind moon.

Stone Wolf and the nephews had the sweat lodge ready the following afternoon. It proved a good notion, for many of the grief-stricken men entered. It was time to put sadness behind them and restore the harmony of their lives.

For Younger Wolf, the steam held no mystery. Nor did Stone Wolf's words and the medicine prayers they spoke together. The healing came later, with the sharing of remembered tales and the crafting of arrows for boys who had no one else to make them.

"The worst pain a man can know passes with time," Stone Wolf said as the brothers sat beside Hoop Woman's cook fire, chewing roasted elk ribs and remembering days long past. "When my daughter left my side, I thought the world would never again know its old sweetness. But my sons' laughter and Dove Woman's touch renewed my spirit and gave me hope."

"I've lost no daughter, Nah nih," Younger Wolf said, studying the flames. "It's the hopelessness of our life that plagues me. When the world we knew as boys is taken from us by *wihio* tricks, and sickness robs the Tsis tsis tas of good men, what road will they walk?"

266

"The sacred path is always there, See' was' sin mit," Stone Wolf insisted. "It only becomes harder to walk in such times."

"Our way will grow no easier. The ten bands are weak and scattered. Already our enemies come into this country of ours. I saw Rees today, and others have seen Crows. Soon even the Pawnee will ride through our sacred places."

"We've known sickness before," Stone Wolf argued. "The *wihio* fevers strike the Crow, too. We'll be strong again."

"I won't see that time," Younger Wolf lamented. "You dream often, and visions hold no mystery for you. You don't fear what you see. I've always been a man who looks at the road before him and walks each day in its turn. Now my sleep is disturbed. I see terrible things. I see Death."

"As I did?" Stone Wolf asked.

"No, it's no death of the People, Nah nih. Only mine."

"You saw it clearly?"

"Too clearly," Younger Wolf confessed. "It's strange that it should torment me. Even as a boy, I knew I would not count the snows of a grandfather. Cloud Dancer said I would have a choice to make, and I chose."

"To be a man of the People," Stone Wolf whispered. "Yes, and the People have enjoyed your protection and sacrifice."

"Yours, too, Nah nih. Soon it will be others who will guard the welfare of the helpless."

"Years remain to you."

267

"Perhaps," Younger Wolf said, sighing. "Not many of them, though. I haven't yet seen the moment, but my dreams have shown me the place. It's odd, too, for I haven't been there. I see a man with red circles painted on his chest. Three feathers are tied in his hair, and when he laughs, he shows a mouth with no front teeth."

"He would be a strange one to fight," Stone Wolf said, laughing. "I've never heard of such markings, nor of such a man."

"Then it may be a boy's dream, full of fear and having no substance."

"If it was, you would know," Stone Wolf said, growing quiet. "The spirits touch all of us, See' was' sin mit, and you carry our grandfather's blood as I do. I would judge the dream real."

"What must I do about it?"

"Try to forget it," Stone Wolf advised. "If you pass the days to come in dread of this moment, you are dead already. Race your son across the land. Hold your daughters close. Enjoy the comfort of your winter lodge, and leave tomorrow to come as it will anyway."

"It will be hard to do," Younger Wolf said, gripping his brother's wrists.

"You've always done the hard things, little brother."

"Sometimes I wish it were otherwise," Younger Wolf said, staring into the distant hills.

"I, too," Stone Wolf confessed. "But a man might as well imagine he can eat the sun. He is what Man Above has determined. If our road is hard, it has at least offered the consolation that our sons have grown tall and strong. We've known the love of good women. The Tsis tsis tas no longer shake the hills with their numbers, but neither are they ghosts like the Mandans, left to haunt Fat River until they are forgotten."

"It's small comfort, Nah nih."

"I know," Stone Wolf admitted. "But perhaps it's all there will be. And maybe enough for modest men like ourselves."

Twenty-three

As the dirt-in-the-face moon of late autumn hung overhead, scouts brought word of fresh trouble.

"Rees!" Speckled Wing announced. "They are camped a day's ride from us, near Hawk's Egg Lake."

"So near?" Wood Snake asked, scratching his chin. "These Rees are brave men."

"Or fools," Talking Stick declared. "Is it a large camp? Do they bring their women?"

"Only men and pony boys," Speckled Wing explained.

"Hunters," Wood Snake grumbled. "Come into the heart of our country!"

"We must punish them!" Talking Stick argued. "Are they watchful, these Rees?"

"Only the pony boys tend the night fires," Speckled Wing answered. "They have good horses. A hundred, maybe."

"And how many Rees?" Wood Snake asked.

"I counted fifteen, Ne' hyo," Speckled Wing told the Snake. "Others are maybe hunting. They appeared to be expecting company. Their fires were too high for such a small party."

"Even if there are fifty, we'll easily run them!" Talking Stick boasted. "We'll ride them into the ground!"

"A hundred ponies?" Thunder Coat asked. "It would be good to have them."

"We have horses enough!" Wood Snake barked. "You speak of a small band, but why then would they bring so many horses into our country. We've passed their men often. They know we camp here. I don't feel good about this."

"No," Younger Wolf agreed. "Rees don't come often into Noahvose's shadow, and now this small party rich in horses camps close. It must be a trick to lure our warriors away so that they can strike our camp."

"It's possible," Iron Wolf said. "Their scouts have ridden close to our lodges."

"It's difficult to know what to do," Younger Wolf said, pacing before the others. "We must ask Mahuts. The Arrows will warn of danger."

"And while we are sitting with Stone Wolf, smoking and pondering what to do, the Rees will get away," Talking Stick grumbled.

"We've acted carelessly before," Wood Snake declared. "We are too few to risk the loss of our young men. If this is a trap, we must know it."

"We must carry a pipe to the Arrow Lodge, Brother," Thunder Coat said, sighing. "The old men are right. We are too few to strike the Rees and guard our camp adequately."

"I'll ready a pipe," Wood Snake offered.

271

"No, it's for me to do," Thunder Coat insisted. "This will be my raid to organize. Too often the old men have led. It's for a younger man to do."

"*Ayyyy!*" the handful of men who followed the Stick cried.

They were mostly Crazy Dogs, though, and the Foxes turned their eyes to their shield-carriers, Wood Snake and Younger Wolf.

"It doesn't matter to me," the Snake announced. "Take up the pipe if you want, Talking Stick. I'm content to safeguard the helpless ones."

"*Ayyyy!*" the Foxes howled. "He's a man of the People!"

Talking Stick glared at the Snake, then marched off to find a pipe.

"That one's changed," Wood Snake told Younger Wolf afterward. "I remember him as a boy. *Ayyyy!* He was a brave heart then, and he was reliable. Now he sees only himself. He's blind to his obligations."

"He's confused," Younger Wolf declared. "He should have remained with my brother, walking the medicine trail. His heart longs for the peace he knew there, but he is driven by his dreams of war. He should take a sweat and restore his reason."

"Yes," Wood Snake agreed, laughing. "But in these crazy times, perhaps he's the man who should lead the young men. It may take a crazy one."

"Not to fight Rees," Younger Wolf objected. "My Lakota cousins tell of hard fights made against those people. They have more tricks than the Crow, and there are many of them."

272

"Fifteen?"

"Would you ride Crazy Woman River with fifteen men? No. The Rees are not fools. There are others nearby."

When Talking Stick had prepared a pipe, he carried it first to Younger Wolf.

"I go to fight the Rees," Talking Stick announced. "Come, Uncle, and join me."

"You were to ask Mahuts," Younger Wolf replied.

"I'm going there this moment," the Stick explained. "It's necessary I have the good will of the Foxes, though, so I would invite their chief to sit at my side."

"I'm no chief," Younger Wolf grumbled.

"Perhaps," Talking Stick admitted. "But if you go, they'll follow."

"I won't encourage them."

"You will. When you walk a road, others follow. I only ask you to come and sit with me in the Arrow Lodge, smoking and listening to what Mahuts can tell us."

"It's not much to ask," Younger Wolf admitted. "I'll go."

Thunder Coat, as was expected, accompanied his brother as well. Speckled Wing came, too, for it was thought the Arrow-keeper might wish to question the scout. They greeted Stone Wolf outside the Arrow Lodge, expressed their need, and followed the medicine man inside.

"First we smoke," Stone Wolf said, instructing them

to sit. As he performed the pipe ritual, the old man scanned the eyes of his guests. His gaze lingered on Younger Wolf in particular. Surprise and confusion filled the older man's eyes.

"What presents have you brought Mahuts?" Stone Wolf asked when the smoking was finished.

"These eagle tail feathers," Talking Stick said, offering three feathers.

"These bear claws," Thunder Coat added, passing over a claw necklace.

"They are acceptable," Stone Wolf said, tying them to the medicine bundle spinning overhead. "Ask your question."

Talking Stick described the Ree camp with the many horses and told of the contemplated raid.

"Will our efforts meet with success?" the Stick asked.

Mahuts turned, and the feathers danced in the faint light cast by the fire. A single feather broke away and drifted to the earth.

"You will take the horses," Stone Wolf said, frowning. "But there's danger. If you're not careful, the price may be great."

"It's as Ne' hyo said," Speckled Wing declared. "A trap."

"Silence," Stone Wolf said, staring angrily at the young man. "You are here to answer questions. Not to speak out as you choose."

Speckled Wing hung his head in apology, and Stone Wolf gazed once more at the Arrows.

"It will be difficult," the Arrow-keeper said. "But it

can be done. Two nights of good weather will pass. Then clouds will hide the moon, and a wind will unsettle the horses. On such a night a party of fast riders might run the Ree ponies. Only three should try it. They may escape notice if they wear the invisible paint. I'll prepare them myself."

"Three men?" Talking Stick asked. "What of the rest of us?"

"Half will remain here, guarding our camp," Stone Wolf answered. "The others will stand ready to pounce upon the pursuing Rees. Hear this, though. No Tsis tsis tas may strike the first blow. It must be a Ree who starts the fighting. If a Tsis tsis tas violates this instruction, the invisible medicine will fail, and Ree arrows will find us."

"We understand," Talking Stick said, nodding reverently.

"It's wise you've come to Mahuts before undertaking this raid," Stone Wolf observed. "It's the old medicine that will lead us from this troubled time."

"Yes," the Stick said, nodding. "I remember when you took me here so that I might learn the medicine cures."

"It's a good thing to put aside hard feelings," Younger Wolf noted. "To rekindle friendships."

"Yes," Thunder Coat agreed. "Perhaps our People will know greater harmony."

"It's necessary," Stone Wolf agreed. But his brother read doubts in the Arrow-keeper's eyes.

The raid was carried out as planned. Two nights

275

the dirt-in-the-face moon glimmered brightly over-head while the Tsis tsis tas made medicine and sang their brave heart songs. Finally, as storm clouds turned the air heavy, Stone Wolf painted the chosen three with buffalo horn powder and marked them with the old symbols that would melt their images into the night.

Twenty men left the camp that night, riding quietly toward the waiting Rees. Only Thunderbird's Crooked Lance fire lighting the heavens overhead disturbed the darkness, and even that subsided when the raiders approached the Ree ponies.

"Go now," Talking Stick urged the three young riders.

Speckled Wing led the way, for he knew the country best. Bent Leg and Mountain Heart followed. They were the invisible three, and their approach evaded the sharp eyes of the Ree guards. Suddenly they shouted and waved their blankets, startling the ponies. Again Thunderbird struck the skies with his crooked lance, and the horses raced off onto the prairie.

"*Ayyyy!*" the raiders howled. It appeared an easy task. Suddenly, though, from a nearby ravine, thirty Rees scrambled atop waiting horses and charged after the stolen ponies.

"Now is our time to fight!" Talking Stick shouted.

"Remember the warning!" Younger Wolf cried. "Let them strike the first blow!"

Two pony boys raced forward anyway, but Iron Wolf turned them back, admonishing their disobedience by taking their bows. The skies exploded with light then, outlining Pronghorn against the dark of the opposite ridge. Angry Rees charged the young man, but he refused to break the medicine. Instead he sat calmly, singing his death song. Three Ree arrows struck him down.

The Rees had no opportunity to celebrate their kill. Instead the whole weight of the Tsis tsis tas raiders fell on the killers, driving them back and punishing them greatly. Five fell dead, and many others were badly hurt. Finally the Rees fled even their camp, leaving Talking Stick to burn the lodges and hurl insults at the defeated enemy.

"They'll know hunger in their winter camp," the Stick boasted as he gathered the warriors and prepared to return to the Rope Men's camp. *"Ayyyy!* This has been a remembered fight."

"We'll call it the time Talking Stick ran the Ree ponies!" Thunder Coat announced.

"No," Iron Wolf argued, standing tall as he blocked the path of the chiefs. "We'll mark it as the night Pronghorn gave up his life for his brothers."

"Ayyyy!" the young men howled. "It's appropriate the brave heart be honored."

"Yes," Thunder Coat admitted. "His was the sacrifice."

Already Two Bows and Lone Elk, his age-mates and continual companions, were tying the body atop a captured Ree pony. As the Tsis tsis tas rode homeward, they sang of their fallen brother and celebrated the victory his death had brought them.

Younger Wolf expected the Rees to return to their old country to the north, for they had been punished. Stone Wolf's medicine was clearly overpowering, and a prudent enemy could only retreat from it.

Even as the young men recounted their coups around the council fire, and scalps were hung outside lodges, Goes Ahead and Porcupine brought word of campfires burning on the next ridge.

"The Lakotas have come to share our winter camp," Talking Stick suggested.

"No, the Rees have returned," Goes Ahead announced. "They are half a day's hard riding from us."

"We failed to run them far enough," Talking Stick grumbled. "They will suffer again."

"Come, let's strike their camp!" Thunder Coat urged.

"No," Stone Wolf shouted. Silence settled over the council, and all eyes rested on the Arrow-keeper. "You must do as before," Stone Wolf insisted. "Carry a pipe to Mahuts."

"We've spoken to the Arrows," Thunder Coat muttered. "We've made the appropriate prayers."

"Is your medicine strong enough to carry you safely home from the Ree camp?" Younger Wolf asked. "Heed my brother's advice. He's brought you victory. Consult the Arrows."

"Yes," the young men agreed. "Stone Wolf's a man of power. Rely on him."

"Take up a pipe," Wood Snake urged. "Our band has returned to the old, sacred path. We're enjoying prosperity. Don't break our power by rushing foolishly into a fight."

Talking Stick turned to his brother, but Thunder Coat offered no encouragement. Reluctantly the Stick set off to ready a pipe.

Again a party of four walked to the Arrow Lodge. Goes Ahead came in place of Speckled Wing. The others were as before.

Stone Wolf welcomed them inside, and they smoked and talked of the good horses brought to the camp. Then Talking Stick offered a string of elk teeth and three additional eagle tail feathers.

"These are appropriate gifts," Stone Wolf said, tying them to the medicine bundle. This time the bundle made a solitary turn and stopped. The eagle feathers touched the smoke curling skyward from the Arrow-keeper's fire. Then again one broke loose and floated a moment before dropping into the embers of the fire. It flared and was gone.

"What does it mean?" Talking Stick asked nervously.

"It's a bad sign," Thunder Coat said, shaking his head. "A warning."

"Before, when the feather dropped, it warned us a man must give up his life," Talking Stick suggested. "Am I reading the signs correctly, Uncle?"

"The feather was a warning," Stone Wolf agreed. "Both times. It wasn't intended for Pronghorn, though."

"For whom?" Thunder Coat asked.

"A great man," Stone Wolf said, eyeing the chiefs.

279

"If we ride against the Rees, a chief must die," Talking Stick said, sighing. "This is what you see?"

"It's a warning only," Stone Wolf told them. "Make the proper preparations. Scout the camp carefully. Be wary of tricks, and all will be well."

"We're not riding to steal horses this time," Talking Stick pointed out. "We must punish the enemy so that he leaves this country."

"Will you kill them all then?" Younger Wolf asked. "Perhaps only half?"

"It's necessary," Thunder Coat argued. "Our winter camp won't be safe with the enemy so close. How can we send women out to gather water? Where will the children play? No, we must strike the enemy."

"We must," Talking Stick agreed. "Even if it's necessary for me to give myself up to the Ree arrows this time."

"Understand the danger," Stone Wolf warned. "Prepare yourselves well. It's all I can suggest."

"It's enough," Talking Stick insisted. "We'll make strong medicine and maintain a guard over the helpless ones."

"Yes," Thunder Coat agreed. "They must be protected."

The chiefs left the Arrow Lodge. Goes Ahead followed. Younger Wolf remained a moment. He thought to speak, but in the end he merely touched his brother's arm and departed.

Shortly before dawn, Goes Ahead, Porcupine, and Younger Wolf rode cautiously toward the opposite ridge where Goes Ahead had seen the fires. They heard the yelping of camp dogs first, and the sounds of people stirring later. Leaving their horses behind, the scouts crept closer. Finally they located the camp.

There were no lodges, for Talking Stick had burned them. In truth, few of the Rees were even adequately dressed. The boys were nearly naked, and only half possessed horses.

"They have no animals to carry them north," Goes Ahead observed. "It's why they've stayed."

Younger Wolf motioned for silence. He saw what the young men noticed—and more. Near a small fire a solitary man sat, speaking medicine prayers and painting his chest. He began by marking three red circles on his chest. Afterward he tied three feathers in his hair.

"They're preparing to strike our camp," Goes Ahead declared. "We must hurry back and warn the others."

"Go," Younger Wolf said, sighing. "I will watch them for a time."

"Should I stay, Uncle?" Porcupine asked.

"No, go and keep your brother safe," Younger Wolf urged. "I'll follow."

"Keep Younger Wolf safe, too," Porcupine said, turning to go. "We need him."

The Wolf managed to smile at them before turning back to watch the camp. He spied twenty men and a few boys there, but later, walking among the rocks and trees of the ridge, he saw signs of many horses.

And more.

On the far slope there was a fire-scarred clearing torched by the recent storm. It was a dark place, charred and lifeless. Younger Wolf knew it well. He'd seen it in his dreams.

He rode back to the Rope Men's camp with a heavy heart. When he arrived, he found the young men painting their faces and preparing for war.

"Is it as Goes Ahead has said, Uncle?" Iron Wolf called. "The Rees are preparing to attack?"

"They are making medicine," Younger Wolf admitted. "They mean to kill us."

"Then we'll strike their camp first!" Talking Stick vowed. "*Ayyyy!* We'll run them down."

"It will be easy," Thunder Coat added. "They have few ponies."

"It won't be easy," Younger Wolf said, frowning at the eager faces of the young men. "Will it, Nah nih?"

Stone Wolf turned to them and sighed.

"My brother has seen the truth of it," Stone Wolf told them. "It's another Ree trick."

"No!" Talking Stick shouted. "They are only a few."

"Others wait nearby," Younger Wolf insisted.

"Did you see them?" Thunder Coat asked. "The scouts have ridden that country, and they've seen no band of Rees ready to strike. If such a band existed, wouldn't they strike our camp?"

"I've seen the signs," Younger Wolf warned. "And I've dreamed of it."

"Now it's you who has dreams," Talking Stick muttered. "I dream myself, and I've seen none of this."

"Younger Wolf has always spoken wisely," Wood Snake observed. "Hear him now."

"I've said what I can share," Younger Wolf told

them. "The rest is for me alone."

"Speak it!" Talking Stick cried. "Tell us."

"It's not intended for us to know," Stone Wolf said, stepping beside his brother.

"Who will follow me and strike these Rees?" Talking Stick screamed. Only a handful responded, and the Stick turned to the young Foxes. "Are there no brave hearts left?" he demanded.

"I will go," Iron Wolf said, stepping forward.

"I would go, too," Four Wounds said, "but if this is a Ree trap, we need a wise leader to ensure our safe return."

"Yes," the others murmured. "Let Younger Wolf lead us."

Younger Wolf gazed into the bright young eyes of his nephews, read the honor and respect the young Foxes held for him.

"It's for me to do the difficult things," he told Stone Wolf. "I must lead them."

Twenty-four

Talking Stick was eager to strike the Rees, but Younger Wolf would not be hurried. He insisted the proper prayers be made, and he devoted most of that day to sitting alone on the nearby hillside, contemplating the fight that was coming.

"See' was' sin mit, trouble should be shared," Stone Wolf said as he sat beside his brother on the slope.

"I read your eyes, Nah nih," Younger Wolf replied. "You know the certainty of it."

"You could stay."

"Could I?" Younger Wolf asked. "Look down there at the young ones. My choice is a simple one. I can let your blood ride to its death or do as I've always done, take the burden upon myself."

"There will be many Rees, See' was' sin mit. Too many for one to fight off."

"I know," Younger Wolf confessed. "I saw the place in my dreams. I've seen the man who means to kill me."

"Stay," the Arrow-keeper pleaded. "You're needed. Let Talking Stick match his words with actions."

"He's still young. He may learn. Now he's like Fire Hawk—a cloud full of menace that failed to bring the promised rain. Don't despair. When I reach the other side, old friends will greet me. Grandfather will have prepared a resting place."

"No Ree is worth your death."

"Look after the little ones," Younger Wolf urged. "As I watched over your sons, watch over mine."

"My brother need not worry," Stone Wolf vowed. "His son and daughters are my own."

"Even as yours are mine," Younger Wolf said, smiling. "Come now. We have medicine charms to make and faces to paint."

But after preparing the young men, the Wolf found himself sitting beside the cook fire, watching Hoop Woman and the girls.

"Ne' hyo, you've neglected your own preparations," Little Dancer scolded. "I can tie the charms behind your ears. Let me help."

"You can bring my horses," Younger Wolf told the boy.

"The buckskin?" Little Dancer asked.

"The white mare," the Wolf answered. "She will carry me into this fight."

"No," Hoop Woman objected. "Already your shield marks you as an important man. A white horse will draw the enemy to you."

"He would come anyway," Younger Wolf told her.

"Then the time you dreamed of has arrived," she said, sighing.

"Yes," he said, nodding gravely.

"Ne' hyo, have you dreamed of this time?" Red Hoop whispered.

"There will be a great battle," he told the girls. "A remembered fight. Your father will stand tall and be remembered for what he does."

"As always," Little Dancer said, bringing Younger Wolf a quiver of good stone-tipped arrows. *"Ayyyy!* The Rees will run far this time!"

"And if they don't, know your father is pleased with his son," Younger Wolf said, pulling the boy close.

Later he held the girls and bid them, too, farewell.

"You're young to understand how a man must sometimes do what's hard," he whispered. "Hardest of all is to leave you, knowing I may not see your smiles again or hear your laughter. Nah' koa will help you walk woman's road, and Stone Wolf will be a father to you. It will be hard for you, too. My father left me when I was small as well, and so I know. Help your mother, and respect your brother. He will be a comfort to you, too."

He then sent the girls inside the lodge and walked to the river with Hoop Woman.

"I've spoken with Stone Wolf," he told her. "You will be provided for."

"Don't trouble yourself with concerns for your family," she answered. "You've made us strong. We won't bend under the weight of this new pain."

"It will be hard leaving you," he said, gripping her hands.

"Husband, I would hold you here if I could. Is it possible?"

286

"No," he told her as they embraced. "When your year passes, I would have you give up my ghost and find another husband. Dove Woman found happiness again. I hope you will be as fortunate."

"Iron Wolf had only two sons," she said, trembling. "I will have the children to occupy my time."

"Soon they'll grow tall and leave their mother's lodge."

"Then I'll be free to join you on the other side, heart of my world."

She held him tightly, and he had to break away to join the men gathering around the council fire.

"Don't go," she pleaded.

"I can only walk my own road, Hoop, and it takes me there," he said, pointing toward the distant ridge.

He joined the circle as the medicine prayers began, and many good words were spoken. Eventually Wood Snake stood and offered encouragement to the younger men.

"Follow the experienced warriors," he urged. "Look to them for your instruction."

"Be wary of Ree tricks," Stone Wolf warned a final time. "Watch the rocks and trees. Every shadow there may conceal an enemy."

"Maybe we should wait for dawn," Iron Wolf suggested.

"Dusk will serve us better," Younger Wolf argued.

"You've not painted yourself, Uncle," Goes Ahead observed.

"I have a thing to do first," Younger Wolf said, stepping toward the center of the circle. There, beside old Badger Toe, rested one of the Tsis tsis tas Fox warriors' two medicine lances. "You've grown old, carrying the obligations of a lance carrier," Younger Wolf noted. "It's for a younger man to take your place."

The others froze and stared as Younger Wolf lifted the small painted stake, its accompanying rawhide rope, and the old, stone-tipped lance. To accept its obligation meant to stand fast in battle. If the enemy prevailed, a lance carrier remained to face certain death.

"I'm old to ride to battle, but I can still guard the camp," Badger Toe argued. "So long as I hold the lance, the helpless ones need not fear."

"You may have it back soon, old friend," Younger Wolf promised. "I have need of it but a short while."

"No," Iron Wolf objected. "Yours is a valued life. Give the lance back, Uncle."

"Yes," the others agreed. "Return it."

"You're not afraid for me, surely," Younger Wolf told them. "You've heard Talking Stick. The camp is open to us. It will be easy killing these Rees."

Suddenly the others had grave doubts.

"Uncle, you've proven yourself often," Porcupine declared. "You need no lance to show your determination."

"Perhaps not," Younger Wolf said, returning to his place, lance in hand. "But the Fox lances have been too often absent from our fights. The other is with the Windpipes. I carry this one so that the Rees can see we're Foxes!"

288

"Ayyyy!" the young men howled.

It was only later, when Younger Wolf mounted the white mare, that the nephews cried out again.

"Are you tired of living?" Iron Wolf asked. "Once you told me only a big-talker rides to war on such a pony. The enemy will fight you even if they run from all others."

"It would happen anyway," Younger Wolf assured them. "I want it remembered. The white horse will look strong when it's painted on the winter counts."

As final evidence of his determination, Younger Wolf then took out his medicine pouch and removed a coal. As he painted his face black, the young men grew nervous.

"You wear the death mask?" Porcupine asked, touching his uncle's arm.

"To show I'm fearless," Younger Wolf explained.

"Then I must borrow the coal," Porcupine said, wiping the yellow spots from his face and chest. "I will stand with you."

"I, too!" Iron Wolf insisted.

"I, too!" Goes Ahead declared.

"No, it was Porcupine who asked first," Younger Wolf told them as he finished. Passing the coal, he fought an urge to pull the young man close. The Wolf had never feared dying himself. Now he struggled with the premonition he would not fall alone.

As the sun started its long drop into the western hills, Younger Wolf led the young Foxes out from the camp. Talking Stick and Thunder Coat rode along, but not even the shields they carried drew followers.

Younger Wolf, too, carried a shield, and the sight of the black-painted warrior riding his white mare drew the other brave hearts to his side.

"Many times I've ridden to battle," Younger Wolf told the others, "but never was I so certain of those around me. *Ayyyy!* We're strong!"

"*Ayyyy!* We're strong!" the others echoed.

"We'll run the enemy!" Younger Wolf vowed.

"We'll run them far!" the others added.

They then took up the Fox Warrior song and rode at a brisk pace toward the opposite ridge. Goes Ahead and Two Bows struck out ahead, their keen eyes scanning the country for ambush. They saw no peril, and Talking Stick urged the Rope Men on.

"Their camp is open to our bullets!" the Stick shouted, waving his rifle over his head. "Let's run them!"

"*Ayyyy!*" the Tsis tsis tas howled, charging upon the naked camp.

The charge caught the handful of pony boys and old men by surprise. Some leaped upon their horses and fled. Others tried, only to fall to arrows or bullets. Rope Men leaped down to strike down the enemy. Others counted coup on the corpses or cut off their hair. The camp was taken quickly, and the celebrating began.

"Where is the Ree ambush?" Talking Stick screamed as he raised a bloody scalp skyward. "Where have the feared enemy gone?"

"Nowhere," Younger Wolf said, pointing to movement in the trees. Suddenly the hillside behind them

290

filled with a hundred well-hidden Rees.

"No!" Talking Stick shouted, hurrying to his horse.

"Stop!" Dancing Lance pleaded as his companions began racing away. "Protect your brothers!"

Those who were mounted kicked their ponies into motion, for the Rees were closing fast. Bullets split the air, and their war cries drove the faint-hearted from the camp.

"Uncle, come!" Goes Ahead pleaded as he covered the retreat of two boys. "There are too many."

"I'll ride some," Younger Wolf said calmly. Ignoring the others, he motioned for Porcupine to follow. They crossed the ridge and continued on to the burnt slope.

Half the raiders had formed a circle there, and the Rees were pressing them. Younger Wolf shouted, raised his lance, and fell on the enemy like a hawk. He cut down one and then another. The Rees gazed up at the terrible black-faced demon and fled from the deadly Fox lance.

"Help us!" Bent Leg pleaded as he fended off a Ree lance. Beside him Mountain Heart struggled to free his legs from under a dead pony.

"Ayyyy!" Younger Wolf screamed, charging the Rees encircling the young men. The lance impaled one, and the other two raced away.

"Here, take this pony," Younger Wolf said, capturing the slain Ree's mount. "Ride fast."

Bent Leg hesitated as he climbed atop the pony, but once Mountain Heart was up behind him, Younger Wolf slapped the animal's rump.

The fighting grew fiercer as pairs of Rope men

291

faced parties of Rees. Good men on both sides found remembered deaths. Others struggled on until a friend drove the enemy away and allowed an escape.

"It's time to go," Iron Wolf shouted as the last band of Tsis tsis tas warriors broke out from the encircling Rees. Climbing atop any horse they could find, they scrambled away from the blackened earth, seeking the protection of their camp.

"Go, Nephew!" Younger Wolf called as he rode before the enemy, holding his shield high and taunting them. Then he heard a cry from his left. Amid the carnage, Speckled Wing struggled to his feet. His side was gashed and bleeding, but his eyes were full of life.

"*Ayyyy!*" Younger Wolf shouted as he rode to the young man's rescue. The weary mare shuddered as the Wolf halted her. Climbing down, Younger Wolf pushed the young man onto the mare and stroked the animal's lathered neck.

"Carry him home," Younger Wolf urged the horse. "Remember me to your father, Wing."

The mare raced off after the others, and Younger Wolf turned to face the remaining Rees. The clearing was full of them, and their tired eyes filled with surprise when the Wolf drew out the stake and drove it into the burnt earth. Binding his leg, he turned at last, holding the Fox lance in his powerful right hand as he steadied the shield with his left.

"Come, Rees, and find your death!" Younger Wolf cried.

From among them stepped a solitary figure. His

292

chest was marked by the red circles Younger Wolf had seen before, and the three feathers danced lightly from his hair.

"I wait my death calmly," Younger Wolf sang softly. "Nothing lives long. Only the earth and the mountains!"

The Ree chief approached calmly, quietly. His companions held back, cheering him on. He paused twenty paces away and aimed his rifle. Younger Wolf raised the shield in time to deflect the bullet away.

"Try another!" Younger Wolf suggested. As the Ree reloaded, the Wolf felt the weight of the shield on his arm. He was growing tired. His lance arm was bruised and battered in six places, and blood stung his eyes from a gash in his forehead. Nevertheless, when the Ree aimed and fired, Younger Wolf raised his shield again. The bullet tore into the thick hide but failed to pass through.

The Ree chief stared disdainfully at his rifle and tossed it aside. Instead he took a hatchet from his belt and closed with the lance carrier. Unable to match the Ree's movements, Younger Wolf waited patiently for the first blow to land. The Ree stepped to the right, then swung the ax high and fell hard on Younger Wolf from the left.

The Wolf tried to parry the blow with his lance, but he moved too late. The blow flattened the shield against Younger Wolf's chest and drove him down onto the ground. A second blow struck hard and deep above the left elbow. A third severed the arm. The Buffalo Shield which had so long protected its owner fell away.

"Ayyyy!" the Ree screamed as he lifted the shield by its holder's dismembered arm.

Younger Wolf was ablaze with pain, but he mustered the last of his energy and thrust the stone point of the Fox lance upward. It struck the Ree hard in the belly and drove on into his heart.

For a moment the Rees stood in stunned silence as their chief reeled backward. He discarded the captured shield and fought to hold his bowels inside him. Death flooded his face, and he fell back onto the blackened earth.

"Ayyyy!" a familiar voice screamed from behind him. Younger Wolf turned in time to see Iron Wolf fire an arrow into an onrushing Ree. A second Ree charged, but Iron Wolf struck him down as well. Then Goes Ahead dashed in and climbed down. He drew out his knife to free Younger Wolf from the stake, but his uncle pushed him away. One-armed, and faint from loss of blood, Younger Wolf regained his feet and again faced the Rees.

"It's not for you to do, Nephew," Younger Wolf insisted. "You've not earned the right."

"I will!" Porcupine shouted, charging the center of the Ree line. Arrows and bullets met him halfway, but he continued on, breaking the enemy line and scattering the faint-hearted ones. As Porcupine returned, he rolled off his horse and stumbled to the stake. Blood flowed from wounds in his chest and hips, but he managed to tear the stake from the earth.

"Now you must go, Uncle," Goes Ahead said, binding the wounded arm as Porcupine fell back, chanting his death song.

"I won't leave the enemy this ground!" Younger Wolf shouted defiantly.

"It is not theirs," Iron Wolf said, dismounting. He raised his uncle's shield high, and the sun suddenly dipped below the horizon. The air hung heavy and still. Then a great wind surged over the hillside, stirring ashes into the air. A blinding sheet of ebony fell upon the Rees, and they shrieked to see themselves painted black as death.

Younger Wolf fell to his knees and touched the still warm body of his slain nephew with his remaining arm.

"You knew, Uncle," Porcupine managed to speak, opening his eyes a final time.

"Yes," Younger Wolf said, shuddering. "You stole my death, Nephew."

"You're needed more," Goes Ahead said, helping Younger Wolf to his feet. Dancing Lance and Four Wounds arrived with spare ponies, and the nephews managed to get their uncle atop one. The Lance and Four Wounds remained with Goes Ahead to tie Porcupine atop the other. Iron Wolf, still holding the sacred shield in one arm, led his uncle's horse homeward with the others.

Twenty-five

Three days and three nights Younger Wolf drifted between life and death. Young men saved by his stand or rescued from the enemy gathered outside the Arrow Lodge to chant for his recovery. Stone Wolf, grieving already for a dead son, endeavored to bring his brother back from the shadow world into which he had gone.

For a time Younger Wolf glimpsed Hanging Road. His solitary arm seemed to reach for the Star Boys. He heard old friends whispering from the clouds, inviting him to join them.

"Grandfather, I'm coming," he called often.

Eventually, though, other voices drew him back to the world below.

"Ne' hyo, we need you," Little Dancer whispered as he clutched his father's remaining hand.

"Ne' hyo, Nah' koa and I baked bread for you," Red Hoop said, placing her soft cheek against Younger Wolf's tortured chest. "Little Hoop has outgrown her moccasins. You must wake and make new ones for her."

In the end, it was Hoop Woman's devotion that restored his strength and opened his eyes to his family once again.

"I knew you would come back to us," she said as she fed him turnip and onion soup. "No painted Ree could kill my husband!"

"He took my arm," Younger Wolf said, moaning. "I feel it, but my eyes assure me it's gone."

"You have your heart," Hoop replied. "It's enough."

"Is it?" he asked. "Never again will I walk warrior's road. Who am I now? A burden to my People."

"You're my husband!" she barked. "If it's pity you seek, go elsewhere. You have a son and daughters that need you. Nephews who wait to honor your stand. All the People whisper your name with respect. Don't you know you are Younger Wolf, foremost among the brave hearts?"

"Once I was," he lamented. "Now I'm only half of what I was."

"You were worth two of the others," she boasted. "Even now you are their equal."

He couldn't help returning her smile. And although the pain and fevers continued to plague him, he knew he would live to resume his place at the cook fire.

When Younger Wolf's head cleared enough, Stone Wolf brought in the nephews. Dreamer approached first, offering a warming elk robe.

"Uncle, Ne' hyo lacks the skill to make me a man's bow," the boy explained. "When you're better, will you help me craft one?"

"It's for Iron Wolf to show you," Younger Wolf answered.

"No," Dreamer argued. "It's an uncle's obligation."

"I have only one arm," Younger Wolf explained. "It takes two."

"Mine are small, Uncle, but there are two of them," Dreamer said, holding them out so they could be seen. "We'll do it together."

"Yes," Younger Wolf agreed. "We'll make you a strong bow of red willow."

Goes Ahead next sat beside his uncle.

"We buried my brother," the boy explained. "Before we returned to Burned Mountain, he told me I must some day tell you he, too, dreamed of that day. Even as you sought your death there, my brother fought to save it."

"He said this?" Younger Wolf asked, seeing the truth of it etched on Goes Ahead's face.

"We waited too long to save the arm, Uncle," Goes Ahead continued, "and for this we both apologize. I don't think he feared dying. He only wished to earn a brave name first."

"Names are not much, Nephew. Deeds count most."

"Yes, and he will long be remembered."

As Goes Ahead stepped aside, Younger Wolf regretted not granting Porcupine a warrior's name. So many younger boys had been named! Now no one would speak of him at all, for it would hold the young man's ghost near and hinder his walk to the other side.

"I bring my uncle his shield," Iron Wolf said, sliding

298

into the place Goes Ahead had made for him at Younger Wolf's side. "The arm rests with our brother atop Noahvose, as we thought you would wish it."

"It's appropriate," Younger Wolf agreed. "One day the rest of me will join it. As to the shield, I have no use for it."

"It can rest in its honored place beside your lodge," Iron Wolf argued.

"No, rightfully it belongs to a brave heart who can use it to keep the People safe. It's yours now, Iron Wolf. The arm that held it is gone. You've won its power. Hold it as you did on Burned Mountain. Devote yourself to the welfare of the helpless."

"I will, Uncle," Iron Wolf pledged, sliding his arm through the strap and holding the shield proudly.

"How many did the Rees kill?" Younger Wolf then asked his nephews.

"Seven," Iron Wolf answered. "Three others besides yourself were badly hurt."

"Have the Rees gone?"

"Yes," Goes Ahead said, gazing at his brothers.

"The Buffalo Shield stirred the wind against them," Iron Wolf explained. "They climbed atop their horses and rode north. Even now no one approaches Burned Mountain. Many Rees lay there still, their flesh food for birds. Lame Elk says that he counted twenty of them, and he didn't visit the camp. I know of five killed there."

"It's good they've gone," Younger Wolf declared. "There was enough killing done."

"They won't return soon," Stone Wolf added. "This

place is bad medicine for them."

"Come," Iron Wolf said, motioning to his brothers. "It's time we left our uncle in peace."

"We'll visit again," Dreamer promised, touching Younger Wolf's chest. "And there's the bow to make."

"Yes, there's that," Younger Wolf said, warming as he watched a smile spread across the boy's face.

"I have words to share with you, See' was' sin mit," Stone Wolf said after the boys departed. "Hoop Woman says you despair of living. It's not right. You will not hold a shield again, but you are a man others will heed. You know the medicine cures, and you can show boys man's road.

"You have a son to help grow tall, and daughters to instruct," Stone Wolf continued. "Never have I known my brother to run from a hard fight, and so you must battle this hurt you feel. Who can say why Man Above sent you back to us? Clearly, he recognized the need of the People. Restore your strength. Walk the high places with me again. Be Younger Wolf."

"You ask much, Nah nih," Younger Wolf said, frowning.

"I have always asked everything of you," Stone Wolf replied. "But never more than you had to give."

That winter and the next were cruelly hard on the Tsis tsis tas. Freezing winds lashed at the lodges, and snows choked the skies. Nevertheless, Younger Wolf found solace crafting bows or sharing tales with the little ones. He took great pride in his tall nephews,

Iron Wolf and Goes Ahead, for they now led the hunt. Their generosity was praised throughout the camp, and Hoop Woman's kettle was never without meat.

When fevers overtook the People, Younger Wolf offered his assistance with the healing cures, and many considered his power as great as any.

"Suffering draws the spirits close to a man," Bent Leg observed. "Younger Wolf's power grows each winter."

Younger Wolf participated in the ceremonies, and he was often consulted by young men eager to enhance their own power. Sometimes parties of young Foxes came from the other bands to see the one-armed man and honor his remembered fight. Lakotas even arrived to sing of the battle, and to tell how a Ree captive spoke of the black-face Tsis tsis tas who struck down Three Coups and rose from death to run the Rees.

When Dreamer marked his fifteenth summer by striking down three bulls in a single afternoon, Younger Wolf rode with the young man to Noahvose and sought a vision.

"It's for your uncle to grant you a name," Younger Wolf explained afterward. "Soon you will turn away from warrior's road and walk the medicine trail. It's appropriate, for the People require men of vision and courage."

"Ne' hyo has spoken to me of this," the young man admitted. "I will miss these good times I've shared with you, learning man's road and the ways of a warrior. I will be a man more alone than when riding with my brothers."

"Your brothers will never be far," Younger Wolf assured him. "You know you carried as a boy the name my grandfather owned."

"Yes," Dreamer said, gazing skyward. "I would be honored to walk the world as he did. To carry his man's name."

"It's a great obligation to place on a man," Younger Wolf observed. "Iron Wolf carries such a name, and its burdens are heavy. I would choose another name for you, one that links our grandfather, but brings to your mind other relatives, too."

"Ne' hyo?" Dreamer asked. "Perhaps yourself."

"Would that disappoint you?"

"I would walk proudly bearing such a name, Uncle."

Younger Wolf rested his hand on the young man's shoulder and found it strong. There was little of the boy remaining. A man now stood beside Younger Wolf, and it was time he receive a brave name.

The Foxes were called together, and many good horses were given away. Afterward Younger Wolf and Stone Wolf shared many remembered stories of brave deeds performed by their relations. Finally, when the appropriate moment came, Younger Wolf led his youngest nephew to the fire.

"The boy you've known as Dreamer is no more," Younger Wolf told the others. "He's carried a boy's name, and he needs it no longer. I give it away to any who would take it."

"Ayyyy!" the young men howled. "A new Fox is

302

among us."

"We've smoked and talked of this nameless one, and his father and I have determined he merits a brave name."

"Yes!" the others shouted. "Give him a brave name."

Iron Wolf now led three additional ponies out and presented them to boys of poor families. Goes Ahead offered good buffalo robes as well.

"We honor our brother," they explained.

"He should carry a name that marks him as an important man," Stone Wolf proclaimed as he gripped his son's shoulders and turned him toward the Foxes. "Greet Dreaming Wolf, my son."

"*Ayyyy!*" the Foxes yelled. "It's a good name."

Dreaming Wolf embraced his father, then warmly greeted his brothers. Finally he turned to Younger Wolf and wrapped his arms around the one-armed warrior.

"Uncle, I will carry it well," he whispered. "And always remember who gave it to me."

It pleased Younger Wolf to see the nephews walk man's road, but his heart glowed hot when sitting with Little Dancer, helping him identify medicine herbs or spot animal tracks. The girls, too, were growing, but Hoop Woman took charge of them.

"I've lost my son to you," she stormed when Younger Wolf attempted to instruct them. "It's for me and their aunt to teach them. What do you know of woman's road? Mind your arrows and leave my daughters to my care!"

"Be glad of it, Ne' hyo," the Dancer whispered. "Girls are mostly a bother. My sisters are forever following me to the river and gazing at the boys swimming there. Nah' koa only laughs when I complain. 'They've seen little enough,' she says. 'Who brings man into the world, do you think? Woman does all the important work.'"

"She's probably right," Younger Wolf admitted. "But never tell her that. If women knew of their importance, there would be no living with them."

"It's hard enough anyway," Little Dancer declared. "I'll be glad when I step inside the young man's lodge and am finished with sisters."

"That day approaches," Younger Wolf said, leading the boy to the river. They sat there, tossing pebbles into the water. Younger Wolf recalled how easy it had once been to hold the Dancer on one knee. The boy approached his twelfth summer. Already Iron Wolf had taken him along to hold the ponies while hunting deer. Soon the Dancer would ride to hunt Bull Buffalo.

"I will miss you when you leave us," Younger Wolf remarked. "It's not a thing a father should admit, but it's true. I should be happy my son's growing tall in all the best ways. I should give away horses to celebrate. But winters touch my bones with their chills, and I won't know, as some will, a grandson's touch."

"I could take a wife," Little Dancer said, "but she would be a burden to me. I would have to bring her meat, prepare hides for her to work, and satisfy her other needs."

"Other needs?" Younger Wolf asked.

"Other needs," the boy insisted. "I know such things, Ne' hyo. You taught me yourself."

"Apparently better than I knew," Younger Wolf said, laughing.

"Some boys leave their father's lodge when they join the buffalo hunting," the Dancer said, growing serious. "I would stay another summer. A son shouldn't speak of this, Ne' hyo, but I would miss my father. I would share as many days as he thinks right."

"Yes," Younger Wolf agreed. "Another year. But a boy of thirteen summers should ride with the other young men." Little Dancer grinned, and his father drew him close.

Twenty-six

The rapidity with which a year could pass surprised Younger Wolf. As spring painted the land green once more, the People faced many difficult challenges. Sickness and dying had again emptied many lodges. Wood Snake was gone. Dove Woman had exhausted herself tending the sick and climbed Hanging Road, leaving Stone Wolf to face the world without a wife.

"Who can help make the Arrow renewal?" the Arrowkeeper cried. "She who aided me is gone!"

Younger Wolf provided a simple solution.

"Already Dreaming Wolf is learning the medicine cures," he noted. "As he learns the Arrow ceremonies, so should others."

"Who?" Stone Wolf asked.

"Hoop Woman," Younger Wolf suggested. "She was a sister to your own wife, and she has less to do with the daughters growing older. Soon Little Dancer will join the young men. Hoop can help you renew the Arrows."

"She has a healing touch," Stone Wolf admitted. "I will ask her."

"The girls can learn, too," Younger Wolf said, sigh-

306

ing. "Too few women know even the medicine herbs now. The old knowledge is passing as the old ones die. Teach them, Nah nih. Preserve our power."

"It will be good to have girls beside me once more, See' was' sin mit. A daughter's touch warms an old man."

Other trouble was less easily dealt with. The ten bands were strong now ever, and the neighboring tribes now rode Tsis tsis tas country freely. The Crow and Pawnee stole horses and ambushed hunting parties. Some of the People rode with the Lakotas, seeking the protection of their greater numbers. Others camped beside the *wihio* fort, taking up the trader's road.

"We're coming to a bad end," Stone Wolf often observed.

Others, hot to strike the enemy, spoke for war.

"The *wihio* has brought these dark days to us!" Thunder Coat exclaimed. "We should paint the Shell River road red with his blood."

"It's the Pawnee who are to blame," Dancing Lance argued. "From the time when they stole Mahuts from us, we've known only death and defeat. Brothers, ride with me and run the Arrow-stealing demons! Kill the Pawnee!"

When a Pawnee war party struck the Rope Men's horse herd, driving off fifty ponies, the warriors gathered to plan a counterstroke.

"I've seen their camp," Goes Ahead declared. "Two days of hard riding would get us there."

"How many are there?" Iron Wolf asked.

"Forty lodges," Goes Ahead answered. "The younger

307

men will be hunting, though. We can get our horses back and take captives."

"There are few girls among us to take for wives," Mountain Heart said. "It would be good to take the Pawnee women."

"There are lodges who would welcome little ones, too," Speckled Wing added. His own small daughters had died of a winter fever, and his wife was bent over with sadness.

"I would rather fight the *wihio*," Talking Stick said, "but I wouldn't mix our blood with such crazy people. We'll raid the Pawnee instead."

"Ayyyy!" the young men shouted. "It's good we take to warrior's road."

Younger Wolf had remained silent as the other talked. Now he rose.

"It's an easy thing to make boasts, to speak of taking captives and running horses," he told the younger men. "War is never so simple a thing as we expect. The Pawnee rarely stand and fight as do the Crow. Instead they use feints and deception. We must plan our movements carefully and make strong medicine."

"We?" Talking Stick cried. "When did you last ride to war, old man?"

"You should remember that day!" Iron Wolf shouted. "The day my brother fell. Yours was the voice eager to fight then, too, but you directed us into a Ree trap."

"That was long ago," Thunder Coat argued. "We can accomplish nothing by speaking hard words against our chiefs."

"It's for our chiefs to set the example," Speckled Wing said, stepping beside Younger Wolf. "How many of us

308

walk the earth because this man rescued us? I remember his stand on Burned Mountain. My life was won at the loss of his arm. Whenever Younger Wolf has words to speak, I'll listen."

"I, too," Bent Leg announced.

"And I," Goes Ahead added. "Tell us your feelings on this matter, Uncle."

"I've said what must be done," Younger Wolf told them. "Talking Stick is right to question a man who stays at home, in the comfort of his lodge. I will put my words to the test, as I've always done. I have no shield to carry against the Pawnee, but Younger Wolf will find a lance."

"*Ayyyy!*" the warriors howled. "A great man leads us against the enemy!"

Talking Stick frowned, but he spoke no more. Even a chief's words could not stand against a famous warrior. Moreover, even the youngest among them knew a one-armed man rode to war with little hope of returning. Younger Wolf intended to fight a final time.

Before joining the others in their war preparations, Younger Wolf crossed the camp and summoned the Hoop.

"We must talk," he told her.

"Am I a dog to order about?" she asked. "We'll talk later. I'm working an elk hide. Our son should have a good coat when he leaves our lodge to walk man's road."

"Yes, it's a good thing," Younger Wolf agreed. "But my words need to be spoken now."

She stared hard at him, then softened as she read the intensity in his eyes. Setting aside her work, she followed Younger Wolf from the lodge, past the river, and into the low hills beyond.

"Yes, Husband?" Hoop Woman asked when he finally halted.

"Stone Wolf is without a woman," he told her.

"I don't know this?" she cried. "His loss was no less than my own!"

"This summer he must renew Mahuts," Younger Wolf explained. "A woman is needed to help with the ceremonies. Once we had many relatives to do it, but now there's no one. I suggested you could help."

"It would honor me," she said, growing solemn. "It's a great thing you ask of me."

"I wouldn't ask it of anyone not worthy. I think our daughters, also, should learn of the medicine road."

"Stone Wolf agrees?" she asked.

"Yes," he told her. "It's only for you to say."

"Red Hoop already helps tend the little ones who grow feverish. Little Hoop envies her sister the work. Little Dancer is leaving, and we will want work to make up the loss."

"Then it's agreed," he said, nodding.

"There's more, though," she observed. "Something not yet spoken."

"Yes," he confessed. "I feel a hard day is coming. This body has grown old and wrinkled. It's unfair to feel so young inside it!"

"Old age suits you," she insisted.

"If I had years to pass, I would spend them in your company, Hoop. The best times I have known have been those we've shared. But now time for me is growing short. Already I'm useless as a hunter. My eyes are growing dim. I don't desire to burden my family, to lie feeble, wetting myself like a child. Younger Wolf has earned a better end."

"We none of us choose our road, Husband."

"Perhaps not," he admitted. "But I can choose not to grow old and weak. The obligations of my life have been met, and it's only for you, the girls, and my brother I must provide. It seems to me you may come to provide for each other. Stone Wolf will need you, and you will need him."

"I have a husband!" she objected.

"Yes, but soon you may not," he told her.

"You've dreamed again?"

"Many times, Hoop. It surprises me I've seen our son ride to the buffalo hunt. If Porcupine had held back, perhaps I would not have. The young men are setting out across Shell River to strike the Pawnee. I will take a pipe to Stone Wolf and seek Mahuts' advice."

"Your warrior days are over," Hoop Woman reminded him.

"I carry the Buffalo Shield no longer, it's true. But my lance arm remains strong. I may yet win a remembered death."

"No!"

"It's a gift Man Above may give me," he said, holding her close. "And one you may grant. Release me from my obligation to you. Let me ride against the enemy."

"You'll die," she cried.

"We all climb Hanging Road," he told her. "I've walked the earth too long. Grandfather waits for me."

"You expect me to hurry you to your death?"

"Hoop, there are no secrets between us. All our days death has seemed like a thief, stealing the sweetness

311

that is living. Now it comes close, walking at my side like an old friend to show me a warm place by a good fire. I don't fear it. It's growing useless I can't tolerate."

"You ask me to tear out a piece of my heart," she said, sobbing. "Little Dancer—"

"Will see you have meat," Younger Wolf assured her. "The girls, too, will mourn. But their hearts will be full of the man they knew as their father, of the brave heart who always put the welfare of the People before his own."

"Even now?"

"Even now," he told her. "If I lead, the proper preparations will be made, and skill will be used in striking the enemy. I will ride into no traps."

"And how will you accomplish your end, Husband?"

"In an honorable fashion," he promised, "so that your grandsons will share the tale of it with their grandsons."

"I always expected we'd climb Hanging Road together."

"It would have been a comfort, having you at my side. You have work left to do here, though. When it's time, I'll be there, waiting to welcome you."

They sat for a time on the hillside, recalling other, better days. So much had passed between them. Younger Wolf wondered if he was deciding wisely, though. That night, as he sat and smoked with Stone Wolf in the Arrow Lodge, he saw his road clearly. Mahuts warned of Pawnee tricks, spoke of the need for sacrifice.

"No feather fell this time," Younger Wolf observed.

"There's no surprising some men," the Arrow-keeper explained. "Before, the Arrows offered a warning. Man Above sent you dreams. What you intend now is clear for anyone to know."

"It's all I know to do," Younger Wolf explained, sighing. "I have nothing but myself to offer."

"And when you're gone, who will speak for caution? Who will rescue the young men?"

"Others who have learned as we did, from the example of our elders."

When the medicine prayers had been made, and the young men painted themselves for war, Younger Wolf walked about the camp, speaking to old friends a final time. He walked with the girls beside the river, admonishing them to walk the sacred path and be true to their father's expectations.

Little Dancer appeared with a white mare painted with wolf paws, and Younger Wolf tied the animal's tail.

"You" ____ ____ to tend the ponies," the boy said. "C ____ ____ you, Ne' hyo?"

"____ ere should be a first time," Younger Wolf said, nodding.

"Nah' koa beaded a shirt for me," the boy explained. "But I will ride bare-chested, in the modest fashion of my father."

"Have you a good bow?"

"Dreaming Wolf gave me his," Little Dancer explained. "The last you crafted."

"It's a strong bow, Naha'. It will serve you well."

The boy rubbed his eyes and swallowed a spreading sadness.

"I'll bring other ponies," he volunteered.

313

As Little Dancer hurried away, Goes Ahead and Iron Wolf appeared.

"He wouldn't stay behind with his age-mates," Iron Wolf explained.

"Ah," Younger Wolf said, laughing. "Would you?"

"No," Goes Ahead answered. "Nor would you, Uncle. There are no stay-behinds in our family."

Only Stone Wolf and Dreaming Wolf remained in the camp, for they were occupied making medicine. Younger Wolf spoke but a moment with them.

"You know what's to be done afterward, Nah nih," Younger Wolf said, clasping his brother's right hand with his own. Neither seemed willing to release his grip, but when the young men began their brave heart songs, Younger Wolf nodded and turned away. He shouted a farewell to Hoop Woman and raced the white mare past the girls.

"Strike them hard, Husband!" the Hoop cried.

"Ayyyy!" Younger Wolf howled. "They'll remember it always!"

Twenty-seven

For those who witnessed it, Tsis tsis tas and Pawnee alike, Younger Wolf's death was long remembered. The People had struck the Pawnee camp as planned, driving off the young men and taking many horses. Women and children, too, were carried away. When the Pawnee warriors collected themselves and rode after the raiders, they found a line of men prepared to meet them.

Younger Wolf rode out ahead of the others, his face painted black as night. On the white mare, he presented a terrible image, one-armed and fearless as he waved his old stone-tipped lance at the enemy and dared them to strike.

Crows or Rees might have sent a single man to counter the old man, but the Pawnee charged as a group. They fell upon Younger Wolf, shouting and firing their rifles wildly. But amid the whirling dust thrown up by the ponies, the white mare emerged. Its rider pierced one Pawnee with his lance and unhorsed another by clubbing him across the forehead. Already two others lay in the dust.

315

"Ayyyy!" the young Tsis tsis tas screamed. "See how he runs the enemy!"

The young Tsis tsis tas could hold themselves back no longer. They threw themselves into the fight. Some of the Pawnee saw what was coming and broke away. Others turned and met the charge bravely. There was no stopping the Tsis tsis tas, though. Those Pawnees who were able made their escape afoot or on horseback, even slithering through the high grass like snakes. Their final backward glance was of the one-armed demon who even now sat atop his white mare.

"Ne' hyo!" Little Dancer called as he raced to his father's side. "You fought them all."

"Uncle, you ran them!" Iron Wolf howled.

"Even one-armed, his power was too great!" Speckled Wing exclaimed.

"No, they've killed me," Younger Wolf said, slumping against the mare's neck. The bare flesh of his sides and back was marked by seven wounds. His chest, too, was opened in three places, and an arrow protruded from his right knee.

"Help him down," Little Dancer pleaded. "Bind the wounds!"

"There's no mending them," Younger Wolf said as his nephews assisted him to the ground. "Give my horse to the wind, for she's earned it."

Goes Ahead stripped off the saddle and whipped the horse into a gallop. As the mare sped off, the Foxes howled.

"Ne' hyo?" Little Dancer called as he jumped down and cradled his father's head.

"Man Above has been good to me," Younger Wolf

316

whispered. "He's granted me a rest at last. And he's left behind a son to remember."

Younger Wolf's lips formed a smile. Then his eyes grew vacant, for death was hurrying him elsewhere.

Epilogue

Stone Wolf accompanied his brother to Noahvose a final time. There, on that sacred mountain where Sweet Medicine received Mahuts, a scaffold was erected near the spot where old Cloud Dancer had been placed a lifetime before.

"Rest well, my brother," Stone Wolf said as he and his sons raised the figure of Younger Wolf above the earth. Already his shade was climbing Hanging Road.

"*Ayyyy!*" Iron Wolf howled.

"Here was a man of the People!" Goes Ahead screamed.

"This was my father," Little Dancer said, stepping out from his mother and sisters. He stood as straight and tall as a grieving boy of thirteen summers could manage.

"Here rests the best of us," Dreaming Wolf added.

"Yes," the Dancer agreed. "He was an example to us all."

THE SEVENTH CARRIER SERIES
By PETER ALBANO

THE SEVENTH CARRIER (2056, $3.95/$5.50)
The original novel of this exciting, best-selling series. Imprisoned in a cave of ice since 1941, the great carrier *Yonaga* finally breaks free in 1983, her maddened crew of samurai determined to carry out their orders to destroy Pearl Harbor.

THE SECOND VOYAGE OF THE SEVENTH CARRIER (2104, $3.95/$4.95)
The Red Chinese have launched a particle beam satellite system into space, knocking out every modern weapons system on earth. Not a jet or rocket can fly. Now the old carrier *Yonaga* is desperately needed because the Third World nations—with their armed forces made of old World War II ships and planes—have suddenly become superpowers. Terrorism runs rampant. Only the *Yonaga* can save America and the Free World.

RETURN OF THE SEVENTH CARRIER (2093, $3.95/$4.95)
With the war technology of the former superpowers still crippled by Red China's orbital defense system, a terrorist beast runs rampant across the planet. Outarmed and outnumbered, the target of crack saboteurs and fanatical assassins, only the *Yonaga* and its brave samurai crew stand between a Libyan madman and his fiendish goal of global domination.

QUEST OF THE SEVENTH CARRIER (2599, $3.95/$4.95)
Power bases have shifted drastically. Now a Libyan madman has the upper hand, planning to crush his western enemies with an army of millions of Arab fanatics. Only *Yonaga* and her indomitable samurai crew can save the besieged free world from the devastating iron fist of the terrorist maniac. Bravely, the behemoth leads a rag tag armada of rusty World War II warships against impossible odds on a fiery sea of blood and death!

ATTACK OF THE SEVENTH CARRIER (2842, $3.95/$4.95)
The Libyan madman has seized bases in the Marianas and Western Caroline Islands. The free world seems doomed. Desperately, *Yonaga's* air groups fight bloody air battles over Saipan and Tinian. An old World War II submarine, *USS Blackfin,* is added to *Yonaga's* ancient fleet and the enemy's impregnable bases are attacked with suicidal fury.

TRIAL OF THE SEVENTH CARRIER (3213, $3.95/$4.95)
The enemies of freedom are on the verge of dominating the world with oil blackmail and the threat of poison gas attack. *Yonaga's* officers lay desperate plans to strike back. Leading a ragtag fleet of revamped destroyers and a single antique World War II submarine, the great carrier must charge into a sea of blood and death in what becomes the greatest trial of the Seventh Carrier.